Captive  King

Silya Barakat

To all the fae lovers out there who dream of being whisked away by a Fae King and have their wildest fantasies fulfilled...

From one fae lover to another, this one's for you. Manifesting it into reality, one book at a time.

Contents

Copyrights 1
1. Chapter 1..2
2. Chapter 2..19
3. Chapter 3..34
4. Chapter 4..55
5. Chapter 5..76
6. Chapter 6..94
7. Chapter 7..109
8. Chapter 8..134
9. Chapter 9..146
10. Chapter 10..163
11. Chapter 11..182
12. Chapter 12..203
13. Chapter 13..223
14. Chapter 14..251
15. Chapter 15..274
16. Chapter 16..297
17. Chapter 17..315
18. Chapter 18..330
19. Chapter 19..344
20. Chapter 20..364
21. Chapter 21..385
22. Chapter 22..405
23. Chapter 23..420
24. Chapter 24..442
About the Author 465

1.
2.

3.
4.
5.
6.
7.
8.
9.
10.
11.
12.
13.
14.
15.
16.
17.
18.
19.
20.
21.
22.
23.
24.
25.

Copyright © 2023 by Silya Barakat

All rights reserved.

No part of this publication may be reproduced, distributed, or transmitted in any form or by any means, including photocopying, recording, or other electronic or mechanical methods, without the prior written permission of the publisher, except as permitted by U.S. copyright law.

The story, all names, characters, and incidents portrayed in this production are fictitious. No identification with actual persons (living or deceased), places, buildings, and products is intended or should be inferred.

one

Hard Lessons of Cheating

Money has a way of speaking to people like me, and I had no intention of ignoring what it was trying to tell me.

Rats scurried around my feet, seemingly in agreement; this was an opportunity I couldn't pass up.

I had to make a living, after all, and swindling a nobleman out of a few coins sounded better than washing dishes for the rest of my life.

Lord Ralston kneeled before me in the murky sewer water, his red hair matted to his forehead. He waved a small sack of coins at me, desperation radiating off of him.

Bowing before a peasant to ask for a favor, one that would cost him his daughter's life.

My siblings' faces danced in my mind, their bellies empty and fingers entwined. Hungrily, they stared at me, awaiting my answer.

Ten years had passed since I'd seen most of them, sending what little money I could back home.

But it was never enough. Not to make up for the past.

A smile crept across my lips as I plucked the bag from his hands. "Gold shrines and shiny coins," I said, my tongue tasting the words with relish. "The Summer King has never let a single one of his brides survive longer than a night and yet, here I am to slay the beast."

I opened the bag and glanced inside, counting the coins with a practiced eye.

The gold would buy me passage away from here, far away into lands untainted by the cruel ways of the Fae.

But there was something I had to do first - something that would likely get me killed if I didn't finesse it: lie. Lie about being willing to fight the Summer King and slay him.

Lord Ralston looked up at me with a mixture of hope and fear in his eyes. "Can you do it?"

I met his gaze steadily, my heart beating faster with each passing second.

I thought of my siblings and their future.

Let them flog me if they must. What are a hundred lashes on the back compared to a lifetime of servitude?

"Yes, my lord. I can do it," I said, the lie coming easily to my lips.

I wouldn't be slaughtering any Fae king, but Lord Ralston didn't need to know that. I'd take the gold, make my escape, and be done with this deal before anyone noticed.

Lord Ralston bowed his forehead to the ground, his shoulders shaking with gratitude.

His lips touched the tips of my muddy shoes. "Thank you," he said hoarsely. "My innocent daughter's life is in your hands."

I looked away as my throat closed up with emotion.

This was a city of two worlds. The red stone facades of the upper class perched atop their mountain fortress and the muddy, stinking slums lined with ramshackle buildings along a river that threatened to swallow them whole.

And here I was, standing in between them, my feet firmly planted on the edge of uncertainty. The eyes of hundreds of people pierced through me like daggers, judging me for daring to defy.

He stood up and wiped his face with a trembling hand. "Half up front and the other half upon completion," he said. "Shakira, I will never forget what you will do for my Eluned."

Zareena. My name is Zareena.

But that didn't matter.

Not anymore.

His misguided belief that I was somebody else, somebody he wanted me to be, was all that mattered.

I had a purpose, one that didn't bear my name, but his.

Shakira, someone brave enough to take on a challenge no one else would dare attempt.

Men easily missed what lay in plain sight, and they easily forgot those who didn't fit into their plans. Fools and heroes made bold choices, while the rest of us just tried to get by.

That's what I was doing - getting by.

I stepped back; the coins jingled softly in the sack.

I took a deep breath and nodded again, my eyes meeting his one last time, before I turned away. "It shall be done. The Summer King will never harm your daughter."

He would drag her away screaming, just like he had done with the last one.

Rats scattered as I walked. I glanced over my shoulder and saw him still standing there, his red hair illuminated by the faint light of a nearby streetlamp.

My damp hair fell heavily onto my neck as I approached the shrine, its golden petals glimmering in the moonlight.

Spouts of water flowed from its mouth. A jade sunflower atop it glowed in the darkness.

The flickering lights of the temple beckoned me closer. The sweet scent of summer drifted through the air along with the sound of worship, as if to pay homage to the power and abundance of eternal summer.

I stepped inside and the carved doors closed behind me.

Tall windows on either side of the room lit up the sacred space with their red and yellow glow.

I dug into my pocket, searching for a penny to drop into the fountain. Azair was not my God, but I wanted to pay my respects.

Today was a blessed day, and I was about to make use of all the blessings it had bestowed upon me.

A chill ran through my spine as a cold steel blade pressed against my throat.

"So, my little mouse," a man purred in my ear. "Is this how you plan on taking down the Summer King? You'll have to do better than that if you're going to get away with it."

The voice laughed mockingly, and the blade pressed harder into me.

"I'm warning you, one false move and it will be your last. Play your cards right if you want to survive this little game of yours."

My hand slowly inched its way toward my sleeve, my fingers brushing against the cold metal of a razor blade.

I hid it there for emergencies like this one, and now it was time to put it to use.

"I'm no mouse." My fingers wrapped around the hilt before slowly pressing the flat side against his groin. "Now, unless you want to become a eunuch, I suggest you back off. No more games."

I didn't want to use this weapon, but if push came to shove, I would do it without hesitation.

He held me tight by the neck with his blade, forcing me to stay still and silent.

A trickle of blood ran down my throat, the tip of the blade searing like hot coal.

The voice hissed in my ear. "You mortals think you can beat us with your pitiful weapons, but you forget your rules and laws do not control us." He laughed darkly, the blade still pressed firmly against my throat. "We are eternal and untouchable, and you are just a mere speck in our presence."

My heart beat faster, my breathing coming in short, ragged gasps.

Now, with the cold steel blade pressing against my throat, the intricate details of his cloak visible even in the dull light, I knew I was up against something more powerful than any mortal.

The immortal Fae.

Shit.

His hooded cloak was made of glimmersilk threads, each one intricately woven together to create a shimmering masterpiece.

My mistress possessed a single fan made of the same material which I had thought was beautiful, but this was something else entirely. The colors glowed in harmony and the threads moved in the light like a dance.

It was mesmerizing.

When the king visited her chambers, she would gracefully wave it in front of him, showing off her extravagance.

That fan was her most prized possession, and she kept it hidden away so that no one could steal it or tarnish its beauty.

Shit. Shit. Shit.

I clenched my jaw, unwilling to give him the satisfaction of seeing me cower. "Maybe so." Standing straight and tall, I held his gaze. "We mortals do not have the advantage of immortality, but we aren't bound by your rules and laws, either." The razor blade in my hand was a reminder of that.

The Fae's grip on my throat became tighter, and the sharp edge of the blade dug painfully into my flesh.

I swallowed hard, feeling his power pressing against me. But I refused to give in and instead stared him down.

Blood ran down my skin as his eyes studied me carefully. "Your little iron blade will not work on me," he said in a low and menacing tone. "Only Fae iron can pierce my skin. You can wave your petty weapon around all you want, but it will not help you in the slightest. Amusing, but ultimately pointless."

A chill ran down my spine as his words sunk in. How was I to defeat this Fae who seemed invincible and untouchable?

"Pray tell me," he said, his voice dripping with amusement. "How did you plan to murder the Summer King?"

I closed my eyes and took a deep breath. "I didn't plan to. But if I had, it would have been with something no one expects - a kind deed."

For a moment, he just stared at me, as if trying to understand what I had just said.

Dark hair peeked from beneath his hood, the only part of his face I could see.

I couldn't make out any other features, but it was clear that he was tall and muscular from his broad shoulders, silhouetted in the darkness.

"Explain yourself," he said, shaking his head and sheathing his blade.

"I never intended to harm your king." I watched him carefully, not sure if he was about to attack or retreat. "Lord Ralston laid his cards on the table; all I had to do was bluff my way into a royal fortune."

The hooded figure nodded slowly, as if understanding something he hadn't before.

He stared off into the distance. "Kindness can be a weapon too," he whispered. "A sharp one, at that. But your actions are contradictory. Why accept payment if you did not intend to fulfill the contract?"

I swallowed hard. "I have no intention of being another forgotten casualty in this city. Lord Ralston's offer seemed like my best way out."

"You must have a reason for such desperation."

Oh Badis, I thought bitterly. If only you had been a better husband, none of this would have happened.

Women were supposed to be cherished and protected, not cast aside like rubbish.

Not work abroad and leave their families behind. Not have to resort to desperate measures to survive.

"My father is a man of honor, if you can believe it. A strict man of a family that values reputation above all else and he taught me the importance of doing what's right, no matter the cost. I will not beg for mercy or lie about my motives. I will not be a coward or a disgrace to my family's name."

My voice cracked, but I forced myself to keep going.

"Honor doesn't put food on the table, and my father is too prideful to accept charity. I have no choice but to take matters into my own hands."

Please believe me.

He pulled his hood back, and it was as if the sun had suddenly burst through the sky.

His features were otherworldly perfect - his golden eyes shone like the stars, his chocolate brown hair tousled around his high cheekbones, and his skin glowed with a golden summery hue.

A thin scar traced the side of his eyebrow, giving him an air of ferocity and danger.

He was fierce and handsome, and something stirred within me I never experienced before.

Something primal, powerful, and irresistibly attractive.

The moment we locked eyes, I realized why he guarded the Fae king. A weapon of beauty so dangerous, it would take an entire kingdom to break it. No one could look upon him and remain unchanged.

Was this how the Fae entranced mortals?

If so, I understood why they were so feared - beauty could be just as powerful as any blade in their hands.

He smiled at me, his lips upturning into a wicked grin. Pointy white teeth peeked out from beneath, and my breath hitched in my throat.

The spell was broken as he bowed his head, and I was left with a strange feeling in the pit of my stomach.

"Your eyes dance with the fire of a thousand stars," I blurted out without thinking.

He looked up at me, an amused expression on his face. "Are you trying to flatter me?"

A faint blush rushed to my cheeks. "Maybe a little," I admitted.

"I am no star. I'm merely a humble servant of the Summer Court," he said darkly, his gaze never wavering. "Don't let my beauty distract you from the fact that any move against me will be met with extreme prejudice."

As if to punctuate his point, a bolt of lightning tore across the night sky, echoing in a thunderous roar.

Its power reverberated through me, and I shivered. "I understand."

He stepped forward, sizing me up, searching my face for any sign of weakness or betrayal.

I held his gaze, determined to show him I was not here to defy his lord, but to save my family from poverty.

He stepped closer, slowly and cautiously. He was so close I felt his breath on my skin. "Your loyalty is commendable."

"And you know the power of kindness."

He nodded, almost wistfully. "Perhaps there are more weapons in this world besides violence and money." He inclined his head. "I am intrigued. What was your strategy for outsmarting the mortal lord?"

I tilted my head back. "My plan is simple. There is a list of eligible brides and his daughter will be chosen in seven days. I intend to sneak away on one of the trading ships during the wedding ceremony and escape with the money."

"The royal guards will patrol the ships to make sure no one escapes."

"They are looking for runaway noble brides, not a kitchen maid. I can slip away unnoticed."

"There is still one more obstacle. He will know you are responsible for the theft. He will send his servants after you, and they won't stop until you are caught or dead."

I smiled, feeling more alive than I had in years. "They won't catch me. I'm resourceful and fast. Where do you think I learned to survive in the first place?"

He smiled and shook his head as if he was impressed despite himself. "I see you have some fire in your veins, after all."

His smile widened as his finger ran down the line of my neck in a gesture that was both intimidating and strangely endearing. A soothing warmth spread through my body, healing the sting.

"Now, let's see if you can outsmart an entire kingdom... or if you will become another forgotten casualty."

Before I could reply, he reached into his pocket and pulled out an exquisite gold bracelet with pearls adorning it.

He grabbed my wrist gently and placed the bracelet around it.

Goosebumps spread across my skin as his fingers brushed against me.

His hands lingered on my skin for a moment before he stepped away, a knowing look in his eyes. "A token of luck," he said softly. "May you find fortune on your journey."

I instinctively stepped back, not wanting to take something so valuable from him. "I cannot accept this."

The clasps snapped shut, and he patted my hand as if amused by my innocence. "Take it and keep it safe. I will retrieve it just before you leave Calan."

I stared at him, unable to comprehend what was happening.

What kind of game was he playing?

Dangerous or not, I needed to play along.

"Aren't we friends?" He smiled dangerously and brushed his fingers against mine, as if daring me to deny our newfound friendship. "And friends don't hand each other into the guards, do they? A little trinket to remember me by will have to do."

The gold alone was worth a fortune.

"If friendship is what you want, then I am happy to oblige," I said slowly, feeling as if I had been tricked into accepting his gift.

There was something about this whole situation that gave me an ominous feeling, like a bad omen that I should have heeded.

My mother's words echoed in my head - *'The Djinn always get their due.'*

This Fae Lord was no Djinn, but I feared that his power was just as dangerous.

Scheming and cunning, I didn't know what he was up to and something told me I should have begged for mercy. Begged for an escape from this madness.

But it was too late.

This strange game of chance had begun, and there was no turning back now. I only hoped the cost of playing wasn't more than I bargained for.

I sighed and tucked the bracelet into my pocket, accepting the consequence that came with taking something so precious and valuable. "You have my word." I swallowed hard. "I will keep it safe."

He gave me a long, appraising look before finally nodding. "Pearls of luck," he said, a slight smile playing on his lips. "Perhaps you'll need them."

He stepped back and bowed deeply.

"Good luck, Outlander. You'll need it." And with that, he turned and disappeared into the night as if he had never been there at all.

I shivered slightly as I remembered his words - keep it safe for me.

Did he mean the bracelet or something else?

two

HENNA HANDS, HEAVING HEARTS

Lemon juice and turmeric mixed as my sister painted intricate patterns on my palms with a brush.

"You're a fool," she muttered, shaking her head as she worked the henna into my skin. "Getting mixed up in the affairs of nobles will only lead to trouble."

Revelers in bright cotton whirled around us, their laughter and music mocking me. Their light hair and pale skin made my dark features stand out in the crowd, making me feel all the more out of place.

"What you're doing is dangerous." She finished up my henna and tied a ribbon around it. "You could end up in the dungeons, or worse, Zee."

Here I was trying to escape a life of servitude, and Salma was trying to stop me.

From beneath her kaftan, she pulled out a small mosaic tile on a hemp necklace. "This is from back home." She placed it in my hand and smiled sadly.

"Keep it close. It will remind you of the people who love and care for you."

My throat tightened. "Salma."

Her fiancé stepped forward, his brown eyes serious.

He leaned close. "My grandfather was a sailor," he said with a quiet intensity. "He used to tell me stories of smugglers and pirates. He said that the best way of escaping is to do it confidently."

I nodded, looking in front of me, understanding his point.

Lanterns hung from poles in the center of the square, their light casting an orange glow over the festivities. A man slushed beer from a barrel, while vendors hawked sweets and toys.

"You have a plan and you are brave," he said. "You may just make it out alive after all."

"I can't wait to go home," Salma said with a soft smile, her dark eyes twinkling as she looked at Aeric. "I think you will love the blue city by the sea."

Aeric smiled, his gaze softening as he looked at her. "I will love Almazigha, simply because you are there."

His arm tightened around her waist, and she blushed at his words.

I looked away, feeling a warmth spreading through my chest.

Even though I was about to embark on a dangerous mission, the love between them gave me hope for my future.

A husband who would love me like that, a home to call my own - all that was possible.

Just thinking of it made my chest tighten, and I swallowed hard.

Love was something I had given up on a long time ago, not believing that someone like me could ever be worthy of such a precious gift.

But now, I realized that deep down, I still yearned for it. That perhaps a love like Aeric and Salma's was something I deserved too.

Maybe one day, I'd find someone who loved me for who I was and wouldn't forget me when someone better showed up.

My heart ached for a love that I knew would never come but still wanted desperately.

Maybe it was time to make peace with the fact that some things were just not meant for me.

Salma looked up at me, her gaze softer than usual.

The affection I felt for my sister was undeniable. With her almond-shaped eyes, she looked like a younger version of myself.

Her long, dark hair was pulled back in a braid, framing her sharp features and olive-toned skin. I saw the same height and curved shape of our noses, the same arch eyebrows, and even the same crooked smile.

Even though she was nine years younger than me, she had a way about her that made her seem wise beyond her years.

"Just be careful, Zee," she said softly. "I want you to come back safe and sound so we can all reunite in Almazigha one day soon."

My heart swelled with emotion as I hugged her tightly, feeling a deep appreciation for my sister's love and support.

"My love follows you wherever you go. Farewell." I stepped back, blinking away tears. "Keep the coin hidden and kiss the children for me. Momma and Baba too."

She nodded, a hint of sadness creeping into her eyes. "I will remember your name until we meet again, my beloved sister." Standing on her toes, she kissed my forehead and stepped back. "May a thousand stars light your way."

Aeric placed his hand on mine, his grip firm and reassuring. "Go forth with the blessings of Azair's summer wind at your back. May we meet again."

I nodded, the lump in my throat making it hard to swallow.

I closed my fingers around the mosaic tile, as Aeric and Salma weaved their way through the square, the crowd parting around them.

The square was alive with music and laughter as couples spun around each other, faces lit up by the lanterns.

A powerful gust of wind blew in from the north, bringing with it the smell of unwashed bodies and smoked pork.

Aeric swept Salma into his arms, twirling her gracefully, as the sounds of drums and lutes filled the air.

The muddy ground was pocked with footprints, the dirt thrown up by dancing feet.

The people around the dance floor were all smiles and laughter, clapping along to the rhythm with their feet.

Children ran through the square playing games and chasing each other in circles, while mothers swayed gently with babies in their arms.

Why worry when the Summer King only wants noble brides?

But I knew better.

Behind the cheerful music was a truth that no one wanted to acknowledge. The Summer King was a cruel man who could take any woman he wanted. Regardless of their social status.

His madness resulted in the deaths of hundreds of brides, his desire for them extinguished just as quickly as it began.

My stomach churned as I thought of all the innocent lives that had been sacrificed on the altar of his appetite.

Prejudice and a disregard for human life were his trademarks. His selfishness and greed knew no bounds.

And the Calanian noblemen weren't any better, looking away from the injustices that occurred in their own backyard.

It was times like this when I wished I could do something, anything, to make a difference in this world.

But for now, all I could do was watch as Aeric and Salma danced together, oblivious to the world.

Goodbye, Salma. May we meet again.

Goosebumps ran down my arms as I felt someone's breath on my neck from behind, sending a shiver down my spine.

Startled, I whipped my head around — just in time to catch the faintest glimmer of bright gold eyes watching me from the shadows.

"Zareena, my friend! Come dance with me!"

A tall woman with wild blonde hair and bright blue eyes smiled widely at me. Her rosy cheeks were flushed from dancing around, serving drinks to the revelers.

"Marja!"

She handed the tankards off to a nearby patron and grabbed my hands, pulling me onto the dance floor.

"Come on," she said, spinning me around. "It's time to forget our worries and enjoy the night!"

The clang of drums and the twang of lutes filled the air with a cheerful tune as Marja twirled around me with grace, her yellow skirts swirling around her.

She was a natural dancer, moving with ease and a sense of joy that was contagious.

Soon, I felt myself relaxing into the music, my worries fading away as I embraced the moment.

We twirled and spun around the square, our feet barely touching the ground.

Marja had been my guide in Calan ever since I arrived. Not only did she teach me the ropes of Calanian society, but I could always count on her to make me laugh and help me forget my troubles.

As we twirled around the square, my sister and her fiancé slipped away from the edge of the dance floor.

Marja laughed loudly as she spun around me. "Look at those two!" She winked and then pointed to Aeric and Salma. "Pleasure awaits them tonight!"

"To be young and in love," I murmured, watching them as they disappeared into the night. "May they be happy forever."

Little did Marja know that this was all part of the plan; tonight would be the last night I would see Salma before she left for Almazigha.

My heart ached at the thought of not seeing her for a while, but I knew she would be safe in Aeric's care. He was a brave and honorable man. He would keep her safe and make sure she arrived home in one piece.

Swallowing my emotions, I grabbed Marja's hands and twirled her around, a grin spreading across my face. "A proper Calanian goodbye!"

She laughed and spun me around, our feet pounding against the ground with a steady rhythm. She twirled me around her gracefully, her skirts fanning out as we swayed.

With each turn, we moved faster and our laughter grew louder, echoing across the night sky.

Sweating, I waltzed to a stop, bowing my head in exhaustion and gratitude.

Marja smiled at me with joy in her eyes. "You are an excellent dancer! For a moment, I thought you were a Fae straight from the Otherworld!"

I smiled, panting softly. The obsession Calanians had with the elusive Fae was something I could never understand.

Why did they have to seek escape in the Otherworld, when right here on earth was an entire kingdom of beauty and enchantment?

My people had no need for the Djinn, preferring to seek solace in the beauty of our own lands. It was a peaceful way of life, free from worries and strife.

Why then did Calanians seek escape in another world?

The answer eluded me, as it had so many times before. Glorifying the Fae had only brought them pain, and yet they persisted in their belief.

A loud commotion erupted from the side of the square.

I stiffened beside Marja, my heart pounding in alarm as a group of guardsmen menacingly pushed their way through the crowd.

Heavy iron shoes sunk deep into the mud as they grabbed a nearby reveler and shoved him to the ground.

Marja's grip on my hand tightened. "It's time to go."

Both of us ducked our heads, scurrying away from the group as quickly as we could.

A tug on my braid made me spin around.

A guard had grabbed it, a sneer on his face. "Where do you think you're going?"

Wincing, I tried to twist out of his grip. But he was too strong and the pain of his fingers pulling tightly on my hair was unbearable.

"Let go of me!" I shouted, struggling to free myself.

Marja trembled beside me. "Please," she begged. "Forgive us. We were just leaving."

The guard snorted derisively and yanked on my braid again, a bored gleam in his eye. "Move along unless you want to join your friend in the dungeons."

"Dungeons?" Marja paled as she stared at me wide-eyed.

The terror in her expression only made my heart race faster. "Go." I pushed her away gently. "I'll be alright."

I cast one last look at her, silently thanking her for all she'd done for me. Loyal friends like her were rare in this world.

She hesitated for a moment before turning and running away, leaving me alone with the guardsman.

The guard grunted and pushed me towards the edge of the square. "Move!"

My stomach twisted in fear as I stumbled along after him.

All around us, people whispered and averted their gazes, afraid of getting involved.

The guard released my braid and grabbed his sword hilt menacingly. "Now, what do you have to say about this?"

"I was just leaving the celebration." I trembled, looking down. "I didn't commit any crimes."

Don't make eye contact. It will only make him angrier.

The guard snorted and stepped closer, his sword rattling against its scabbard. "That's what they all say." He sneered and leaned closer. "You think you can get away with anything in this world? Not here! This is the King's city, and by the Sun God, we will uphold justice!"

He reached down and grabbed my wrists, clamping a set of cold iron chains around them.

A larger guardsman stepped forward and grabbed me roughly by the arm, dragging me away. Roughly shoving a gag in my mouth, he pulled a burlap sack over my head, the smell of pig shit filling my nostrils.

Shackled and gagged, the guardsmen dragged me away, my feet barely touching the ground, the weight of the manacles oppressively heavy on my wrists.

I thought of my family and homeland. Places that I would never see again.

The tangy smell of oranges, the laughter of my siblings, the whisper of the wind through the palm trees—all of it seemed so far away now.

The blue city of Almazigha slowly disappeared into the distance as they dragged me to my fate.

Salma.

Salma had been my last hope, and I knew I made the right decision.

The heavy iron cuffs around my wrists made the knowledge that my sister would save our family feel empty and hollow.

What would become of me now? Where were they taking me?

The loud screeching of rusty hinges filled the air as the guardsmen pushed open a thick wooden door.

My stomach sank as I heard voices; people shouted in terror, making me wonder what was happening on the other side.

As they dragged me through the corridors, whispers and hushed mumbling followed us until, finally, the guardsmen stopped.

The ominous sound of metal clanging against stone made my heart stop in fear.

Roughly thrown inside onto the cold jagged floor, a guardsman slammed the door shut with a loud thud.

My throat tightened as I heard bolts locking in place, sealing me inside. The sack was pulled away from my head, and I blinked, finding a large stone chamber lit by torches.

The walls were adorned with tapestries of ancient battles, and shelves lined the walls, filled with ancient weapons.

Not a dungeon, I thought. The royal prison.

Kneeling in the center of the room were two hooded figures, their faces partially hidden in shadow.

The silks of their robes were embroidered with a symbol I recognized—a symbol of power.

The royal family crest. Sunflowers encircled a single golden sun, the mark of the Calanian royal family.

Only blood royals could wear that symbol.

What were they doing here? And why had I been brought before them?

"Well, well, look who it is." Gold shoes stepped forward and a melodic voice filled the room. "My little mouse has returned."

three

Silver Chains, Golden Boons

"What, no witty retort? No smart quips? I'm disappointed."

His golden eyes were still the same, but everything else about him had changed.

His dark hair draped around his face, reaching down to his broad shoulders, and a crown of delicate antlers adorned his head.

He was decadent royalty at its worst, a symbol of everything that was wrong with the world, and he was here, sneering down on me.

He was no longer a weapon of beauty - he became the embodiment of it.

Seeing him in all his glory took my breath away.

He shed the guise of a guardsman and revealed his true form, a being of immeasurable power.

The Summer King.

His smirk returned, only this time it was more playful than before, as if he knew the secrets of all eternity and was daring me to discover them.

Why did he present himself like a guard before? Why the mystery?

Unless... he was watching me, testing me to see if I could penetrate his disguise.

The mortal guardsman removed my gag.

The realization that I was going to die hit me hard. I had been so close to freedom, only to be pulled back in by the sardonic glare of this strange creature.

No, I would not die begging or cowering. I would face this creature head-on and die with my head held high.

Swallowing hard, I looked up and met his gaze. "I was about to say the same of you," I said in a firm voice. "You don't look like much without your disguise. The King of Summer? More like the King of False Appearances."

The shackles binding my wrists chafed against the cold floor as I waited for his response.

He took a step closer, his nose wrinkling slightly in disgust as the smell of pig shit filled the room.

"Ah, but that's why I like you so much. You always have something to say."

"Why have I been brought here, Your Highness?" I asked.

His lips curled into a cold smirk, and he stepped even closer.

The torchlight glinted off his skin, highlighting the golden tones that pulsed beneath his skin.

"You can try to hide it, but you carry yourself like royalty. A peasant's body, but a queen's heart. I think that suits you well. It will help in the days to come."

Was he planning something? What did he mean by "the days to come"?

Why was he calling me a queen? I had no royal lineage, no claim to power or wealth. Only a small family that was struggling to survive.

As I tried to make sense of it all, a shiver ran down my spine. Maybe some rumors were true—maybe he was mad.

His eyes shifted—a wild glint that was almost animalistic in its intensity.

At that moment, I truly feared for my life.

He seemed to talk more to himself than me, as though he was inventing a future as we spoke. A future that I had no plans to be a part of.

"You can call me a queen, but I know my place in the world and it's not as far away from the peasants as you'd like to think."

My cheeks flushed as I realized what I'd said. I was too frightened and exhausted to think straight.

He cocked his head to the side and studied me for a few moments, something strange flashing behind his eyes.

Kneel before the King. Kneel and obey. A voice in my head urged me to demean myself, to bow down and submit.

I fought against it, my body growing tense as I resisted the urge.

The others in the room were frozen in place, their eyes looking down and never meeting his gaze.

They never questioned. They never spoke.

Proud mortal royals succumbing to the will of a Fae king. How far we had fallen.

The Summer King stepped closer and gave a small chuckle, as if he could read my thoughts.

He slowly paced the room, his robes trailing behind him. "My subjects seem to be rather well-behaved today. They know better than to look upon me without my permission."

His eyes lingered on mine for a moment.

He was challenging me.

Test me, he seemed to say. Dare to challenge the Fae king.

The others shuffled uncomfortably, and I heard a few gasps of disbelief.

The oppressive tension in the room was suffocating, and beads of sweat formed on my forehead.

I stared at him, refusing to look away.

He arched an eyebrow, and his lips twitched in amusement.

His piercing gaze had me on edge, like he was searching for something that I was not sure I wanted to relinquish.

Heat swelled and crawled up my body as if the sun was trying to smother me. An invisible hand gripped my neck tightly, trying its best to force me to kneel and look away.

I struggled against it, my body shaking as I tried desperately not to succumb to it.

Honor your King. Obey without question.

I heard this over and over.

My knees trembled, and my breath came in ragged gasps. I was so close to breaking, so close to submitting.

Honor your King. Obey without question.

I wouldn't kneel. Not now, never.

The room seemed to shrink as he appraised me with a strange intensity, and I fought against the urge to cower.

Slowly, he stepped back and smiled. A genuine smile, one that reached his eyes and lit up the room.

"So brave, so unpredictable. I like that about you. Your arrogance and your lack of submission." He stepped closer until he was standing mere inches away from me, his voice dropping to a whisper. "Never forget who you are."

"Pervert. Murderer. Monster." The words slipped out of my mouth before I could stop them.

He didn't flinch or look away. "You will never know what I am capable of," he breathed. "And you should be grateful for that. For yes, I'm all those things. But I'm also so much more. Summer King, protector of the realm, keeper of the ancient laws. Call me what you will, but never forget that I am the one who holds your fate in my hands."

He gestured for me to stand and I rose to my feet. The chains binding my wrists clanked, and I winced in pain.

"Your reign might extend far and wide, but your authority over me does not," I said, unable to keep the bitterness out of my voice. The lies rolling off my tongue tasted like poison. "You will never own me."

He cocked his head to one side and studied me for a few moments. "It will surprise you what I can accomplish, even from far away."

There was something in his voice that made me shiver, and I looked away quickly.

"Summer reaches far and wide, my dear. It is a power that cannot be contained."

I desperately tried to think of a way out of this mess. Never in my wildest dreams did I expect the Summer King himself to intervene in my scam.

I cursed my stupidity — if I had known the Fae could interfere, I never would have tried to scam Lord

Ralston. Only a fool would take on one of the most powerful beings in the world.

I had no choice but to face this Fae king's wrath and hope that he would offer me some kind of mercy, however slight it may be.

The chains clinked as they shifted with the movement, and I winced as pain shot through my wrists.

He took a step forward, and I could smell the sweet scent of summer on his breath. It was almost overwhelming, a hint of sweetness, like honeysuckle in bloom.

He reached out and gently touched my arm, his thumb running along the length of it before coming to rest on my wrist.

I tensed as he unclasped the chains, feeling the warmth of his touch as he freed me from my shackles.

"You question me far too much for a mortal that bleeds so easily."

The others in the room looked down, too afraid to meet his gaze.

"It must be difficult to rule a kingdom when all you can do is kill."

He spun around and my heart skipped a beat. I had pushed him too far this time.

"There is more to ruling a kingdom than just killing."

He ran the back of his finger along my cheek, and I shuddered at the wave of warmth that raced through me.

"My power lies in understanding my people. For me to lead, I must be able to see through their eyes and into their hearts. Knowing when it's best to be merciful, and less so." The gold of his eyes glowed in the dimly lit room as he looked at me. "You are to be my wife. You are to be my queen."

Blood rushed to my face.

I was to be a sacrifice to the altar of his insanity.

Blood-soaked robes, a crown of terror, the nightmarish shouts of dead brides long gone.

All of this was to be my future, the fate I had been chosen for.

But why? What was his purpose?

I couldn't imagine what he saw in me that made him pick me to be his latest victim.

Only noble brides had been chosen before me, daughters of powerful families from all across the Calanian Empire.

What made me so special that I was deemed worthy to be his bride?

Rumors flew around the kingdom about why this had happened. Some said that it was a curse laid upon him by an enemy of his long ago, others that he had done it for some kind of twisted pleasure.

A few even suggested that he was looking for something specific, some kind of secret hidden in the souls of these young women that only he could uncover.

Whatever his reason, I knew one thing: that I would not differ from all those who came before me. That this time too, this Summer King's reign would bring death.

But this time it wouldn't be just another victim; it would be me. A stupid girl with foolish dreams of freedom.

"A wife? How intriguingly unconventional," I said, my voice shaking, as I carefully tried to mask my fear. "Am I supposed to be grateful? What makes you think I would agree to this union?"

The Summer King's expression shifted subtly. "Your sister looks a lot like you." A sphere of light appeared in his hand, showing my sister and Aeric on a trading ship.

My breath caught in my throat as I watched the scene unfold before me: Aeric bartering with a merchant for supplies while my sister patiently waited by his side. Her green kaftan was a stark contrast against the dull colors of the merchant's wares.

My heart thudded in my chest as I realized what he was implying. That it would be all too easy for him to take her away from me if I refused his offer.

It was a subtle threat and one that I had no choice but to acknowledge.

I looked up at him, my expression carefully controlled. "I understand. But I've been wedded before, my lord. I'm not sure how you'd feel about a ruined bride."

An abandoned wife was a blight in the eyes of many, and I knew that this alone could be my salvation.

Please don't take her away. Please, please.

But the Summer King only smiled and shook his head. "Ruin brings a certain beauty, one that I find utterly captivating. Not a ruined bride, no. A bride who has seen the world and tasted its sorrows and joys. That is what I seek in a wife."

I nodded slowly, my throat tight with emotion. "How could I refuse?"

My mother's smile, the way my father's eyes lit up when he saw me, my siblings' laughter, all flashed before my eyes.

I had to protect them, and this was the only way.

The Summer King smiled, his lips stretching into a satisfied grin as he gently brushed his knuckles against my cheek. "Good girl."

He stepped away, and the world seemed to shift back into place.

The servants regained their composure, and the hooded figures bowed their heads in deference. The gold rings on their fingers glinted in the dim light as they moved around, shuffling and murmuring.

"Fortunately for us both, I don't have to resort to harsher tactics. You already agreed."

Reaching into his pocket, he pulled out a delicate gold band secured by two pearl charms.

With gentle movements, he grabbed my wrist and carefully placed it around me. He then snapped the clasp shut with ease, holding my gaze as he did so.

"Your token of allegiance." He traced his finger along the bracelet before looking deep into my eyes. "You accepted."

For a moment, I could not think or speak.

It was the same bracelet I buried deep under the ground in a hole so no one could steal it. That bracelet he tricked me into accepting.

The pearls glimmered in the light as if they were laughing at me for my foolishness.

But then, something inside me stirred - a tiny flame of defiance. "You tricked me."

"Tricked you?" He cocked his head and raised an eyebrow. "Little mouse, I have done nothing of the sort. You chose me."

The urge to scream grew stronger, yet I remained silent and composed.

Breathing slowly, I looked away and nodded in agreement. "Is that what power means to you? To take whatever you want?"

He stared at me for a few long moments, his eyes unreadable. "Power is so much more than that."

His voice was soft like velvet as he looked away and stepped back, giving me some space to think.

"It's something greater—a responsibility to be respected, guarded, and cherished. Power can change the world for either better or worse; it can build empires or destroy them in an instant. It is a delicate force that needs to be handled with care."

My gaze shifted from him to the bracelet on my wrist.

Controlled. Manipulable.

He took away my choice and made his own terms, binding me with an oath that could never be broken. But even oaths had gray areas.

Now, it was up to me to use those to my advantage.

"Deals can be renegotiated," I said slowly, deciding how I wanted to play this game. "Power can be used for more than just taking things."

He raised an eyebrow and cocked his head. "What else can you do with it?"

I stepped closer, my gaze never faltering. "Build trust," I said firmly. "Earn loyalty. Create something greater than yourself."

He stared at me for a few moments, and then a slow smile spread across his face. "I have chosen well. Our shared ability to deceit and manipulate could prove interesting in our marriage. It could even be fun. You are right. Power is not just about taking what you want, but also the ability to protect those who deserve it."

"Am I undeserving of your protection? As your wife, will I be treated as nothing more than a possession?"

"Are you not still alive?"

His eyes blazed with an intensity that made me take a step back.

"Then I must be protecting you in some way, shape, or form. Mice do not survive in the wild for very long."

Each word felt like a hammer pounding away at my will and pride until only bloodied shards remained.

Was this what the Summer King wanted? To trap me in his kingdom with an unbreakable bond before he slaughtered me?

But I knew he was right. Power was a game, and sometimes you had to play it if you wanted to survive.

Images of the poor girl who had been found hanging in the town square filled my mind and I shuddered.

Her silk dress torn and her face pale and lifeless as crows picked at her body. The stench of rotting flesh and desperation lingered in the air around the area for days.

I didn't want to be like her. I wouldn't be like her.

This marriage would happen whether or not I liked it, and if I was going to die, I might as well make sure that his power would save others in the future.

Mercy from a Fae felt like a dream, a beautiful hope that seemed too good to be true and was unlikely ever to be realized.

"I accept your proposal," I said solemnly. "But there is something that I need from you in return."

My culture did not require a dowry, instead, it was tradition for grooms to provide a bride's price. A sum of coins or goods meant to give a bride security and prosperity in marriage.

I wanted something from him in return. Gold coins and jewelry be damned. I had something else in mind. A promise that he could not break.

Delight spread across his face as he recognized my request. "Name your price, little mouse."

"As your bride, I want what is owed to me."

He stared at me in silence, his gaze penetrating my soul as if he could see the depths of my heart.

A true gentleman would provide a bride's price to his intended, and I had every expectation that this king would adhere to tradition.

Despite their manipulative tendencies, the Fae still held close to their values. Marriage was a sacred vow and the Summer King wouldn't take mine lightly.

Murdering a bride was one thing, but breaking a vow? That would be an act punishable by death.

Rules and contracts were sacred to the Fae, and while they could be bent or broken in certain circumstances, marriage contracts were set in stone.

The Fae held marriage in high regard, and the Summer King would do everything in his power to uphold this unspoken law.

I just had to make sure I was the one who wrote the rules of our contract.

Gold eyes glinted in the light as he nodded his head. "Greedy little thing, aren't you? Name your price."

"No bargain will be struck without a bride's price that is fit for the Queen of the Summer Fae."

Twitching his lip, the Summer King nodded slowly. "You are to be queen of the most powerful nation in the realm, and you will be well provided for. What more could you possibly ask for?"

In his eyes, he almost begged me to make a request.

Despite his arrogance and strength, he wanted my approval, and I had every intention of using that to my advantage.

Stepping forward, I cocked my head. "Boons."

Low laughter vibrated from his broad chest. "You want boons?"

His cheekbones were prominent, and his face held a mischievous glimmer.

"Greed and power, what a deadly combination. Three boons, my little mouse. That is your bride's price. Three boons dripping with the power of my kingdom."

I raised an eyebrow. "What are the limits of your generosity? What boons can you grant me? And how do I know they will be honored?"

"My boons are only limited by your imagination. You can ask for anything, and if I can give it to you, I will do so. But," he said, his voice taking on an almost sad edge, "you cannot use my boons to save your life."

My heart plummeted as my eyes widened. I had expected as much, but to hear him say it aloud made it so much more real.

"Your generosity is appreciated," I said, although my voice faltered slightly.

He clasped his hands together and gave me a slow, almost regal bow. "You can't save yourself, but you can still help others in need. Those are my terms, and I will honor them as long as I live."

I nodded slowly, understanding finally dawning on me. Despite his reputation as a ruthless ruler, the Summer King offered me a kindness that went beyond material wealth.

He gave me the hope of saving others, even if I couldn't save myself.

The warmth of gratitude swelled within my chest. Then it was gone, replaced by the icy chill of fear as I realized what this meant for my future.

Death.

I bowed my head in deference, accepting his terms and the ultimate fate it would bring upon me. "My King, I accept your proposal."

He cupped my chin with one hand, lifting my face until our eyes met. "You know, this fake cordiality doesn't suit you. Your power lies in standing up for yourself and demanding what you want. Demand, my little mouse."

The coolness of his fingers on my skin sent a shiver down my spine, but I forced myself not to show it.

He may offer me boons and kindness, but he was still a Fae king. And kings could never truly be trusted. Not this one, not any of them.

"I will remember that," I said, bowing my head again. "May your bride's price be a reminder of your generosity, and may you never forget what it truly means."

For I wouldn't. Never.

He nodded once, solemnly. Then, with a wave of his hand, the room became still and silent as if we were the only two people in the world.

"What is it you desire? Power over your enemies? Riches beyond compare? Or maybe just one night with me?"

four

BOUDROMOS

"I'm sure you think spending a night with you would be a gift," I said coolly. "But I want something more lasting than that."

The corner of his eyes crinkled and his lips curved into a wide smile that lit up the entire room. He looked genuinely pleased with my refusal, as if it was something he expected all along.

"Nights with me are for lovers. What you want is something grander. Tell me, little mouse, what is it you truly desire?" He leaned in, the warmth of his breath tickling my ear. "A woman's power is in her desires. I want to know what truly drives you."

His breath against my neck sent a shiver through me, and I stepped away.

Allurement and manipulation were two of his most powerful tools, poisons that he used to twist the desires and thoughts of others.

Be careful. You don't want to be caught in his trap. The Fae are clever and devious, but you must be wiser. Don't let your curiosity get the best of you.

The Summer King stepped forward. "Remember, your existence hinges upon tasting what I hold in my hand."

Before I could ask what he meant or what was going on, strange music played from unseen sources. It came from everywhere at once, emanating from the very air around us.

Strings sang in a wild melody, a deep bass drum provided an intimidating beat while horns and flutes entwined in a beautiful chaos.

It was both strange and familiar, as if I could dimly remember it from some distant dream.

The Summer King danced, spinning me around in a dizzying waltz.

Fireflies swirled around us, a dazzling array of lights that illuminated the dark hall.

I followed his lead effortlessly, as if we had danced together countless times before.

He twirled us through the air, his feet barely touching the stone floor beneath us.

As we moved, the world changed, and the seasons shifted, even though it was still early spring. Summer blossoms bloomed in our wake, and the scent of honeysuckle and wild roses hung in the air.

We moved faster and faster, until I no longer felt like myself, my mind free and filled with wildness.

Heat engulfed me like a raging inferno, my skin tingling as if it were on fire.

Gripping my shoulders, the Summer King held a blue-tinged fruit in front of my mouth. It glowed with an unearthly light.

It pulsed.

"Taste this fruit. The fate of your future rests upon it," he commanded, and his voice changed.

Older. Deeper. Ancient. A voice that spoke of millennia and the secrets of Fae.

My screams echoed off the walls as I tried to resist, but his grip was firm.

"Taste it. This is the only way you can reclaim your freedom and your power."

A sweet, honeyed liquid trickled down my throat, and my mouth filled with a strange energy that coursed through my veins.

The sweetness was so intense that it almost burned through me. As if every cell in my body was remade.

The unbearable heat evaporated in an instant, leaving me feeling strangely refreshed.

Awe rose in my throat as I beheld the breathtaking sight before me.

An extravagant city built on six islands connected by golden bridges and waterways glittered before me.

Red jade walls sparkled in the sunlight, and glass towers stretched their spires towards the heavens. Jewels adorned every building, radiating a richness and luxury that was nearly overwhelming.

He released me from his grip and stepped back, a satisfied smile on his lips. "Welcome to Garnet Isles, wife." His thumb slowly went down my cheek as heat raced through my veins. "Be prepared to be spoiled beyond your wildest dreams."

The music lingered in the air, but now it was wilder, louder, and more alive.

Slammed by a wave of inferno, I looked down.

The smell of pig shit had been replaced with the musky scent of jasmine, and the simple kaftan I was wearing had been replaced with a luxurious kaftan of gold and silver.

My diamond-studded wrists and elaborate braids sparkled in the light, while my hands were decorated with a golden, intricate henna.

I was still me, but I felt as if something from another world had been woven into my very being - a sensation that made me tremble.

His dark hair shimmered in the molten light, a stark contrast to his sun-bronzed skin, as he smiled. "Your first boon, what shall it be?"

The possibilities ran through my head, and I knew I had to decide. I thought of the people who depended on me.

There was only one choice.

One thing that coin couldn't buy, and no amount of power would grant me.

I allowed myself a moment to steady my nerves. "My initial plea is small. Your word, King of Summer, that no harm or misfortune will come to my loved ones in you or your court's name."

Gold eyes flashed in the torchlight as he looked at me. "You believe I would harm them?" he asked, his voice taking on a frosty edge.

I thought back to the stories Marja told me about the Fae. Stories of cunning tricksters, of beauty tainted by cruelty, and a wildness that could turn even the most innocent soul into prey.

I was standing before such a creature now, and my throat felt dry.

Should I lie? Could I even keep up the charade if I did? I had heard stories of the Fae's uncanny ability to smell out untruths.

Shivers ran down my spine, and I took a deep breath.

No, honesty was the only way to stay safe. I had to remain as close to the truth as possible. To protect myself and my family.

"You have threatened my sister and are now forcing me to marry you. What else am I supposed to think?" I said carefully, watching his expression closely. "No one else needs to suffer because of this arrangement. Please, grant me this boon."

The Summer King held my gaze for a long moment. Then he sighed and stepped away, the coldness gone from his expression.

"I grant your request. As long as I live and reign, no harm will come to yours on my behalf."

He reached out and gently touched my henna-stained hands. His long, elegant fingers danced lightly over my skin as if he were trying to memorize the shape of them.

His touch was soothing, and the sight of my name—*Zareena*—carefully drawn in intricate swirls on my skin, was a small reminder of the future I longed for but never would have.

I grieved for what could have been. For the life that would now forever be denied to me.

Beloved. Wife. Mother.

Everything I wanted, and yet far beyond my reach.

Tenderly, he brushed a single tear from my face. "Your name will be remembered, even after you are gone."

I swallowed hard. "How do you know my name?"

"I know you, Zareena." He kept his gaze fixed on me, not blinking or looking away. "I know your dreams, your fears, and the battles you fight every day."

I pursed my lips. "You may think you understand me, but that doesn't mean you actually do."

For what did a Fae king know about human struggles? What could he possibly understand about the strength it took to keep going when life kept taking away everything you had?

Something in his gaze shifted. It was subtle, almost unnoticeable, but I saw it. Calculating, assessing, understanding.

He gestured to one of the golden bridges with a flourish. "Come. There is still much to see here."

It was a bridge of terror and beauty, of magic and dreams.

Gold and silver shimmered from the walls and arches, creating an intricate web of patterns that could take one's breath away.

But the height of the bridge, and my fear of heights, made me hesitate.

The bridge was eerily silent and, even though it glowed brightly, a darkness emanated from it. I saw something squirming there, something that made my skin crawl.

Snakes, I realized with a shudder. Hundreds of them, writhing in and out of the gold and silver threads.

He smiled knowingly. "Do not be afraid. This is a safety measure, of sorts. Those who are unworthy will die here."

My feet felt as if they were rooted to the ground and my breath came in shallow gasps. Was I really about to take that first step?

I wanted nothing more than to turn around and run away from this place. But where would I run? I had nowhere to go.

Taking a deep breath, I took that first step onto the bridge. The moment my foot touched the ground, an earthquake shook the Garnet Isles and thunder roared around me.

For a split second, I feared that the bridge would collapse underneath me. But then it was still again.

The Summer King now stood right beside me, his breath hot on my neck. "Your second boon, Zareena. Name it."

For a moment, I hesitated. What could I possibly ask of him? This creature, so powerful and distant from my own struggles, yet so attuned to the needs of those around him.

The wind whistled in my ears and my stomach twisted as I looked down. The bridge seemed to stretch on for eternity, yet it was barely a few steps wide.

Far below me, the ground shimmered like a pool of molten gold.

Fear flooded through me, and my grip tightened around the handrail as I took another step forward.

My head spun as everything around me turned into a hazy blur.

Sensing my fear, he placed a steadying hand on my shoulder. "Courage, Zareena. You can do this."

His voice was soft yet firm, and it soothed the panic that had taken hold of me.

I took another step forward, focusing on the steady warmth of his hand. "Your word," I said slowly as an idea took shape in my mind, "that no one, except for noble Calanian women, may be chosen as your brides from this day forward."

He cocked his head, his gaze settling on my lips. "The intent behind your second boon is commendable. Titles or bloodlines do not always define nobility." His throat bobbed ever so slightly as he swallowed. "I accept and will honor this wish."

No more would peasants and foreigners be sacrificed to appease the Fae king. Instead, only noble Calanian women would be chosen to share his bed.

I had done what I could to protect those who couldn't protect themselves.

The nobles wouldn't be able to sacrifice the rabble to save their own. Because they would, when they found out I was the newest bride.

Opening my mouth to thank him, I hesitated. For a moment in time, something wild and ancient saw the beauty in my plight and *chose* to protect it.

I bowed my head, not trusting myself to speak. Snakes slithered beneath my feet, their scales making a soft shushing sound as they moved.

My gaze raked over him as he turned away.

His shoulders slumped, and the slight tremble of his hands belied his composure.

The iron-clad facade of a powerful figure crumbled in front of me, exposing the vulnerable beneath.

Mortal.

He seemed so broken, so fragile, that I almost forgot who he was — the monstrous being whose threats had landed me here and whose power might destroy my family.

On this bridge of fear, he had shown me a glimpse of kindness.

Despite everything that had happened, I couldn't help but feel sympathetic towards him. He was the Fae king, but he was also a man.

I knew that whatever sadness he felt in that moment had nothing to do with me and everything to do with his own sorrow.

Maybe there was hope yet, a faint glimmer of possibility in the darkness. Maybe he wasn't just a beast or monster, maybe, underneath it all, he was a man too.

But as he turned back to me, all traces of emotion were gone and his face once again wore a mask of rigid indifference.

My breath caught in my throat, for even if the illusion had been fleeting, it was one that would stay with me forever.

The Summer King had a heart. It was just hidden behind the many masks he wore to protect himself from the world.

Or was it part of his manipulation? Was this bridge of terror and beauty a way for him to lure me in? To make me think I could trust him?

It didn't matter. He had given me my boon and the safety of my family was assured. I had done what I needed to do.

We took careful steps as we walked across the bridge.

Every few feet, I felt a shudder rumble through the structure as more and more snakes slithered beneath our feet.

The cracks between the stones grew larger, until finally, there was an unmistakable hole in the center of it all.

Tentatively, I peered down into the darkness, my heart thudding in my chest as I saw the bottomless abyss beneath us.

My palms were slick with sweat, and my legs trembled with fear.

There seemed to be no end, just a never-ending darkness.

A chill ran up my spine as I realized that if I took one wrong step, the chasm would swallow me whole.

"Walk," he commanded, his voice echoing through the void. "Fall and you will not escape the snakes."

Snakes twirled in and out of the crevices, their tongues flickering in the darkness.

Fear gnawed at my heart as I forced myself to take one shaky step after another, knowing if I faltered, I would be lost forever.

My eyes never left the Summer King as we walked across the bridge, and with each step I took, his gaze seemed to grow more intense.

It was almost as if he were daring me to step wrong or falter.

"Now, what is your third boon? Surely you must want something for yourself?"

I bit my lip, considering the distinct possibilities.

A part of me wanted something spectacular. Something impossible for anyone to offer. But what would be the point of that?

Hollow dreams could never take the place of reality. And I had a feeling that nothing, not even a king's power, could give me what I truly desired.

"Will I not be the queen of the most powerful and wealthiest kingdom? Surely that would be enough to satisfy me? As for freedom," I murmured to myself, the word freedom carrying a weight of desire, "I have come to terms with the fact that my fate was sealed the moment our eyes met. For now, I'll leave my third boon unspoken. I am content with what I have already asked for."

A mirthless smile crossed his lips. "I accept your demands. However, you will need to pay a price for the blessings I granted you. As is tradition in Calan, every woman who seeks to marry me must offer me a dowry. I require a boon from you as well."

My hubris at making a demand now came back to haunt me. It had blinded me to the potential consequences, and now I was left to pay the price.

Gold stones turned to white sand beneath my feet as I hung my head in defeat. "What is the price of my requests?"

For Fae tradition dictated that a price must be paid, and in this, I was no exception.

He stepped closer, the warmth of his breath on my neck. "Look into my soul, for that is what I wish to know. What do you see in me?"

The intensity of his stare sent shivers down my spine as power emanated from him. A strange, invisible force barely contained in his gaze.

Swallowing my fear, I nodded my head in agreement. "As you wish."

The Summer King smiled, satisfied with my response. He stepped back, giving me a moment to collect myself.

Demanding. Ancient. Powerful. Wild. I saw all these things in him, and something more, too. A hint of something that I could not quite put my finger on, but that was oddly familiar to me.

The sensation made my heart ache, for I knew this feeling.

"I once attempted to nurse a soldier back to health who had been struck by illness. He spoke a language I could not understand, but he seemed to find comfort in me being there."

I looked away from his intense gaze. Despite the fear that coursed through me, I could not stop my words.

"In the end, he died with his hand in mine. I was helpless to save him, and yet he still chose me as his last grasp of life. His last breath spoke of me as if I were something abhorrent, one single word in his native tongue. Boudromos. Devil."

A deep rumble vibrated from his chest.

My body was telling me to run, but my feet refused to budge.

Jade walls materialized around us, pushing out the edge of darkness and enveloping us in a chaotic beauty.

Pleasure swirled in my veins as music poured from somewhere unseen, its cadence both familiar and foreign at the same time.

Houses of gold glimmered in the distance, and colorful creatures flew above us, blinking in and out of existence as we passed.

"I hoped that by granting you the three boons, I could prove to you I'm not a monster," he said, with a hint of bitterness in his voice. "Do not think for one moment that I am the villain in this story."

Wife killer. Terror. Misery. Despair. Fury. All these words rushed to my mind as I thought of him.

The blood on his hands, the torment embedded in his soul - it all seemed so obvious, yet he wanted to deny it completely.

No matter what secrets lay hidden behind those eyes, no matter what pain he felt and chose not to show, a man who murdered brides after a single day was still a monster.

He was a danger to all those around him, and to think he could ever be anything else was naïve.

But I saw something else, too. A hint of humanity in his eyes, and an underlying vulnerability that made me want to believe the impossible.

Perhaps there was something more to this Summer King than what meets the eye.

"Did I imply such a thing?" I arched an eyebrow. "What I told you is an example of how so often tragedy can come from misunderstanding. We judge one another without truly knowing each other. If I am the soldier, then you are the unknown and I cannot see your soul. Only glimpses of your true nature can be seen, but nothing more."

He shifted his weight back, the hard edge of accusation fading from his gaze. "Your story has given me enough insight to know what sort of person you are. I think you know what must happen now."

"When will it take place?"

A faint smile played on his lips as he took my hands in his. "It already did. The moment you tasted the fruit of the Summer Tree."

"The other brides?"

He shrugged nonchalantly. "They will not bother us anymore. I have seen to that."

A chill ran down my spine as I looked into his eyes, and I wondered if this was what it truly meant to be face-to-face with the Boudromos.

The soldier's last word echoed hauntingly in my mind. Was he right? Was I really the devil in this situation?

"Do you usually dress your victims in finery before killing them? Do you take pleasure in their pain?"

The Summer King's mouth curved into a cruel smile. "No. But then again, you are no ordinary victim. You are my wife now and deserve the finest things in life."

He brought my hand up to his lips and kissed the tips of my fingers.

"I eagerly await our reunion in three days for dinner."

My nose scrunched up. "And what, pray tell, is the purpose of this unusual generosity? What have I done to deserve such a grand gift?"

"Killing a wife every day?" His lips twisted into a sardonic smile. "Such a chore for a Summer King. Time runs differently in my realm. You will understand. In my court, everything has a purpose. Even you."

My mouth opened and closed again. "What purpose could I possibly have?"

He brushed my cheek with the back of his hand. "That I took the trouble to select you myself should be considered a compliment. You possess something I need, something valuable."

His gold eyes shimmered as he looked into my soul. It was like he could see everything that I was and all the things I would become.

"And with that, I give you the chance to be a part of something bigger than yourself. To make your mark on the world."

"What do you mean?" I asked cautiously.

He grinned, pointy teeth flashing white in the fading sunlight. "You'll find out soon enough." He stepped back and let go of my hands. "This is your home now. Welcome to the court of the Summer King."

Unhinged. Unsettled. Uncertain of what was to come, I stared at the beauty of Garnet Isles in disbelief.

Why was he so certain that I had something valuable to offer? What sick game was he playing?

Shivers ran down my spine as I thought of the consequences of standing up against the Summer King.

But death was certain, and if I was going to die anyway, then I wanted to do it on my terms and not play a sick game with him.

The only way I could ensure my death was by plunging my blade into his heart first.

five

Reverence

"Welcome, my dearest dear," the Summer King drawled sardonically as I stepped into his chambers. "If you plan on murdering me today, you'd better do it quickly, as I have a lot to attend to."

I raised an eyebrow and crossed my arms. "Didn't you invite me here for dinner?" I asked, my voice low and icy as I turned to face him. "I hardly think that my presence here is for any other purpose..."

I stood dumbstruck by the sight of him in all his glory.

Laying sprawled out on his bed, he looked at me with a judgmental gleam in his eyes.

His fingers absently toyed with a golden goblet that was perched atop the bedside table beside him. Dark hair fell in an artful cascade over his shoulder, framing his sharp features and giving him a wild, untamed appearance.

"Admiring the view?" he drawled in the same languid tone as before.

The words rolled off his tongue, beckoning me closer.

I wanted to resist him, but slowly took tentative steps towards the bed.

There was something about the way he spoke, the way he looked at me - as if I were a plaything to be toyed with and discarded when no longer entertaining - that kept my feet shifting forward against my will.

His strong fingers dug into my skin as he dragged me down onto the bed with him.

Falling into the softness, I could smell honeysuckle and summer sun, a scent that made my heart flutter wildly.

His lips brushed against my neck as he whispered in a dark voice, "You want to play? My heart is yours. Take it if you can."

My ears rang as I lay there in shock. The frivolity of his words belied the danger they held.

Gathering all my courage, I pushed myself away from him and stood up. "I might not like you, but that doesn't mean I want to kill you."

I met his gaze steadily, thinking that he had forced my hand. I didn't want to kill him, but what choice did I have? I was here because he had summoned me, and I knew that if I didn't do something, I would inevitably be killed myself.

A roar of laughter erupted from him, and he gave me a lazy smirk. "That's good, because I think you are the one who needs protection in this arrangement."

"Your presence alone has been enough to put me in danger."

He shrugged. "Perhaps, but I think you can hold your own."

His lips twisted into a sardonic grin.

The goblet clinked against the bedside table as he raised it in a salute. "To your courage and cunning. May they never fail you in the Summer court."

"To truth." I met his gaze with my own and lifted my chin. "No matter what happens."

His room was as beautiful and treacherous as the Summer King himself, and I couldn't help but be a little intimidated by it.

Silk curtains hung from the ceiling, and the walls were adorned with fine tapestries. A grand fireplace blazed in one corner of the room, casting a smoky haze over us. Blue-white marble floors gleamed in the dim light.

He smiled at me, a curious glint in his gold eyes. "Mortals may be incapable of telling the truth," he said, "but the Fae make an art form of it. We never tell a lie."

But they knew how to twist the truth so that it became something unrecognizable. Cruel words disguised as kindness, false promises hidden in plain sight.

My cheeks flushed as I struggled to find a response.

"It makes little difference." His gaze flicked to the window, watching silver clouds drift by in the sky. "Brides come and go, like the seasons."

My fingers curled into fists as he spoke. How could he be so callous?

"But you," he said slowly, his voice low and gravelly. "A plain, mortal girl… you have something that none of them do."

"Stupidity," I muttered.

He flashed me a toothy grin and laughed. "No, it's more than that, my dear." His voice was soft with amusement as he reached out and stroked my cheek. "It's something far more valuable."

I raised an eyebrow, the question unspoken but clear.

His gold eyes glinted with amusement as he looked at me. He seemed to savor the moment, as if he was taking pleasure in my curiosity and confusion.

My stomach flip-flopped nervously as I waited for him to explain himself. But he simply continued to smile, his gaze never wavering from my face.

I stepped closer, and he quirked an eyebrow as I reached for his goblet.

Our fingers brushed briefly as I plucked the goblet from his grasp, and then I raised it to my lips.

"I thought I was the one to get greedy around here?" he said, his voice now edged with amusement. "Seems like you've been taking lessons."

I curled my fingers around the goblet's stem and whirled the smokey liquid inside. The reflections of red and gold shimmered in the cup's depths, mesmerizing me.

"It's not greed if it's deserved," I said haughtily. "And I think I deserve this."

Especially after dealing with someone like you, I added silently.

He chuckled and pushed himself up onto one elbow, grinning wolfishly. "Indeed, you do, my dear. Indeed, you do."

We locked eyes for a moment, and then I took a sip of the goblet and allowed its sweet flavor to roll over my tongue.

I tasted a hundred different spices that were carefully blended together.

The Summer King grinned as he watched me, amusement dancing in his eyes.

I had his attention now, but how long would it last? He was a man of many secrets, and I had to be careful. If I wasn't cautious, he would turn on me in an instant and that wouldn't end well for me.

"So, if you're not here to kill me, what else did you come for?"

My mouth suddenly felt dry as I considered my options.

I could tell him the truth, or I could try to deceive him. Risking his wrath was a gamble.

"Don't you tire of taking? Don't you want to give something back?" I said finally, arching an eyebrow.

"Maybe you should try giving a little of yourself." I sipped from the goblet, savoring it as he smiled at my defiance.

"Fae wine." His eyes never left mine as I set the goblet down. "A rare delicacy. I know you will treasure it and not take it for granted."

"Honeyed words..." I murmured, allowing myself to relax a little. "What do they mean, coming from your lips?"

He chuckled and rose from the bed, stretching languidly.

"To me," he said slowly, "Sacrifice means something different than it does for you mortals." He clasped his hands behind his back. "It isn't about giving away something precious; it's about understanding the value of things and taking only what you need."

I nodded slowly, considering his words. They made sense, in an odd way.

"Do you think I can learn something from this?"

He smiled and ran his fingers through my hair. Tugging gently, he brought my face close enough that I saw the flecks of green in his eyes.

"I think you already have," he said. "This is your chance to prove yourself worthy. What happened to the brave girl who would do anything to keep her family safe?"

My breath caught in my throat, and he let go of my hair.

He stepped away from me, his expression now a mask of neutrality.

"She never left."

He laughed, a deep and throaty sound that filled the air. "It's strange, isn't it? How often we find ourselves in situations that frighten us."

His words were heavy and oppressive, like the swirling gold and silver clouds that illuminated the sky outside.

"But in those same moments, we realize we can be more than what we thought. That if we just dare to take a chance, everything could change."

Closing my eyes, I thought back to my family and the way they had looked at me before I left. I could still see the worry in their eyes, but there was something else too - a silent understanding that even if this journey ended badly, they would always love me.

I opened my eyes and met his gaze.

Leaning against the bedpost, he watched me with a quiet intensity.

"It doesn't matter what happens next," I said softly, my voice shaking with newfound strength. "I have already won."

My family was safe.

The gold rings on his hand glinted in the soft light as he clapped them together slowly, a mocking smile on his lips.

I'd come here for a reason, and it was time to make it known.

Standing up straight, I cleared my throat and squared my shoulders. The blade hidden below my sleeve shifted against my skin, a reminder that I was still in control.

"Finally, your true purpose," the Summer King said, his voice edged with amusement. "I won't hold back. If you have violence in your heart, then I will be the one to give it a home. Feed me your rage, your desperation, and I will give it purpose, Zareena."

Reaching down, I pulled the blade free and held it before me. Charging forward, I aimed straight for his heart.

The razor blade wouldn't hurt him. Only Fae iron could. But that didn't mean I wouldn't try.

Fear and desperation tingled through my veins, but I kept going because if I stopped now, what would happen?

Maybe I was suicidal after all. Maybe this was the only way to end my suffering and release myself from the gilded prison I had been thrown into.

But he never moved. Never flinched.

He just watched me with a steady gaze, as if he already knew what would happen next.

Stopping inches away from him, I felt the heat radiating off his skin.

His lips twitched into a faint smile, and he nodded once in acknowledgment. "You were going to kill me with kindness, weren't you?"

I opened my mouth to answer, but he silenced me with a finger pressed against my lips.

"Making promises you can't keep, little mouse?"

I swallowed and looked down at the razor blade in my hand. It seemed so small now, almost insignificant. Was that why he'd allowed me to keep it, because it wouldn't hurt him at all?

But then, why had he let it go this far?

The Summer King pulled away from me and crossed his arms over his chest. He made no move to attack or even defend himself.

My fury rose as I thrust forward, but he easily blocked my attack with a single hand. With the other hand, he grabbed my wrist, keeping me pinned in place as he looked into my eyes.

"You can fight with all the strength and anger you possess, but in here." He tapped his heart. "I will always be one step ahead of you. You must accept this or lose your way entirely."

The razor blade dropped to the floor with a clatter as his other hand traveled up my arm, caressing the exposed skin until it reached my neck.

My breathing grew ragged as I felt the heat of his body against mine. Every muscle in my body tensed, and I could feel my heart pounding in my ears.

Anger surged through me, clouding my vision and blurring the boundaries between right and wrong.

He stepped back, his hands still on me but not pressing down like before. Instead, he was almost caressing me, as if trying to soothe my rage.

"Kill me with kindness?" I repeated, the words coming out as a snarl. "You can never understand what it would be like to actually receive genuine kindness from someone," I hissed as he grabbed my other wrist and pinned it against the wall.

I tried to break free from his iron grasp, but it was no use. He was too strong for me.

He smiled, his lips just a breath away from mine. "Do you think so? It's interesting how kind you mortals can be." Brushing away a strand of hair from my face, he cocked his head. "I suppose if you worship something enough, it's only natural to show it kindness. Even when I don't deserve it."

"Worship you?" I spat as he released my wrists and stepped back. "You're not worth my worship, Summer King."

He laughed again, a sound that filled the entire room with its warmth. "Ah, but I am. You just don't know it yet. Every prayer, every offering, and every act of kindness you show me will be returned in kind."

"You delu-"

He did not let me finish, cutting me off with a shake of his head. "Oh, Zareena, you'll learn soon enough."

"As if anyone would want to worship the likes of you!"

He stepped closer again, his face inches away from mine. "I think you'll find that there are many who do."

My pulse quickened as he caressed my chin with one finger. An intense heat flooded through me, and for a moment all I wanted was to scratch his pretty face until it bled. I wanted to scream and fight until he was nothing but a broken shell at my feet, but I stayed quiet.

The Summer King stepped back, a knowing smirk on his lips. "You can't win every battle you fight, Zareena. But the ones you do... those will be worth it in the end."

Zareena. Zareena. Zareena. Stop using my name like you know me.

My eyes narrowed as I looked away, unable to take the intensity of his gaze any longer.

"Don't tell me you don't even know the name of your husband?"

My jaw tightened as I clenched my fists to stop them from shaking. Wicked thoughts flooded my mind, images of what he could do if I said the wrong thing at the wrong time.

"Very well then. I will tell you who I am. I am the Summer King -"

"Get to the point, you pompous ass."

Shit. He was going to kill me.

But the Summer King just laughed, his voice tinged with admiration. "It appears you may be more of a challenge than I expected."

He stepped closer, and for a moment, I thought he was going to strike me down right then and there.

Instead, he reached up and brushed my cheek with his fingertips.

"Your courage is admirable, Zareena. I am the Summer King, ruler of all that is sacred and magical in this land."

Gold light shimmered from his fingertips, radiating outwards and wrapping around us both.

"I have been watching you, and I see great potential in you. And so it is with pleasure that I offer you my name."

His voice was gentle, a stark contrast to the hard expression on his face.

He leaned in closer until his warm breath tickled my ear. "Azair."

Bow down to your King, a voice in my head urged, and I blinked, taken aback by the sudden realization.

Azair. God King of the Calanian people. The Sun King.

The golden light around us faded away as he stepped back, a satisfied smirk on his lips. "And now you know who I really am underneath all this pomp and circumstance." He gestured around the room with one hand, his eyes never leaving mine.

I swallowed hard. A king among men. A man among gods. Fae beyond compare.

"Worship me, Zareena. Show me the respect and adoration you owe to me as your husband and king. And I will offer you a world of wonders beyond your wildest imagination."

My heart pounded in my chest as I stood there, speechless.

The Calanians had long worshiped the Sun King, and he had always been a distant figure - an unreachable symbol of power.

But now here he was, standing before me in the flesh. Azair, the Summer King.

The Calanians revered the Fae, but I hadn't realized they worshiped them too. How could I have known?

"I am your husband, and I will not be denied."

It was then that I realized he had not been asking for my obedience but demanding it. Demanding my loyalty and worship - expecting me to bow down in reverence. Telling me to accept the destiny he had chosen for me.

My lip curled in contempt. "What, you think I'm going to show you 'kindness' now? After all of this?"

He didn't utter a word, but his unflinching stare spoke volumes.

My mind was a whirlwind of thoughts as I battled to contain my rising anger. I could accept his 'kindness' and be his obedient wife, or I could reject him and risk the consequences of defying a king.

The choice was simple.

"Are you that desperate for my submission, Azair?" I asked through gritted teeth.

"Desperate?" He shook his head, a small smile playing on his lips. "No, I am not desperate for it. But I will have it all the same."

He stepped closer and reached up to caress my face again.

This time, I didn't flinch away from him as I had done moments before. Instead, I held my ground and met his gaze head-on.

"You will submit to me, Zareena. And you will do it willingly. You know it in your heart as well as I do." He leaned in, his voice barely above a whisper. "Because, deep down, you want to be mine."

"You'll never understand what it's like to be truly respected. To have someone do something for you that isn't motivated by fear or reverence. Just because they want to. Just because of who you are," I said.

His eyes burned into mine as if searching for some hidden truth.

"It grieves me to think that you've never experienced genuine kindness."

The smile on his face faded away as he stepped back. "So you're saying that I'm not worthy of receiving kindness? That my people aren't worth fighting for? That they don't deserve the same respect as everyone else?"

I hesitated, my throat tight. "For all the atrocities you have committed, your people do not deserve condemnation for your wrongdoings."

"I shamed the proud Astridr, shy Halldora, and countless others. Their suffering is my burden to bear. I fully agree with your sentiment."

Shivers ran down my spine as I thought of the other brides he had killed - the proud Astridr, shy Halldora, and countless others.

It was an unspeakable horror to think of him taking away lives so callously, and I couldn't help but feel a sense of dread in his presence.

He may have been powerful, but he had no right to take away what belonged to these women.

But why admit to his wrongdoings? Why murder and torture innocent people in the first place?

"Why did you choose to build your empire with violence and cruelty?"

six

THE PLUCKED PETALS OF POWER

He sighed and stepped away from me, turning his back. "I promised you a feast and I intend to keep my word."

I turned around.

Honeysuckle and sunflowers bloomed around the edges of a magnificent gold and gemstone dining table, jewels glittering in the sunlight.

It was an opulence I had never seen before.

On top of the table were dishes overflowing with succulent seafood. Juicy tiger prawns, plump mussels, and sweet clams, all cooked to perfection in a fragrant coconut broth.

Gemstones sparkled in the dishes alongside slices of exotic fruits and vegetables.

He pulled out a gilded chair. "Join me."

I trudged towards the table.

Azair stepped forward and pulled out the chair for me. He then pushed it in, a gentlemanly gesture I hadn't expected from him.

After taking his own seat opposite me, he smiled and gestured toward the feast before us. "Feast your eyes and fill your soul with the flavor of my kingdom."

I was so mesmerized by the sight that I didn't realize Azair had filled my plate with generous portions until I heard him chuckle.

I looked up to find him watching me, one hand resting on the armrest of his chair while the other moved in a slow circle around the rim of his goblet. "You look like you've just been presented with the world."

I took a deep breath and shook my head slightly. "It's only food."

The lie felt heavy on my tongue and I knew he could see through it.

But instead of calling me out, he just smiled and nodded. "You will never have to go without again. Feast and be merry, little mouse. Enjoy the gifts I have offered you."

I stared down at my plate, overwhelmed by the gesture.

I felt like a mouse in the presence of a lion. I had grown up in poverty, subsisting on scraps as a kitchen maid.

The feast before me seemed far too extravagant for me to partake in - it was not something I was used to or comfortable with.

Yet as I looked around at the opulence surrounding us, my mouth watered and my stomach growled in anticipation.

I tentatively reached for a prawn, savoring the juicy sweetness as it melted in my mouth.

A hint of garlic, the sweet tang of honey and spices that lingered in my mouth long after my last bite was gone.

We ate in silence for several minutes, savoring the flavors of each dish, until finally, I broke the silence. "Why do you cause so much suffering?"

Azair paused, his fork hovering above the plate. "What do the Calanians whisper about me in the dark?"

I was going to die anyway, or worse, be tortured for the amusement of Azair's court. So why not tell the truth? Even if it was a truth that would cost me my life.

"They say you're cursed." I placed my fork on my plate. "That you can never love without destroying it in the end."

I looked up at him, my eyes searching his face for some sign of understanding or remorse.

"They say you take away what is most precious from the Calanians. That in your lust, you leave a trail of grief and heartache."

I paused, not wanting to go on but knowing that I had to continue.

The words were like poison on my tongue, but I forced them out, anyway. This was my last chance, and I had to make it count.

It would have been far easier to keep my mouth shut and pretend that I didn't know any better. But I thought of the destruction he had caused, and how many lives he had ruined.

"And that your power has made you a lonely, isolated figure. That you'll never know the love of another, for none would dare to challenge your reign."

Azair went still, as if an arrow had struck him.

I couldn't speak; my mouth was dry with fear. I had said too much and now all I could do was brace myself for his wrath.

This was it.

I had chosen my fate and would accept the consequences no matter what they were.

But instead of anger, his expression softened, and he leaned back in his chair.

He reached for his goblet and took a long sip before placing it down gently on the table. "Is that all they say about me?"

Slowly, I shook my head. "No. They say that you have become what you once sought to destroy. That the power you so desperately chased has consumed you and left behind a cold, ruthless ruler. But your people love you still."

He looked away, his face unreadable as he stared off into the distance.

He remained that way for several moments, before finally turning back to me with a hint of sadness in his eyes. "And what of you, Zareena? Do they speak kindly of me in your presence, or do you hate me too? Do you believe the lies they spread?"

I glanced away, not daring to meet his gaze. But then, despite my fear, I slowly looked up. "I would like to ask you a question, if I may."

"Ask."

"Do you have any capacity for love?" I asked, my voice trembling. "Is it possible for someone like you to feel something as human and pure as love?"

"I have caused great suffering in the past."

He rose from his chair and walked around the table, pausing beside me.

He extended his hand, and I took it in mine, allowing him to lead me away from the dining table and out into the night air.

Lava streams glowed around us, and two suns blazed in the sky, bathing us in warm light and a sweet summer breeze.

"The Fae, we feel emotions just as strongly as you. We love, we hurt, and sometimes we destroy things." He looked out across the landscape, his eyes far away. "But we create, too. We create beauty in destruction."

The heat enveloped me, thick and heavy, like molten honey oozing across every inch of my skin.

My eyes fluttered as sweat slid along my brow like a stream of tears.

And then, floating above us, was a single flower - its petals as delicate as spun glass and its color an impossible shade of indigo.

My lips curved into a soft smile. "It's beautiful."

Delicate tendrils of steam rose from the flower, and its petals quivered in response.

The flower slowly burned, its petals transforming from delicate indigo to vibrant oranges and reds. Heat rose, and the steam thickened until finally, with a crackle of thunder, it burst into flame.

Fire consumed the flower completely, reducing it to nothing more than smoldering ashes in a matter of seconds.

Gold dust hung in the air, catching the light of the two suns and creating a glorious display.

Azair turned to me. His expression was both solemn and resigned. "Beauty is often born in destruction. It is a lesson we Fae must learn to appreciate - for without destruction, there can be no transformation."

I looked at the smoldering ashes of the flower and thought of my pain. I understood all too well how destruction could lead to transformation, but I also knew that it could be a painful process.

He had taken what was most precious from his mortal brides; their hopes, dreams, and loyalties were stolen in an instant.

Which woman could ever trust a man who had caused so much suffering?

I certainly couldn't.

A man like Azair could never love and be loved in return, for he had proven himself to be a destroyer of all things beautiful.

He was no different from the flower, destroyed by his own power and transformed by the ashes.

Bitter, yet undeniably capable of creating beauty.

The thought of my own ashes filled me with sadness.

My family would never know what happened to me, and the pain of their grief would be unbearable. Wondering what happened to me would consume them, and I couldn't bear the thought of causing them any more pain.

I looked up at Azair, my head bowed in humility. "For my last boon, I ask you this," I said, my voice trembling ever so slightly. "When you take my life, please grant me the mercy of returning my body home to my family unharmed."

I bowed my head and waited, my heart pounding in my chest.

He waved his hand, his gold ring glinting in the light. The ashes rose into the air, forming a glittering cloud that swirled around us.

The flower was reborn, but the petals were now a brilliant blue. Its stems were longer and its colors brighter.

"I cannot grant you life, but I can give your loved ones peace of mind." Azair handed me the flower. "I will not grant you this boon, but I will honor it. You have my word."

I took the flower in my outstretched hands.

The petals were still warm from the fire, and it pulsed in my hands like a heartbeat.

I gave what I thought was a polite bow and stepped back. My heart raced as his gaze followed me, my skin tingling from his proximity.

"Why haven't you left your rooms until today? You're not a prisoner."

I cocked my head. "Am I not? You forced me to marry you. A gilded cage is still a cage."

His eyes darkened as gold sparks danced across his skin. "Theatricality is my lifeline. That's what I thrive on, and you have become my most prized audience. I only seek to capture you with my presence, never to cage you."

Glancing away, I took a deep breath. "Pretty words."

"In this cage, we are both prisoners," he said. "We all wear masks. Mine just happens to be different from yours. The cruel hand of fate has cursed us both."

His voice was low and melodic, his words weaving around me like a lullaby.

"But there is beauty in the curse, if we choose to find it." A wry smile curved his lips. "We could be like two lost birds in a caged sky, trapped yet still free to fly."

He paused, as if savoring the moment.

"Sometimes, in this darkness, I feel that hope is just within reach and I can almost touch it." He looked away. "But then I remember it is only an illusion."

A heavy silence fell between us, and I felt a sudden urge to take his hand in mine and tell him that everything would be okay - that there was still hope, no matter how faint.

But I stayed rooted in place, afraid of breaking the fragile spell he had woven around us.

"This kingdom is my life," he said finally. "It's what I must do. But I can still show you kindness and understanding if you'll let me. I can be a friend, a confidante. My best self."

I stared into his eyes, searching for any sign of deceit.

But all I saw was sincerity and a hint of vulnerability. He wanted me to stay by choice, not because he was forcing me to.

How unexpected, and yet how comforting. Men like Azair, rulers, rarely showed such vulnerability.

"There is honor in your words, even if I can't be entirely sure of your motives."

"Honor?" He shifted his gaze away from me, his jaw clenched tight. "What honor? Little mouse, I am a king. We know nothing of honor."

"But you do." My lips curved upwards, but the smile was hollow. "Otherwise, why would you have spared my life?"

He could have struck me down for my insolence or dealt out a swift punishment for attacking him, but instead, he chose to show mercy.

Mercy was a rare trait in a man of his station, and one rarely extended to those beneath him. The Fae were a proud race, and the thought of showing mercy to an outsider was unheard of.

He didn't answer, but he didn't need to.

I saw the answer in his eyes. It was a question of honor - an unwritten code of unspoken rules, a type of respect that ran deeper than words.

"Sometimes even kings can show mercy."

"Despise not thy foes, but seek to reduce their animosity," I said, repeating my father's words as he had taught me all those years ago. "And remember, if you cannot bring yourself to love those who oppose you, then be kind in your actions."

The air around us seemed to thicken, the heat seeping into my bones and warming me from within.

"This is not a fairy tale," he said. "Rose-colored dreams will not save you."

"I never claimed that you are the epitome of chivalry," I said. "But you are capable of kindness and mercy, if you choose."

"I will formally introduce you to my people, and I will have them understand you are my wife. No one will ever threaten your safety."

"Unless it's by your hand."

He stepped away, the heat of his body fading from me along with his proximity.

"You are free to explore my kingdom as you wish, and I shall be your guide. You will never be a prisoner here, only an honored guest."

"Why play these games?" I asked, my eyes focused on the volcano in the distance. "End me now, if you wish."

"The games are little more than a distraction. You may not understand now, but someday you will. The rules of this kingdom are ever-changing, and one must learn to adapt. But I swear to you, I will not take your life without warning. That much I can promise."

Relief and gratitude flooded my body.

Despite the risk of death looming over me, I found myself eager to explore this strange new world.

Even in such dire circumstances, I decided to make the most of my time, to take solace in the moments and cherish them no matter how brief they were.

I was no longer a prisoner in this kingdom; instead, I would be an honored guest with access to things many people would never see.

No matter what happened, I vowed not to waste this chance. I would take every opportunity to experience life to its fullest, and when the time came for me to go, I would be grateful for having lived at all.

The Gods had blessed me with this chance, and I would honor them with my actions.

"Thank you," I said as I picked up the flower and tucked it into my hair. "I will never forget your mercy."

The intensity of his gaze made my stomach twist in knots, but I held his gaze and didn't look away.

A slow smile spread across his face, and my heart leaped in response. "You will be an asset to this kingdom. A Summer Queen is never without her court."

I swallowed hard. "And this court will be mine?"

He gave a small, self-satisfied smile that hinted at a deeper meaning. "Should you choose to accept it. You do not need to fear in my court, but I would advise you to remember your place. A host of Fae will be there to meet your doom, and it will be my solemn duty to bid you farewell."

"Then I will not forget that power lies on the side of the Fae."

His eyes narrowed and his lips quirked in a half-smile. With a slight tilt of his head, he said slowly, "Sometimes it is best to let the truth go unspoken."

His voice was low and sultry, sending shivers down my spine.

He didn't take his gaze away from mine even for a moment. "Our hunger sets us apart. Beware of trusting too much, for fire can consume even the strongest of hearts." His gaze lingered on me a few beats longer before he slowly turned away.

seven

THE DANCE OF DAMNATION

No one knows it is a bridal dance.

Strange instruments crafted from bone rattled and jangled in time with the drums, while high-pitched voices rose in a wild song that seeped from the very stones beneath their feet.

It was a refrain of high spirits and wild joy, of untamed freedom that threatened the balance of even the oldest rules.

I stepped forward, my bare feet barely making a sound on the smooth marble floor.

The eyes of the crowd followed me, the anticipation barely contained in their faces.

I knew what was coming and my heart pounded in time with the drums.

Azair lounged on his throne, one arm draped casually over the back of it as he watched me with an arched eyebrow. His long legs stretched out before him while one hand rested lazily on the armrest.

He was a bastard for calling me out in front of everyone like that.

If he thought he could intimidate me, he was mistaken.

"A Summer Queen should present herself worthy to her court."

His words echoed in my head as I stepped forward.

No matter how much I wanted to look away, I couldn't - he made it clear that this was a test and one I could not fail.

I had no doubt I could show this arrogant king a thing or two. He wanted a performance? I'd give him one that would haunt his dreams.

The music swelled and the drums beat faster as I stepped forward. With a slow bow to Azair, I danced.

My arms rose to the air in graceful arcs, dipping low before rising again as my feet glided across the cold floor.

Drums and rattles echoed around me, their beats setting the pace for my dance as I spun in intricate patterns.

The firelight glinted off the jewels on my dress, and the coins around my waist tinkled in time with the drums.

Azair leaned forward on his throne, the sardonic smirk on his face slowly slipping away.

His gaze burned into me, and even though I kept my eyes locked on the horizon, a little smile tugged at my lips.

This was no bridal dance. This was an act of defiance.

Courtiers watched in rapt attention, their eyes never leaving my form as I spun faster and faster.

The orange and yellow flames rose with each beat of the drums, as if they too were entranced by the music.

There was something magical here. Something that held us all in its thrall.

Almost ritualistic, I allowed my body to be taken over by the music. My movements became more intricate and demanding as the rhythm rose in intensity, and a surge of power ran through me.

Ornate masks of gold and silver lined the balconies, following my every move with their eyes.

As I spun and twirled, I noticed the wide eyes of a pink-haired lady with pointed ears, her angular cheeks illuminated by the dancing flames. A Fae with scales glittering like newly minted coins stood beside her with auburn hair that cascaded down his back, while a lord with goat's legs hovered in the shadows, his fine bone structure highlighted by a mask of pure white.

Tall, willowy figures with gossamer wings and luminous skin flitted around the dance floor like sprites from a dream, while hulking creatures with scaly hide and horns lurked in the shadows.

The sheer diversity of the Fae was astounding, and it made me wonder what other secrets this kingdom held.

Azair shifted in his seat, adjusting himself ever so slightly. His fingers tightened around the armrests of his throne, his gaze never leaving me for a moment.

He appeared enthralled, almost forgetful of the others around him, as if unaware that he was in danger of losing control.

Good.

I threw my head back and let out a wild laugh, challenging him with my eyes.

His jaw tightened and his gaze grew cold, but I saw the hint of admiration in his eyes.

He had underestimated me, and he knew it.

The drums thumped louder and faster with each passing second, the rhythm drawing me ever deeper into its embrace.

I could have danced until dawn, but all too soon, it was over.

For a moment, the entire court held their breath in anticipation.

Azair slowly lowered his arm from the throne and stood up. He crossed the space between us in one single stride and seized my hand, pressing it against his chest.

"I suggest you remove your hand," I said, my voice low but cutting through the silence like a blade. "Your position in this court does not give you leave to do as you please."

"You are bold for one so small," he breathed. "But then again, I suppose that is what a Summer Queen should be."

He released me with a bow, and I felt the power of his gaze along my back as he stepped away.

"You suppose?" I snatched up my skirts and bowed low to him. "After hundreds of failed marriages, I would think you have more of an idea than that."

"Accepting compliments gracefully is a lesson you should learn, my Queen," he drawled, amusement dancing in his eyes.

I smiled sweetly at him before stepping away. "I'm sure I will, with more practice. But in the meantime, your appreciation is noted."

His pointed ears twitched, and the corner of his mouth quirked up. "Did you really expect anything less than my undivided attention?"

He stepped closer and ran a finger down my cheek.

"The sway of your hips, the twinkle of your eyes, and that fire in your voice... I could watch you all night long."

The heat of his touch made my skin tingle, and I stepped away from him. "I'm sure you didn't call me forward to see my dancing," I said, my voice light. "So what is it you wanted?"

He stepped back and ran a hand through his dark hair. "Can a husband not show appreciation for his wife's talents? I'd like to think a king can do as he pleases."

My heart thumped in my chest.

I wanted to reach out and touch him, but I knew better than to do something like that.

The Fae were known for their whimsical and mercurial nature, and I knew that if I touched him now, it would be more than a simple touch.

Bowing my head, I stepped back. "Of course." As he leaned in, I instinctively leaned away. "If that's all."

He smiled and nodded. "That is all for now." His hand flicked towards the courtiers, and they bowed their heads in respect. "They seem to have enjoyed your performance, my Summer Queen."

I raised an eyebrow and met his gaze head-on. "It was for them, wasn't it?"

"Mortals can be so unpredictable. I'm sure they found your show quite captivating."

"I hope they did," I said with a smile. "For the Summer Court's sake and my own."

He laughed softly but didn't reply, his gaze lingering on me for another moment before he gestured to the court.

The court erupted into applause, and cheers of joy echoed through the hall.

I would survive another night. I had made it—for now.

The last few days had been a whirlwind of extravagance and luxury. Soft beds, clean linen, and sumptuous feasts filled the days.

Evenings were spent in whispered conversations with courtiers and other nobility, where I was treated as an equal.

For the first time in my life, I had a taste of what it meant to have privilege. To do as I pleased without fear of punishment or reprimand. It was a feeling that I wouldn't soon forget.

And I would never take it for granted.

I couldn't help but notice the way he leaned in slightly, his gaze never leaving mine.

"Ruling a kingdom," he said, "is like controlling the optics of a painting. See both the beauty and the flaws to understand what must be done. A wise man understands that he must never forget the tiny details, even if they are invisible to others." He tapped my shoulder lightly. "I've got another surprise for you, little mouse. Let's see if you can handle it."

The smile on my face faded, but I nodded. Whatever he had planned, I was ready to face it head-on.

He stepped away and gestured to one courtier, who bowed low and presented a box wrapped in gold paper with an ornate ribbon tied around it.

Azair handed me the box with a sly smile. "A Summer Queen shouldn't be walking around without her crown, don't you think?"

I carefully untied the ribbon and opened the box.

Inside was a delicate golden crown with six gemstones set in it—two gold, two white, one red, and one yellow. Henna symbols were etched into the metal, shimmering in the light.

I ran my hand over it reverently before looking up and meeting his gaze. "It's beautiful."

I breathed out a sigh of relief. He hadn't been testing me after all. He had been trying to give me something.

He stepped forward and gently placed the crown on my head.

The gemstones glittered in the torchlight as I took a deep breath and smiled.

"Allow yourself to bask in the glory of your victory, Zareena," he said. "It's yours."

"But?" I hesitated, as if uncertain what words to choose.

"But nothing." He smiled knowingly, understanding my hesitation. "You are the Summer Queen, and this is your crown."

I stepped closer to him; the firelight reflecting off my golden jewelry. "What are you planning for me, Your Majesty?"

"Husband. No more formalities. A wife should call her husband by his name."

"What are you planning for us, *my darling husband*?"

"You are so full of questions." He paused and ran his finger down the side of my face. "But never fear—all will be revealed in time."

"Can you blame me for being curious?" I said, a hint of amusement in my voice. "You have certainly been full of surprises tonight."

He took my hand in his and brought it to his lips. "I always have more surprises up my sleeve." He winked. "Pleasant ones, of course. That is the Summer Court's way, after all."

"Really?" I said, quirking an eyebrow.

"Truly," he drawled, his gaze twinkling with mischief. "I rather enjoyed that performance. Next time, let's keep the wedding festivities between us two."

I arched an eyebrow. "Are you familiar with the custom?"

His fingers threaded into my hair as he leaned in closer. "I am no stranger to a bridal dance, my dearest dear," he whispered in my ear as he pulled me closer. "I'm sure we could think of something... memorable."

The sound of my laughter reverberated through the courtyard.

Men remained men—Fae and mortal alike.

"Ah, so you propose to dance?"

He grinned, and a flash of white teeth emerged. "That's why it's called a bridal dance. I'm sure we will find some way to make it work."

I stepped away, and his hand dropped from my face. "So here's the thing, there's a small catch. We're not married."

His brow furrowed, but the smile remained on his lips. "You accepted my hand and tasted the fruit," he said slowly, his gaze searching mine for any hint of a lie. "Tell me, little mouse. Do you not feel the connection between us? Do you not sense the power of our union and know that we are bound?"

My heart skipped a beat, and a blush rose to my cheeks.

I had felt it—the connection—though I hadn't expected it.

"Yes," I whispered. "I feel it."

His lips quirked up into a smirk as he stepped closer to me, his gaze lingering on my face for a moment before meeting mine again.

I stepped back.

The idea of being someone's 'wife' in name only, especially this cruel and unpredictable Fae king, was more than I could bear.

Azair may have thought he could win me over with his charm and gifts, but I was not a woman to be bought so easily.

Enjoying his gifts, his attention, and his flattery was one thing. Becoming emotionally entangled with him was quite another.

I had to be careful and protect my heart from the pain of losing something I never even fully owned in the first place.

The fire in my belly reignited, and I stood tall. "We may have married according to the custom of your people," I said in a measured tone. "But to me, you are a stranger. Nothing."

Wildness danced in his eyes, but something else tempered it. Something deeper and more alluring.

"What would you have me do?" he asked, his voice low.

I looked away, my chest heaving with emotion. "You cannot just come here and expect me to accept you as a husband—to trust you blindly—when I know nothing about you. Our connection is built on nothing but falsehoods and lies." I stepped away again, creating a space between us. "It should have never been formed and it will never last."

He opened his mouth as if to speak, but I held my hand up, silencing him.

"I will not be your wife," I said firmly. "You may have married me according to your custom, but I decide for myself whether or not I will accept it."

He stepped back, his expression unreadable. "So you would have me forget the connection between us? To ignore that which binds us?"

His voice was low and full of an emotion I couldn't quite put my finger on.

I refused to meet his gaze and instead focused on keeping my expression neutral. "We are not bound by anything, least of all a feeling."

He nodded slowly and stepped away. "As you say."

His voice was deep and rich, but there was an edge to it I hadn't heard before.

He clenched his jaw as if restraining himself from saying something else. "Your heart will speak in time. Until then, I remain at your service."

"My heart is not yours to keep. Nor my decisions," I said, my voice laced with caution.

He smiled and raised one of my hands to his lips, pressing a kiss against my knuckles. "You have already given it to me, whether or not you realize it. Every beat of your heart belongs to me now."

"Lust fades. It is not sustainable. It is fleeting and can be broken as easily as it can be formed. I have seen it far too often. A pretty face and a clever tongue can only do so much."

He stepped closer and ran his fingers through my hair, sending shivers down my spine. His fingers moved lightly, tracing the outline of my face.

"Oh Zareena," he drawled. "Clever tongues and pretty faces can be your downfall, little mouse." Gold glinted in his eyes as he smiled down at me. "Be careful, or you may even welcome it from me."

My breath caught in my throat as his lips touched mine.

The innocent brush of his lips drew a gasp from me. I felt as if I were melting into him, the heat of his body radiating through me like wildfire.

He pulled away and studied my face for a moment before brushing his thumb against my cheek.

"Do you feel it now?" His voice was barely more than a whisper. "Do you feel the power of our bond?"

The warmth of his breath washed over me and I shivered, my mouth too dry to speak.

Rumblings of laughter rose from the court, and the spell was broken.

I stepped back, allowing some distance between us. "I... I...."

"In time, little mouse. We both have a lot to learn still," he leaned in and whispered in my ear, his voice suddenly serious. "This is not the end of us. Not by a long shot."

And with that, he turned and walked away, leaving me in the courtyard with his parting words ringing in my ears.

The Summer Court had accepted me as their Queen. I should have been elated, but all I could think of was the warmth of his hands and the electric surge I felt when his lips touched mine.

I watched him go, a chill snaking down my spine.

He was dangerous—all Fae were—and he had an uncanny ability to manipulate me and make me question what I knew about him.

I could never be certain who the real him was, and that thought both terrified and exhilarated me.

Courtiers frolicked around the crackling fire, leaving me to my thoughts in a deserted corner of the courtyard.

"You two make quite a pair, don't you?" A voice came from behind me, and I whirled around to see a petite figure standing in the shadows of the bonfire.

A wild mane of spun sugar hair framed her delicate features and illuminated her glowing green skin. Black pearls adorned her neck and wrists, and a gown of fine silver thread glimmered in the bonfire's light.

She stepped closer and tilted her head to one side appraisingly. "I can see why he chose you," she said with a pointed look. "You are strong-willed. You will not be an easy bride for any man."

"Thank you." I took a moment to study her features, and her eyes met mine with a knowing smile. A beauty in the way all Fae were, she was a sight to behold. "Lady?"

"Catriona." She inclined her head gracefully. "You don't think I'm a servant, do you? The other brides all seemed to think so. I must admit, it insulted me greatly."

I chuckled. "No, the stitching on your dress, the jewels around your neck. These speak of power and wealth. As a former servant, I'm well aware of the distinctions."

It was the minor details that gave it away. The pearls around her neck were a deep black, not the usual white.

Her dress was crafted with a fine glimmersilk thread, far more expensive than the gold or silver thread the other courtiers wore.

Even her gait was different, a regal bearing that marked her as someone of rank.

It was clear she wasn't a servant. It had been my job to notice the details that others missed, and this time it had paid off.

She turned away from the bonfire and motioned for me to follow her. "Sharp eyes, sharp mind. I can see why he chose you to be his bride."

I sighed and glanced over my shoulder towards where Azair disappeared into the crowd.

"But what about love?" I asked softly, more to myself than to anyone else in particular, as I followed Catriona away from the bonfire.

"Love," she said without turning around. "Are you capable of loving him?"

"Love is a risk," I murmured, recalling the emptiness I felt when my husband left me.

It had been a hollow pain, one that I hadn't wanted to let anyone else in to fill.

I had thought I was happy before, but now all of my experiences mocked me. I knew what it felt like to be let down and taken for granted, and the fear of history repeating itself made me hesitate.

"That it is, my dear." Catriona glanced back at me with a knowing smile. "But sometimes it's a risk worth taking."

Men were fickle creatures, and I had no intention of putting my heart on the line again.

We stopped in front of a small waterfall, cascading over rocks and into a shallow pool at the base.

As I listened to the tranquil sound of the water, my tense shoulders relaxed. "I may have been forced into becoming his wife, but I will never be tricked into loving him."

"No one could ever trick your heart. Only you can decide what is right for it." She patted my arm gently as we sat down in the shadows, both of us looking out over the pool.

I sighed and ran my fingers through the water, watching as the ripples spread outwards in concentric circles.

"Choose to love him and you will experience a love that transcends everything. The curse of Azair is not so easily broken, but love can conquer even the darkest of forces."

Curse? What did she mean by that? Were the rumors true?

"Is his heart cursed, unable to love without the destruction of something precious?"

Drums pounded, and the fires roared as the court danced and sang.

Catriona looked away, her expression unreadable in the darkness. "That is a story for another time. His heart is as free as yours, but it has been kept locked away for too long." She tilted her head towards the crowd of people around us. "It's up to you to unlock it."

"Do the Summer Fae love talking in riddles?" I asked, my brows furrowing as I tried to make sense of her words.

Catriona laughed softly and shook her head. "It's not a riddle, it's an invitation. But you must decide if you will take the risk and unlock his heart. His heart may be cursed, but love has the power to break the spell."

The corners of my mouth twitched as I chuckled softly, barely containing my laughter. "He might as well kill me now if he's cursed to find a woman who will love him. Because that will not be me."

The very idea of loving him was as absurd as the thought of him loving me.

"Do not be so quick to turn away from the potential of love," she advised. "The Summer King's curse is formidable, but one thing can only break it. His willingness to open himself up and embrace love."

She gestured toward the revelers around us, who continued to dance and laugh despite the darkness that surrounded them.

I looked around, my gaze lingering on Azair in the center of the crowd, his long hair glinting in the firelight as he laughed with a group of courtiers.

Brawny arms reached out to embrace him, and the laughter of those around him was contagious.

Could a man like that ever be tamed? Could I truly unlock his heart, or would I simply be setting myself up for disappointment and heartbreak?

The questions whirled through my mind as Azair glanced in my direction, his gaze intense and heavy with emotion.

"If he cannot love you with all his heart, our court will be doomed to an eternity of darkness and despair."

Shivers ran up and down my spine as I thought of the curse's implications.

Wiping a hand across my forehead, I tried to clear my head and focus. "Who is capable of cursing a Fae king?"

She smiled enigmatically. "You are asking the wrong question." Pausing, she put her other hand on my shoulder and looked into my eyes with a serious expression. "The question you need to ask yourself is, how will I survive this curse?"

My stomach churned.

Dangerous curses and powerful kings were no joking matter, and I feared what might happen if I didn't make the right choices.

But there was also a spark of excitement that flared to life in my chest. I had been raised to believe that there was always a solution, no matter how daunting the problem may seem.

And if Azair's curse could be broken... Well, I wasn't as powerless as I thought.

A flutter of hope welled up inside me as I considered the possibilities. Not trying would be so much easier. But I had never been one to take the easy way out.

"How can I make him love me? What do I need to do?"

She smiled and patted my arm. "You will find a way. You have already taken the first steps by opening yourself up to him. Now it is up to you to take the next steps."

"Seduction?" I suggested, without thinking.

She laughed, a low and throaty sound that sent shivers down my spine.

"No. You must not rely on seduction." Her eyes were piercing as she looked into mine. "Your body may be a powerful tool, but it is not the only one. Winning the heart of Azair requires more than physical seduction. You must show him your heart. He will know the truth of it, and he cannot resist it."

Badis would disagree with Catriona - I had never unlocked his heart. Even after years of marriage, he left me without a second thought.

Not worthy of his love. Not enough woman for him.

I was not sure I had the strength to try again.

The truth was that I had given my heart away freely, but it had been broken and battered in return.

Men seemed to think love was something they could take and discard at will. A pretty bauble to be toyed with until they were done.

Why would Azair be any different? He was a Fae king, and I was but a mortal woman. He could have any creature he desired - why would he choose me?

And yet, Catriona had said it could be done. That love would conquer the curse.

She squeezed my shoulder gently. "Do not be afraid. Love can bloom in the most unlikely places."

"A seduction of the heart," I murmured, thinking of all I had to do if I wanted to break the curse. "A man who has been isolated for centuries may find that difficult to accept."

But the challenge in his eyes, the way he challenged me to match him step for step - perhaps there was something there. Something that could be unlocked.

Staring into the night sky, I knew that if anyone could break this curse, it would be me.

My family counted on me. The Summer Court depended on me. And Azair, whether or not he knew it, needed me too.

She nodded. "But it is a necessary step if you are to break the curse." She took my hand in hers and squeezed it tightly. "He chose you. However, what he truly desires remains to be seen. Show him who you are and his response may surprise you."

eight

MISLEADING LINES IN LACE

"Ah, now this one is quite stunning," Maevar remarked, gesturing to a deep blue velvet gown, his black wings ruffling in the breeze. "It complements your eyes perfectly."

I moved closer to the dress.

It had been a week since my conversation with Catriona and I had been determined to take her advice.

Cultivating allies within the court would be essential for my mission. By creating bonds with the courtiers, I hoped to weave my way into the Summer Court and gain information.

Azair still hadn't shown his face since his speech, giving me the perfect opportunity to make a name for myself amongst the courtiers.

Public opinion often swayed kings and rulers, and I had to be sure that my reputation was strong enough for me to be considered a viable option.

Risks had to be taken, but enjoying myself in the process didn't seem like such a horrible idea.

I traced my fingers along the intricate embroidery on the bodice of the dress.

"It is beautiful," I murmured, as the stitchings around the neckline sparkled in the light. "But I'm not sure it's suitable for court. It's too... flashy for my taste." I glanced at Maevar, who gave me a delusively sly smile. "It would be more appropriate for a ball, don't you think?"

The backless style was too bold, and the pattern was too intricate. Though beautiful, it was unsuitable for my personality or court situation. The frivolity of the gown didn't match my purposes, and I wanted something that represented me better.

No, there had to be something else. Something that represented me in a more subtle, but no less powerful way.

"That's the point." Silyen's four eyes blinked in tandem. "Each color, each stitch, each gemstone has its meaning that the other members of the court can interpret. Do you see the runes here? They spell out the wearer's intentions."

I peered closer, trying to make sense of the strange symbols.

Curling my fingers around the fabric, the delicate curves seemed to form into words, as if they were whispering secrets to me.

Unconsciously, my hand stroked the fabric, feeling its power through my fingertips.

"Boldness? Confidence? Courage?" The runes seemed to answer my questions, as if they were guiding me towards the truth. "A language of sorts, spoken through fabric and gems."

Maevar nodded. "One that can be deciphered by every single Summer Fae."

I traced my finger along the gem-studded runes. The pearls and rubies glinted in time with my movements. "And what does this say?"

"Blood lust and vanity," Maevar said without hesitation. "It is a powerful display of power for those who know how to interpret it. You must be careful with how you use it."

I was used to dressing plainly and blending into the background. But here, I was expected to be bold and make a statement, and that was something completely new for me.

I found myself inexplicably drawn to the idea of wielding such power without ever having to utter a single word.

I could be seen. I could be heard. And I could make a difference.

"Blood lust is not something to be admired, Maevar," I said.

The corner of his lips lifted in an almost imperceptible smile. "But it is an emotion that all Fae understand." He leaned closer and his voice dropped to a whisper. "We feel deeply, and our emotions are powerful. Use them to your advantage."

I fingered the fabric one last time before turning away from the dress.

Frivolous adornments of clothing suddenly took on a whole new meaning. I was no longer dressing for aesthetic purposes, but to make a statement, to show my intentions.

There was power in that - and it was something I had never experienced before.

Softer colors, bolder patterns, and intricate adornments. I could use them all to achieve my goals - and break the curse.

Talon-tipped fingers rose to Delros' lips as feathers of silver and purple danced around her face in a soft halo. "Subtle messages can be just as powerful as the loudest of words."

Maevar stood up, his wings sliding gracefully along the ground. "Powerful statements attract powerful attention. You must learn to wield these weapons if you are to survive. You will be tested, Summer Queen."

I sipped on the cup of thyme tea that Maevar had provided. Taking a deep breath, the warmth of its steam filled my lungs and settled in my chest.

"What image do I need to convey? What are you looking for in a queen?"

Maevar's gaze softened, the hard edges of his face softening. "No one knows what a Fae truly desires - not even I. We are creatures of passion and emotion, but our needs are often hidden beneath layers of duty and obligation."

That didn't answer my question, but I nodded anyway.

The light glinted off Maevar's wings as he turned to me. "You must be yourself," he said simply. "You can never please everyone, nor should you try. You are the Summer Queen, and what matters most is that you stay true to yourself and your own unique sense of style."

"What image speaks the truth to you?" Delros looked me up and down, her gaze appraising. "The runes on the dress are only a reflection of what lies inside your heart, and if you wear them truthfully, they will speak volumes to those who understand."

I took a moment to consider her words. I did not know what kind of image I wanted to convey, and I wasn't sure how to go about finding it.

But perhaps the key lay in being myself and expressing the values that were most important to me.

"Honor. Humility. Compassion. Strength. Royalty should embody these qualities."

The three of them exchanged looks, and then Delros' sharp features softened into a gentle smile. "Then find the dress that speaks to these qualities." She nodded towards the gown. "And wear it proudly."

Maevar stopped in front of me, his wings folded neatly behind him. "Now all we need is the right dress..."

Silyen's hair turned from soft pink to a deep purple and back again in a matter of seconds. "I think I may have just the thing."

And with that, she was out of her chair in a flash, scurrying over to an enormous wardrobe in the corner.

I followed close behind.

Gold and silver lockets hung from the wardrobe doors as she pulled back the heavy wooden doors.

The walls were lined with shimmering gowns of every imaginable color, embroidered with intricate patterns, and adorned with gemstones and charms.

Some were delicate and airy like a summer breeze, while others boasted flowing capes and cascading trains befitting a queen.

Tiny pixies danced around us, tugging at our clothes, beckoning us to explore.

At the center of it all was a magnificent tree with branches of emerald green and a canopy of bright yellow flowers.

Following Silyen, I watched as a peacock spread its feathers, creating an elegant gown of deep blue velvet and lavender silk.

Nearby, a family of otters transformed a delicate lace dress with pearls glimmering along the neckline into something more regal and refined.

"Are they paid?" I asked cautiously, my eyes wide with wonder. "For their services?"

Were these magical creatures being taken advantage of?

Silyen laughed. "No, my friend! They are not sentient creatures. They are merely enchanted by whatever magic we choose to employ. See?"

She gestured towards the tree as a small hummingbird appeared on one of its branches.

"We have imbued them with the magic of Summer itself. Their craftsmanship is unparalleled, and you will be hard-pressed to find anything like this in the other courts."

The hummingbird flew up to me, its wings beating in a blur of motion.

Its beak gently plucked one lock of hair from my head and returned to the tree, weaving the black strand into a tiny lock atop one of the branches.

An elegant gown manifested around me.

The fabric spun in circles, showering me with a dazzling mist of blue and gold.

Rich teal and lavender hues swirled together to form intricate patterns along the hems and cuffs, while glass beads glimmered across the neckline.

Carefully crafted drapes flowed gracefully from my body and sleeves trailed behind me like delicate butterflies.

As the hummingbird finished its work, I realized that this was the dress I had been searching for.

It was simple yet elegant and spoke to my spirit like no other garment ever could. I knew at that moment that this would be my signature look as queen - an expression of my true self.

Mortal conventions no longer mattered. It was time for me to embrace my new identity and take my place in the Fae court.

Flawed. Unconventional. Powerful.

The hummingbird perched atop one of my shoulders as I looked up to meet Silyen's gaze, who was looking at me with a delighted expression on her face.

She nodded slowly in understanding. "We've found the perfect dress."

I smiled at the hummingbird and stepped back, stunned by its craftsmanship. "Thank you for your service."

I watched as it flew away and vanished among the trees.

My fingers traced the runes and sunflowers that had been delicately stitched along the fabric. "What do the symbols mean?" I asked, turning to Silyen for answers.

"The teal and lavender colors signify a softness in your power. An unspoken truth that speaks louder than any words could ever say." Azair stepped forward, shoulders back, and head held high.

His lips turned into an arrogant smirk. He gestured to the symbols on my dress with a flourish of his hand.

"The glass beads remind us of your infinite strength and courage, while the lock of hair ties you to your people in a way that no words ever could. The sensation will be impossible for them to ignore."

Silyen bowed her head, her lips curling into a gentle smile. "It is the perfect dress for the Summer Queen."

He smiled in agreement and turned back to me. "The runes represent groundedness, stability, and tradition. Something all outstanding leaders should strive for."

"And the sunflowers?" I asked, tracing my fingers along the shimmering petals.

"Bloodshed and courage," Azair said softly. "A reminder that you must make the tough decisions to protect your people and safeguard their future."

I arched an eyebrow as Silyen slipped away, her tail wagging with each step.

The Summer King stepped closer, his lips twitching in a smile that reached all the way to his eyes. He held out his arm, and I hesitated for a moment before taking it.

"Two days from now, I'd like to invite you for a night out. Nothing too formal, of course, but I think you'll find the activities most enlightening."

Raising my chin, I looked up at him. "I look forward to it, Your Majesty."

A spark of amusement flashed in his eyes. "Husband. Not Majesty."

I couldn't help but chuckle. "Husband it is then."

He leaned in closer, his gaze searching my face. "Until then..."

He stepped back and bowed slightly, a mischievous glimmer in his eyes. Reaching out with one finger, he lightly brushed the edge of my dress before turning away.

My, my... what is the Summer King really after?

nine

Pretend Wife

The sun glinted off the endless expanse of crystal blue water as I stood atop a cliff that overlooked the beach.

A chorus of seagulls soared above while their distant calls echoed in my ears.

The sand gleamed like gold beneath my feet and moved on its own in a strange sort of choreography.

Strange creatures of all shapes and sizes marched around the beach, performing intricate dances.

Some spun in circles, while others moved their feet up and down in sync with one another.

At the far end of the beach was a large stage made up of what seemed to be an infinite number of colors - purples, blues, greens, reds, and oranges, blended seamlessly together to create a vibrant kaleidoscope of color.

Brightly lit torches lined the edges and illuminated the performers as they danced in perfect unison with one another.

I looked up from the beach to find Azair already leading the way.

His long cloak trailed behind him like a black shadow as he marched across the sand.

We followed a winding path that led us through fragrant gardens of exotic flowers and tall trees with strange fruit dangling from their branches.

The path opened up to reveal a small, secluded area surrounded by an array of wildflowers.

A soft blanket was already laid out on the ground and a basket sat in the center as kittens scurried around preparing the food.

The furry creatures chattered cheerfully as they laid out fruits, juices, and cakes on silver platters.

He gestured for me to sit down.

Silk pillows and delicately embroidered blankets lined the ground, creating a cozy atmosphere that beckoned me to relax.

He followed suit, gracefully folding his legs and resting against a pile of pillows.

Smooth muscles flexed beneath his skin, and I shivered at the sight. The hint of skin peeking out from beneath his brocade shirt was a cruel tease.

"Tell me." He leaned forward to grab a handful of strawberries from one platter. "What do you want out of this life?"

Arching an eyebrow, I considered his question.

Yes, I wanted to stop the curse - but doubt crept into my mind. Could I really do this? After all that had happened so far, it felt almost too good to be true.

I would try, but I also wanted something else.

"I've already accomplished my goal. I wanted to save my family, and I have done that. Now..." I took a deep breath. "I want to enjoy life as much as I can. Fate brought me here, and all I can do now is make the best of it."

Bands of bright colors illuminated the night sky as performers danced beneath the shimmering stars. Beads and sequins glittered like diamonds in the darkness, while feathers and ribbons floated around like petals from a flower.

The music carried on the breeze, intoxicating my senses with its melodic allure.

He grabbed another strawberry and held it up to my lips, his gaze never leaving mine. "Then let us hope fate will be kind."

I opened my mouth, biting into the sweet berry. It was tart and juicy, bursting with flavor that melted on my tongue.

His finger lightly pressed against my lips, and I heard the soft sound of his breath as my tongue brushed against it.

"Can we be truthful with each other?" I asked, looking at the kittens playing nearby.

The light of the stars glinted off their fur, and their tails swished back and forth as they explored.

"The games and secrets are tiring. I want us to speak plainly, without fear of reprisal."

He smiled and nodded, setting the strawberry in his hand aside. "Yes. We can be honest with each other."

"It takes a powerful leader to defend their court from such a dark curse, and you have my respect."

He shifted closer to me, leaning close enough for our noses to brush against each other. "I didn't expect you to be so forthcoming. But I can tell that you have something else in mind."

I shrugged, my cheeks heating with a flush of embarrassment. "It's just —" I hesitated, searching for the right words. "I want us to talk freely without having to worry about secrets or courtly etiquette. I don't want either of us to have to hide who we are. If I'm to die here, I want to be remembered for my real self."

He nodded slowly, eyes calmer than before. "Then let's start with an honest question. What do you wish to accomplish as the Summer Queen?"

His gaze never wavered, and a surge of determination washed over me.

No more secrets or lies - only truth.

I took a deep breath and looked him in the eye. "I want to be remembered. I don't want fame or riches. Just a legacy of my own. A legacy that survives beyond my death."

"I despise mortals who set such ambitious goals," he said, his voice low and velvety. "But I can appreciate your audacity."

His gaze seemed to penetrate my soul, as if he saw straight through me and knew exactly what I was thinking.

I couldn't help but feel that he was well aware of my knowledge of the curse and perhaps even planned for it.

I cocked my head. "I said nothing about breaking the curse."

He chuckled and leaned back, his arm brushing against mine. "Ah, but I think you did. You simply haven't realized it yet."

"A wife isn't a legacy. Another bride will take my place, eventually. Calan has no shortage of eligible ladies."

His broad chest expanded as his eyes narrowed, like a lion sizing up its prey. The thunderous power under his taut skin threatened to erupt at any moment.

"Have you given up? Are you truly content to let your story end here?"

Was he challenging me?

Every bride before me had died. He had asked me what I wanted out of life, but all I could think was that my fate was already sealed.

Death was inevitable. Seducing him was a way to make it easier.

I met his gaze, fire flashing in my eyes. "Your kingdom is beautiful," I said. "The gardens are meticulously tended and the people don't have to work. Saving Garnet Isles would mean saving all of this. I can't let it disappear into the night."

His fists clenched and unclenched as if struggling to contain himself in response to my words.

"I appreciate your admiration." His jaw tightened before he finally relaxed, a hint of a smile playing on his lips. "But it is the will of the people, not mine. I merely provide them with a safe haven and an opportunity to prosper."

My face softened as I looked around at the majestic gardens, the lush greenery, and bright flowers reminding me of home. The home I would never see again.

"You provide more than that. You provide hope. That is your legacy. One that will last far longer than any name or title." I sighed, feeling a measure of peace settle over me. "I understand why you must do this, and I wish to help in whatever way I can."

He smiled, his eyes taking on a distant glint. "The naivety of youth," he murmured. "But I appreciate your sentiment."

I swallowed back. "Being wed and bedded changes a woman. I'm no longer a young girl with rosy dreams of knights and true love. I have seen what this world can do, and I will sacrifice anything for my family. I have sacrificed everything."

I paused, taking a moment to look up at him, and let my words sink in.

"Who am I to fault you for wanting to protect your people the same way?"

He looked away, his jaw tightening. "This realm is mine to govern. It's my sacred duty to make tough decisions and ensure the safety of those under my watch in my role." He looked back at me, emotion in his eyes that he had concealed before. "And sometimes those decisions require sacrifice. No matter the circumstances, killing brides is never justifiable."

That he regretted his actions only made him more real to me.

All those brides, all the lives lost... It was heartbreaking.

"It's a necessary cruelty," I whispered. "It's the only way to keep Garnet Isles safe. I understand that, and so do all those who live here."

He nodded, his jaw tightening. "You're willing to die for that? To be just another casualty in the never-ending cycle of life and death?"

I met his gaze and shrugged lightly. "My story may not have the happiest of endings, but it's been an adventure. I always expected to die young - that was something I accepted long before I ever met you. But I have no regrets over dying for my family and for Garnet Isles."

He nodded and smiled, though his eyes betrayed a hint of sadness. "You are a remarkable woman," he said. "I understand why you strive for a legacy of your own."

"If I am to be remembered, it will be for the things that I do in life - not for what happens after my death."

A dimple appeared on his cheek as he smiled, and it was like the sun had broken through the gray clouds.

A dazzling warmth filled my chest, spreading slowly throughout my body as I drank in his beauty.

The meow of a kitten interrupted the trance, and I blinked, pulling myself away from his gaze.

Its small paws pawed at the basket of food, the silver platter glinting in the fading sunlight.

Azair chuckled and stood up. "It looks like we have a dinner guest."

I watched as he scooped the kitten into his arms and brought it to my lap. Its soft fur brushed against my skin as Azair smiled down at us both. "What do you think, wife? Shall we share this feast?"

The kitten purred as I ran my hands along its blue fur. Soft and warm, as if it were made of silk. I smiled up at Azair, feeling a surge of warmth flood through me.

"I wish to court you."

I was stunned by his confession, barely able to form the words. "For what purpose?"

He tilted his head, his expression unreadable. "You understand the gravity of this situation and the sacrifices required of us both. A pretend courtship between us provides me with an opportunity to investigate the curse without suspicion, and you with a chance to see your family again."

I bit my lip, trying to make sense of his words.

I could only assume that this fake courtship was meant to make the Summer Fae think that their king was capable of falling in love - and, with it, breaking the curse.

A charade, then.

A charade that had the power to save us all.

My heart raced as I looked up at him, my mouth dry. "Do you think it will work? Would it be foolish of me to agree?"

He clicked his tongue. "It would be a foolishness shared by two, but I think it is our best chance. We can work together and figure out how to save our court without sacrificing innocent lives." White pointed teeth flashed as he smiled. "What do you say? Will you become my pretend bride?"

The kitten purred softly between us, as if on cue.

Why was I different?

The thought bubbled up from the depths of my heart and soul, penetrating my every thought.

Why did he choose me over all the others?

The others who were more beautiful, more obedient, and more willing to do whatever it took to please him?

Unless there was something more to this than I realized.

I looked at him, studying the intensity of his gaze and the determination in his expression.

He wanted this, and he was willing to put his life on the line for it.

That changed everything. All I had to do was make him fall in love with me, and maybe—just maybe—I would get to go home.

Proximity would be our ally, and I would do whatever it took to make this courtship a success.

It was the only chance we had.

For my family's sake, and for the Summer Court's too.

I looked down at the little bundle of fur in my arms and smiled. "Yes, I will be your pretend bride."

"It is settled then."

I straightened my spine, my gaze still locked with his. "But I need something in return. A promise."

Music and laughter reached my ears as I glanced at the glittering shore.

Dancing couples, their silhouettes illuminated in the orange light of the setting sun, twirled and spun with joy.

A few children played near the water, their squeals of delight echoing in my ears.

"Greedy little thing, aren't you?" He smiled and tucked a strand of hair behind my ear as I stared into his eyes. "Demanding a token like this."

"Is it greed if I'm asking for something I deserve?"

"To the Fae, greed has many definitions," he said. "Name it and I will decide whether you are entitled to it."

My heart thudded against my ribcage.

I wanted so much — freedom, security, a chance to be loved — but in the end, I settled for one thing. Something more attainable and perhaps a bit selfish.

"I want your word," I said slowly, "that I get to see the real you, not some deceptive version of who you think I want you to be. I want us to be in this together, and for that to happen, you have to show yourself not just as the King of Garnet Isles, but also as a man."

"What if you don't like what you see?" he asked, his expression guarded. "What if I am not the man you want me to be?"

"I want you to be who you are," I answered firmly. "I don't want to change you. I just want to understand you. If we are in this together, then let us truly be in it together."

He looked at me intently, his gaze searching my face as if trying to see into my soul.

After a moment, he gave a single nod. "That is a fair request," he said finally. "You have my word that I will be the man that I am. That is all you can expect of me, and all I can promise."

I nodded, trusting his word.

I knew the Fae kept their promises, but they were also known to be crafty with what they said. They could omit details or twist words in such subtle ways that it was hard to distinguish between what was said and what wasn't.

This was the best I could hope for, and I accepted it without hesitation.

I didn't ask him to be perfect. I only asked for his honesty, and that was something he seemed willing to give.

We could work with that.

The kitten purred between us, a silent witness to our agreement.

He grinned, a satisfied expression on his face. "I insist you do not fall in love with me. No matter what happens during our courtship, I must always remain the one who is out of reach."

I raised an eyebrow, feeling the soft fur of the kitten against my cheek. "Don't you think you're being presumptuous?"

He chuckled and stood up. "I think it's inevitable," he said, his gaze never leaving mine. "But I will not take advantage of your naivety. Our courtship shall remain strictly professional, and nothing more."

"You should know that it's not very gentlemanly to tell a lady she will fall in love with you. Or, you know, to choose her as your bride and then imply that she has no chance of winning your heart."

My tongue found its way between my lips as I smiled coyly. Why choose me if he wasn't willing to give me a chance?

His eyes flared with heat, and he leaned closer. "Just make sure that you don't break the bargain."

I nodded, my breath hitching in my throat. "If you say so, my lord."

"I do say so," he said, his voice low and husky. "My wife."

He took one step back as if to break the spell, then glanced down at the kitten in my lap.

The kitten mewled softly from my lap, its tiny body nestling in the crook of my arm.

I glanced up to find him watching us both, a thoughtful expression on his face. "In all honesty," he said quietly, "my heart is not something I plan on giving away. But I wish you luck in your endeavor."

His words and the way he looked at me betrayed a need for more than just a pretend courtship between us.

He didn't realize it yet, but by admitting that his heart wasn't up for grabs, he was inviting me to win it.

Deep down, he wanted it.

For the first time, I felt a spark of hope. With this, maybe I had a chance. Maybe he wasn't as far away as he seemed.

My eyes narrowed, and I couldn't help but burst out laughing. "I'm not a woman to be trifled with." I stood up, cradling the kitten in my arms while its tail brushed against my arm. "If you think this courtship will be easy and predictable, then you don't know me very well."

He chuckled, the sound low and deep. "I know it won't be easy or predictable, but I think it's worth a try. After all, there are two of us here, and if we can fool our people with this charade, then we shall both benefit."

He paused, his intense gaze boring into me.

"Trust me in this, little mouse. I will make sure our people are fooled…and that you get everything you desire in the end."

ten

THE ART OF CREATING CONFUSION

"Remember that the Summer Court is more than just a kingdom," Azair said, as we sailed our palanquin across the glittering canals of the city.

Red jade walls glowed against white marble columns, while gold-tipped spires reached high into the air.

"It is a living, breathing beast that has to be fed stories to keep it alive."

His fingers twitched almost imperceptibly, and I could tell that his words were directed toward me. If only to remind me of what I already knew.

We passed under a bridge made of white marble and rubies, its reflection shimmering like a prism in the water beneath us.

"Back home, gossip is our way of keeping peace." I leaned forward, my hands clasped in front of me. "It's how we know who to trust, and who not to. It's how the unwritten rules of society are formed and maintained."

The sound of drums and horns echoed through the air, and I smiled in spite of myself.

A dragon boat, adorned with white pearls and blue silk banners, glided gracefully through the waters ahead.

"It sounds like your people know how to navigate the delicate balance between what is said and what is left unsaid." Azair's lips curled into a sly smile, and I couldn't help but match it.

The aunties and uncles back home were versed in the politics of gossip, and I'd been taught by them since childhood.

"They called it 'the art of conversation.' It's a skill that comes with practice." Exasperation crept into my voice as I thought of all the pointless conversations and debates I had endured in their presence. "And boredom, too."

He chuckled, a low rumble that sent shivers down my spine. "Ah, but it is through these conversations and this boredom that we learn the most," he said. "Sometimes the best way to understand someone is not by talking to them, but by listening."

I nodded, my gaze lingering on the dragon boat ahead.

His words seeped into my skin, taking root in my heart and mind.

He was right. Hungry gossipers weren't only after juicy stories; they were looking for clues to tell them who was rising and who was falling, which family had the upper hand, or which lord held sway over another.

To understand more, one had to learn how to read between the lines. And that was exactly what I intended to do.

Not because it was my role as his pretend betrothed, but because he deserved to be understood.

I wanted to get close enough to see who he really was, beneath the masks and the layers of expectations.

And maybe that was the key - not seduction, but connection. Not flattery, but honesty and understanding.

The kind of trust that could bridge any gap, no matter how wide or deep it might be.

To truly win his heart, I had to go beyond the surface of things and dig deeper. To understand what made him tick and accept it in its entirety.

That was the only way to gain a genuine connection with him—one that could survive even in times of conflict or disagreement.

Azair smiled, but it didn't reach his eyes. "In the Summer Court, gossip is more than just a game. It's a way of life. And if you want to survive here, learn how to play the game. Wars are won and lost with words, not swords." He looked me in the eye and his voice softened. "Do you understand?"

We should never underestimate the power of words. Tread carefully, I reminded myself.

Tilting my chin up, I met his gaze and gave a small nod. "During a time of crisis, even the smallest whisper can become a deafening roar. This kingdom is built on stories, but it can also be destroyed by them."

He looked away, and I wondered what secrets he was hiding.

I thought back to the stories I heard of kings and queens who had fallen from grace in the blink of an eye.

How the smallest mistake could have devastating consequences.

I shivered, despite the warmth of the summer air.

One wrong word or one wrong move could spell disaster for us both. But if we played our cards right and kept a level head, who knew what stories we might write together?

"How do you navigate such a dangerous sea?"

He smiled, and this time, it reached his eyes. "The same way you navigate rapids and whirlpools. With grace, a steady hand, and a little bit of luck." He winked at me, then turned to face the dragon boat ahead. "And with an eye for what makes a story worth telling. Sometimes I'll spin a tale, and sometimes I'll speak nothing but truths. No matter what, I know stories are our only anchors in this ever-changing world. Mortals and Fae alike cling to them, clinging to the hope that our stories can outlive us."

Mortals are fragile. We can be broken so easily.

The Fae were made of iron and fire. They could withstand so much more. My mortality made me vulnerable in ways they could never understand.

He glanced up at the sky as if searching for something, then turned back to me with a smile.

"Your mortality gives you something that the Fae lack. Perspective. You can look at things from both sides and see the truth in the middle. That, more than anything else, will be your greatest weapon here."

I quirked an eyebrow at him. It almost seemed like he heard my thoughts.

"It sounds like you're trying to say that, despite your disdain for mortals, I could have something to offer the Summer Court."

Pointy teeth glinted in his smile. "I'm saying that your stories can be just as powerful as ours. That they matter too."

He looked out across the water, his gaze focused but distant.

"And I'm saying that, if you play your cards right, they can shape the future of this kingdom."

Perhaps I could learn to play their game after all.

The palanquin dipped and swayed in the gentle current of the canal.

We rode in silence, listening to the low murmur of gossip that drifted over the water.

Glass stalls glinted in the afternoon light, their wooden tables laden with fresh produce and trinkets.

Families crowded around them, their children racing between the stalls and playing tag.

Men and women in bright colors haggled over prices, their voices raised in friendly banter. Tails swayed, feathers fluttered and antlers bobbed as they chatted. Colored gemstones sparkled in their hair, and intricate tattoos adorned their skin.

I watched the scene unfold, taking in every detail.

The Summer Court was alive and vibrant, a mix of beauty and chaos that had to be experienced to be understood.

We passed under another bridge, its archway lit by thousands of twinkling lanterns.

The canal widened as we approached the harbor, and the sounds of merriment grew louder.

Azair leaned forward, resting his elbows against the edge of the palanquin and letting out a heavy sigh.

His brow furrowed in thought, and his lips pursed into a thin line.

Beneath his stoic exterior lay a heart of gold, but it was hidden away from prying eyes. An asshole, yes, but not entirely without empathy.

We were both trying to save people, after all. In this strange courtship of ours, we could both benefit from a mutual understanding.

"Secretly, I've always wanted to cause a scandal," I confessed, breaking the silence. "Maybe even a little chaos."

He arched an eyebrow, his lips twitching into a smirk. "Is that so?"

I nodded, drawing my knees to my chest and wrapping my arms around them. "It would be nice to do something different. To shake things up a bit."

The gold rings on my fingers glinted in the sunlight, as I twirled them absentmindedly.

"I never dared to before, for the destruction it could cause."

"Sometimes, the only way to make a change is by embracing chaos and turning it into something beautiful."

"Have you ever done that? Embraced chaos completely?"

He was quiet for a moment. Then he nodded, a wry smile playing on his lips. "Oh, yes. Once or twice in my life."

"What happened?"

He reached out and brushed my fingers with his own, his gaze still fixed on the horizon. "Let's just say that I was rewarded for my courage." He turned to me and smiled, his eyes twinkling with mischief. "Change is inevitable, wife. And sometimes it's necessary."

The palanquin swayed, and I leaned closer to him.

"I have seen empires fall and rise again," he said, his voice low and distant. "And wars are often won or lost in the words that are spoken."

He paused and reached out to brush a lock of hair away from my face.

"Be careful with your words. They can break even the strongest of hearts."

I stared into his eyes. I knew all too well the cruelty of words. The power they held.

The palanquin swayed as we rounded a bend in the canal, and I let my guard down just enough to let him in. "Words can build walls or tear them down."

The sting of past pain rose in me, and I shuddered as memories washed over me.

All the times I'd been hurt or betrayed, all those moments of suffering that had seemed so unbearable.

The loneliness, the heartache. They were all still there, buried deep within my soul.

I thought of the people who had caused this pain, and the pain that they had caused others. How quickly their words, spoken in anger or spite, could break a person's spirit.

And yet, here I was. Still standing. Divorced, but still alive.

I forced myself to take a deep breath and release the tension from my body.

I survived, I reminded myself. Despite everything, I survived.

My walls were not as strong as they once were, but I was still here.

I was still alive.

He leaned against the edge of the palanquin. His hands rested lightly on his hips, and he cocked his head to the side with an inquisitive tilt. "The Summer Court may be wild and unpredictable, but beneath that chaos lies a hidden beauty. All you have to do is find it."

Boats glided by, each more ornate than the last. Sunlight caught their gilded prows and turned them into liquid gold.

Somewhere in the distance, a horn sounded, its melody echoing off the walls of the canal.

"Do you regret them?" I closed my eyes and breathed in the sweet summer air, letting the sound of Azair's voice fill my head.

"Regret what?"

I opened my eyes and looked into his. "The choices you made?" I said softly. "Do you regret them?"

His brow furrowed as he considered the question.

"Regret is a dangerous thing," he said finally. "It paralyzes, leading one down paths that were never meant to be taken. But it can also provide clarity, allowing us to see the consequences of our actions and learn from them. I choose not to regret anything, for it has all shaped me into the man I am today."

Gold and silver lanterns bobbed in the breeze, their light illuminating the harbor.

Waves lapped against the banks of the canal, as fishes swam beneath its crystal surface.

Azair turned to me. King of the Summer Court, ruler of chaos. "Fear not the chaos," he said, his eyes twinkling in the light of the lanterns. "For it can be your greatest ally."

I grinned, excitement coursing through my veins as I imagined the possibilities. "I think we should make our courtship scandalous enough to make even the most jaded courtiers take notice."

The dragon boat that passed us earlier was now surrounded by a half-dozen mermaid ships with glittering scales and long, flowing tails.

He stepped out of the palanquin and offered me his hand. "And how do you plan to achieve this, little mouse?"

I took his hand and stepped onto the dock, my silk dress billowing in the wind.

My dress was white, but with accents of red that took on a life of their own as they twisted and turned in the wind.

A crown of roses adorned my head, their petals a deep ruby that dripped with the blood of those who had come before me.

I was no longer the mouse in the corner, cowering from the chaos around me. I was a Fae queen, an embodiment of divine femininity.

"In the country of Ura, culture and tradition reign supreme. The noblewoman who can best maneuver her way into the court will be crowned queen," I said, raising my chin and looking out over the horizon. "As a lowly handmaiden, I had an undercover advantage. I could observe the calculated affairs of those vying for power."

Azair smiled and took my hand, leading me away from the dock. "And now you enter the arena as a contender."

"I've learned a few things about courtly politics," I said as we walked, my heart beating faster with each step. "The most determined of these noblewomen was Aiara of clan Vilnas, a beautiful woman with a sharp wit and an even sharper tongue. She had her eyes set on the crown prince, and she meant to make him hers no matter what stood in her way."

Gold eyes watched me closely, his gaze never leaving my face. The intrigue of the court captivated him.

"And what happened next?"

"Aiara was determined," I said. "She would not be denied her love, no matter what obstacles stood in her way. But there's one person she hadn't counted on. Ayala of clan Hessa. In Ayala, Aiara had finally met her match. For she, too, had her eyes on the crown prince."

"It sounds like the start of a tumultuous rivalry."

"The women's rivalry captivated the court."

The bickering between Aiara and Ayala was a source of endless entertainment, and I watched with bated breath as they fought for the heart of the prince.

The dressmakers made fortunes as the two women vied to outdo one another with increasingly elaborate gowns and jewelry, and my pockets filled with iron coins as I was hired to act as a messenger between them.

"They both had their sights set on the same goal, and it became a battle of wits to determine who would be crowned queen. Both women fought valiantly, employing every trick in the book. But in the end, it was clear there could be one victor."

Azair stopped walking and turned to me, his eyes sparkling in the sunlight. "And how did Aiara win?"

"Why do you think she won?" I countered. "She took an unconventional approach to the game, and it paid off in the end. Where her rival was meek, Aiara was bold. Where her rival held back, Aiara stepped forward. In such a strict court, she was a breath of fresh air. Her courage and ambition captivated the court, and in the end, they crowned her queen."

"And so Ayala was outmaneuvered and defeated."

"But she was not defeated," I said. "For in her own way, Ayala won too. She was not made queen, but she gained something even more valuable."

He raised an eyebrow. "What do you mean?"

"She gained the king's respect. Her intelligence impressed him, and even in defeat, he gave her a place of honor in his court. Ayala may not have won the crown, but she left Ura with something far greater: the first woman's place in the court."

"Neither Aiara nor Ayala loved the prince of Ura. They wanted what he could give them. Power, status, and wealth. The trappings of the powerful." Harsh lines appeared around his mouth. "Love is not a commodity to be bargained with."

"Life is never a game of chance. There are always forces at play, unseen currents guiding our lives in ways we cannot comprehend. We must sacrifice our own desires to achieve our goals. The women had no choice but to use whatever means necessary to win his affection."

Azair frowned, but he seemed to understand.

"It is a lesson we all must learn," I finished. "To succeed in life, sometimes, we must give up the things we want most for the things we need most." I looked up into his eyes, and a sudden feeling of profound sadness overwhelmed me. "The nobility use us as pawns in their games, even their own children. Neither Airara nor Ayala were exempt from that."

Azair sighed and ran a hand through his hair, his eyes troubled. "It's difficult to accept that we are but pieces in someone else's game. But accept it, we must. For the Queen of Ura is not only a symbol of power, but a reminder to us all that sometimes we must take our fate into our own hands if we are to shape the future."

This was not just about Aiara or Ayala; it was about all of us who had ever dreamed of overcoming the odds and achieving greatness.

"Hearts can be broken," I said, "but dreams never die."

His gold eyes flashed with a mix of anger and wildness.

There was something feral about him, like he was a beast that had been tamed, but could never truly be domesticated.

"Were you ever betrayed by a nobleman?"

I looked away, unwilling to let him see the pain in my eyes. "No, but I have seen many hearts broken by their desires for power and prestige. *He* could be just as calculating and ruthless as any other nobleman."

"We are all betrayed in one way or another. The only thing that matters is how we respond to those betrayals." The wind blew through his hair, his crown of thorns glinting in the lights of the harbor. "Widowhood is a heavy burden. The strength it takes to bear it is a testament to your courage."

I swallowed hard, the smile on my face brittle and small. "I'm not a widow, Azair. He lives. But I'm no longer bound to him."

Unprotected, unloved, and unwanted. I had been abandoned.

The shame of it burned like acid, but I kept my chin up and met his gaze with all the strength I could muster.

Widows had a certain level of respect and admiration for their courage, but those who had been abandoned by their husbands were viewed with scorn and suspicion.

I was often reminded that when a husband abandoned his wife, he did so for a reason.

It was a heavy burden to bear, but I would carry it with dignity and pride. I had been abandoned, but I would not be humiliated.

"The disgrace of your former husband does not define you," he said, reaching out and taking my hand in his. "You may not be a widow, but you were abandoned just the same. The pain, the suffering. It's enough to make anyone swear off love altogether."

Did someone hurt him too? I wondered. Who betrayed this man who seemed so strong and powerful?

I took a deep breath and let out a shaky sigh. "It's easy to become bitter after being mistreated," I said slowly. "My mother used to say that love is like a rose, with its thorns and petals. We must not forget the beauty of love, even when we are wounded by it."

I blushed and looked away, suddenly feeling shy under his intense stare. But when I looked back up, a mischievous smile had spread across his lips.

"Fortunately, we don't have to worry about that," he said, squeezing my hand in reassurance. "Our courtship will be unconventional, but if we play our cards right, we can still cause a scandal."

My pulse leaped at his words, and a thrill of anticipation ran through my body. "Now that," I said, giving him a sly smile, "sounds like a challenge."

He laughed and released my hand, his eyes twinkling with amusement. "You're not scared of a little scandal, are you?"

"Not here. Not with you backing me."

He leaned in closer until his breath was tickling my ear and the warmth of his body pressed against mine.

"Shall we make them foam at the mouth?" he asked, his voice a low whisper. "How much trouble do you want to cause?"

eleven

THE TAINT OF JADE WALLS

My heart raced as I thought about what we were planning.

We could easily make a scandal of our own, but would it be worth the trouble? What if it ended up hurting us?

Sometimes, even the most daring plans could have disastrous consequences.

But then I thought about Ayala and Aiara, risking everything for a chance at love. If they could be brave, then so could I.

His hands moved to my waist, anchoring me in place, as I tilted my head to the side, letting my dark hair spill over my shoulders. "Enough to make the courtiers whisper my name with reverence."

"I could drag you back to the palanquin and have my way with you."

His voice was laced with a hint of danger, but I felt no fear, only a sense of anticipation.

"Or I could just tear off your dress right here, in front of everyone. No one would dare try to stop us. We'd be the talk of the court."

My breath hitched as his breath brushed my skin and, for a moment, I was lost in his golden gaze.

I wanted to say something - anything - but all the words disappeared from my mind.

He let out a low chuckle, his lips just a fraction of an inch away from mine. "Which would you prefer?" he whispered against my lips. "A scandalous courtship or a wild, passionate affair?"

A warmth settled deep in my belly, radiating outward as if it had always been there but only now revealed itself.

I was aware of every movement he made; the slightest brush of his fingers sent shivers up my spine and a flush to my cheeks.

His eyes mesmerized me, drawing me in and wrapping me up in his intensity.

I felt something else too - a longing I hadn't experienced in years.

For the first time, I realized that this wasn't just a fleeting feeling; it was a real, deep desire burning inside of me for him.

I blinked, my head spinning from his nearness, and realized I had been holding my breath.

He smiled knowingly and leaned closer, his lips just a hair's breadth away from mine.

I wanted both. But it was impossible. A man like him could never be mine.

No matter how much I wanted it.

His lips curved into a satisfied smirk, and he pulled away from me, still holding my gaze.

"Scandalous enough for you, little mouse?" he said, the amusement clear in his voice. "You know nothing of Fae courting. It's wild and passionate, untamed and unrestrained. It doesn't care for rules or proper etiquette; it only knows the language of desire."

I swallowed the lump in my throat and nodded, unable to speak.

His eyes glowed with a dangerous intensity, and I knew he wanted me to take the plunge. To break away from all of my inhibitions and throw myself into the wild, passionate affair he was offering.

This man was dangerous, and I knew it; he could easily consume me if I let him.

From the corner of my eye, I spotted horned Fae women with delicate wings watching from a distance as Azair and I whispered to each other, their curious gazes lingering on our every move.

Some looked surprised by our bold touches, while others seemed captivated. Almost entranced by what was unfolding before them.

"To you, my little mouse," he said in a low voice. "A scandal means gossip and whispers behind closed doors. But to these otherworldly creatures."

He gestured towards the Fae with an elegant sweep of his hand.

"A scandal is a thing of beauty, something to be applauded and admired. Our courtship will be no different - wild, passionate, and untamed. It will be thrilling." His eyes darkened as he leaned in close, whispering against my lips. "And it will make them all talk."

I knew I had to take control of the conversation—and our narrative—quickly, before things got out of hand.

I had to make sure that Azair and I became the talk of the court—for the right reasons.

"If you want a scandal? I'll give you one." I leaned in, my lips barely grazing his neck. The smell of his skin was intoxicating. "But it won't be the type of scandal the Fae are used to."

His breath hitched as I brushed my nose against his, my eyes searching his for a sign of approval.

His gaze smoldered, the intensity of his eyes almost too much to bear.

He looked like he wanted nothing more than to tear off my dress and take me right there on the street in front of everyone.

Instead, he simply smiled and stepped back, his hands still clasped around my waist.

My core ached with longing, and I swallowed hard, trying to keep my composure.

People stopped in their tracks and gawked as we passed by, the light from lanterns strung up between buildings casting an orange glow over the cobblestone street.

"What kind of scandal do you suggest?"

"Don't forget that I've been watching you, Azair. I know your habits and mannerisms. I'm aware of what you're capable of," I said, my eyes never leaving his. "Fucking me won't be enough. It needs to be something more... Something new, something they haven't seen before. Something that will haunt their dreams and leave them craving more of you."

My lips curled into a wicked smile as I stepped closer to him, my body pressing against his.

Azair's breath caught in his throat as I reached up to trace the outline of his jaw with my fingertips. "To truly scandalize the court, we need to make sure they remember us. Forever."

His eyes glinted with amusement as he ran his thumb along my cheek. "And how do you suggest I go about it?" he asked, his voice low and husky. "What do I need to do to make them talk?"

What did he see when he looked at me? I wondered. Was it the same thing I saw when I looked at him?

A shiver ran down my spine as his breath fanned across my neck.

I leaned into him, the warmth of his body seeping into mine. "Make them feel something," I whispered. "Make them feel alive and give them an experience that they will never forget."

I glanced down, tracing circles on the runes on his chest. Stability. Fatherhood. Fidelity. A father of nations.

"Make them feel like they are a part of something bigger than the mundane, that their lives are worth more than dust. Give them an emotion so powerful it will reverberate through eternity."

"You mean... love?"

Wild abandon glittered in his eyes and my stomach flipped as I nodded.

"Feed the beast with your love and watch what happens."

Fae morality was a strange beast, and I knew that if the Summer King was cursed to fall in love with someone or doom his court, then he needed to choose me.

If I could make him fall in love with me, then maybe, just maybe, it would be enough to break the curse.

It was a long shot, but it was worth a shot. People said that love could conquer all, and I believed them.

For this, I was willing to risk it all. And if I failed, then I would accept whatever consequences came my way.

His jaw was clenched tight as he stared at me, his eyes full of a million questions. Then, without warning, he stepped closer and started tracing my lips with his thumb.

"My little manipulator," he said in a voice laced with amusement. "Your intentions are transparent to me, but I can sense your motives. They're not so different from mine. You want to survive; I want to survive. We can do this together."

Tenderly, he brushed my cheek as I closed my eyes. Such power he had over me, and yet it felt so natural.

Roughly, he pulled me to him and buried his face in my hair. "But know this, dear wife... If we are to make it through this wild game of our own making, don't expect me to tame my feral heart. Your inner beast is demanding a feast and I aim to oblige it."

I swallowed hard, my heart pounding against my ribcage.

I was playing a dangerous game. But if there was a chance to survive, then so be it.

Children ran in circles around us, laughing and playing. Trails of gossip floated in the air as they whispered our names.

The Summer King and his consort. What were we up to, they asked? What secrets did we share?

Azair reached out and brushed his thumb across my cheek again. Our eyes locked in a silent challenge. "So, little mouse," he said with a smirk. "Are you ready to feed the beast? Command me."

There was no going back now - it was time to make a stand, and I had to choose wisely.

The roar of the gossip faded away as I stepped closer and reached up to touch his face, my thumb brushing over his sculpted cheekbone.

Gold skin, pale lips. Burning eyes that saw right through me. This Fae was mine.

"Show your people you care for me," I said in an even voice as I observed his face for any sign of emotion. "Show them I am no longer a stranger to you. That I am a part of your life. That I am your wife."

"You're asking me to give them something I can't even give myself, Zareena. Not even to my people," he said. "It consumes me, this feeling that I can't name. But it's there, and it's real."

"Love, Azair. It's called love."

I held his gaze for a moment before turning away, my lips curling into a small smile as I walked toward the market.

"We just have to make them believe it exists between us... and that we both deserve it."

His eyes followed me, his expression unreadable.

But I could feel his longing, as if he wanted to come after me but couldn't bring himself to do it.

I paused and looked over my shoulder, a mischievous grin playing on my lips. "Think you can handle it?"

Grabbing my arm, he spun me around and pushed me back against the cold jade wall, his face inches away from mine.

"You make a convincing argument," he murmured, his breath hot on my skin. "But I think you do not know how dangerous it could be for us both."

His muscles tensed as he looked away, his gaze lost on the distant horizon.

"That's the point, isn't it?" I whispered, taking his face in my hands and tracing circles on his cheeks with my thumbs as wild energy surged through my veins. "A king has to take risks to gain something of value. No manipulations, no games. Show your court that you're willing to let go of everything - even yourself - for love. That's the scandal they won't forget."

His lips twitched, but he didn't move away. Instead, his hands moved to cup my face as he leaned closer, pressing his forehead against mine.

I closed my eyes and let out a deep breath, knowing that this was the moment of truth.

He might reject me or accept me, but I had to trust that he would make the right decision.

Could he really love me? Did I even want him to?

His lips curled up into a smile as he leaned in closer, his breath tickling my skin. "And what about you, wife?" Lifting a hand, he traced the curves of my lips with his thumb. "Do you believe I'm capable of love?"

A million emotions raced through me as I stared at him in stunned silence.

He was asking if I thought he could actually love me - but why?

His words implied he didn't think he was capable of it - so why did he ask?

"My opinion doesn't matter -"

"I want to know," he interrupted, his voice taking on a softer edge. "Do you think I can do it? Do you think I can love someone with all my heart?"

A man incapable of love was now asking me if I thought he could do it.

The jade wall was cold against my back, but I could no longer feel the chill. All I could feel was the warmth of his skin and the intensity of his gaze.

For a split second, I let myself believe that anything was possible, even the impossible.

Even something as extraordinary as Azair being capable of loving another person.

Did he not love his people? A king sacrificing his sanity for his court, a man that had once been so manipulative and distant now asking me if I thought he could love?

I looked into his eyes and nodded, my lips curving into a small smile. "Yes, I believe you can do it."

He stepped closer and brushed his thumb across my cheek again, his eyes never leaving mine. "Then prove it to them. Show them the love that you have for me, and I will do the same, my pretend bride."

Chuckling, I stepped sidewards and drew away from him. "You're up for a challenge, my darling husband?"

"I hunger for it," he replied, a wolfish grin spreading across his face.

We had a plan, a challenge to face, and I felt like it was within our reach. We could make them believe in us.

A farce of a marriage, but one that could prove to be the most real thing either of us had ever experienced.

Azair arched an eyebrow and cast me a sidelong glance, a smirk playing on his lips. "Shall we start with love letters, then? Poetic lines of adoration, that sort of thing? I'm out of practice, but I can feel the words forming on my tongue."

I laughed, feeling the tension in my shoulders ease.

The music swelled around us as we strolled along the canal.

Wild voices and drums echoed off the jade walls, the laughter of children and the clinking of glasses ringing in my ears.

He raised a hand and brushed his fingers against mine, his gaze smoldering with sheer intensity. "Let me describe you as if I were a poet of old," he said in a low voice, his lips curling into an amused smile. "In battles both fair and foul, you are a swordsman of grace. In love, you bring naught but sweet release."

He moved closer, his gaze never leaving mine as he raised an arm and rested his hand on my shoulder.

"And in pleasure," he added, "you bring me to the brink of madness. Though your sword may be stained with blood, your heart is pure."

"Fae romance is an acquired taste. A battlefield strewn with roses and swords."

"And what would you have me write of you?" Biting his lower lip, he smiled. "That you are a beast in disguise, a beauty no man can resist?"

I thought for a moment, feeling a strange flutter in my stomach.

"The poets would not sing my praises," I said. "Neither do I want them to. I want the common people to sing of a woman with thorns, who burns bridges like the sun sets."

"And of her love?"

I rolled my eyes and playfully punched his shoulder, unable to contain my laughter at the absurdity of the situation.

Here I was, in another world, with a man who had once been so cold and distant that it made me shiver just being around him. Now he was talking about love letters and poetic lines.

"You can laugh all you want," he said with an amused grin. "But the Fae need drama, and I intend to give it to them."

"Grand gestures are fine," I said. "But it's the small things that really make a difference. The little moments of tenderness and affection that show them we're in this together. That we are, in fact, a real couple."

His eyes lit up with a glint of amusement. "Ah, so you want me to whisper sweet nothings in your ear?" he murmured, his lips inches away from mine.

I couldn't keep the blush from rising to my cheeks as I stepped back and shook my head. "Well, I don't think that would be quite necessary," I said. "A little more subtlety wouldn't hurt, my King."

He raised an eyebrow and looked down at me with a playful smirk. "Yes, yes, of course," he said in mock seriousness. "I always aim for moderation."

We both laughed as he pulled me close and tucked my hand into the crook of his arm.

"Remember," he said. "We have to make them believe. That is the only way we can get away with this."

"I know," I murmured, nestling closer and unable to repress a small smile. "It won't be easy, but if anyone can do it, it's us."

Azair's skin glowed like molten gold in the soft light, and I couldn't help but wonder if this was what a real Fae love story looked like. Two people, sharing moments of tenderness in the shadows of an ancient city.

Did the people around us know that we were in the midst of a grand masquerade? That our love story was nothing but a show?

Merchants in boats floated past, hawking goods and services. Jade walls and golden spires encircled us, illuminated by the warm glow of the lanterns.

The suns had already set by the time we reached our destination: a small bridge that overlooked the city. Azair's hands were tight around my waist as we gazed out over the lights below.

Handcrafted ships and ornate decorations lay on the banks, the lanterns casting the entire city in a warm glow.

Azair reached for my hand, his thumb tracing gentle circles on my palm. "What now, master strategist?" he asked, his voice a low rumble. "What do we do next?"

I smiled and inhaled deeply, the scent of spices and flowers filling my lungs. "Now." I leaned against him, my fingers trailing up his arm. "You tell me why we are here."

Azair looked over the city, his face illuminated by the soft light of the lanterns. "The power is in the story and whoever can tell it best will be the one who comes out on top."

"Liar. You're too calculating for your own good."

"Why do you think I brought you here, then?"

"Your goal is to break your curse. You need to prove to your people that you can love."

Biting my lip, I looked out at the city beneath us, people living their lives and going about their daily routines.

"But you could have proved that in your court. So why did you choose to bring me out here?"

"What is your theory?"

"My theory," I said slowly, savoring the words as they formed in my mind, "is that you brought me to this place—these canals, this city—where your story began. The birthplace of your curse, and the place where you will prove to yourself and everyone else that you can choose your happy ending."

Azair remained silent, his eyes following the group of pixies that flew by us.

I watched as their wings fluttered like delicate butterflies in the soft light of the lanterns.

"It's a beautiful theory. Do you believe it?"

I stepped away from the bridge and glanced back, my gaze lingering on the flickering lights. "It's a theory, but it's something to think about."

More boats floated by, carrying merchants and entertainers, while others had small stages set up for plays and music.

Teenagers ran around the boats playing games with pieces of boldly colored fabric.

Azair gave me a sidelong glance, his expression unreadable. "Do you not want to know what I'm doing here?"

Cocking my head to the side, I watched as a boat filled with musicians passed by us. "No," I said. "I trust that you have a plan."

He stopped. Madness swirled in his eyes, a wildness that I'd never seen before. He stepped closer, and for a moment I was almost afraid of him.

But then he smiled, and the fear evaporated as quickly as it had come. "You really don't want to know, do you?" he murmured in disbelief. "You're content with just trusting me?"

"Trusting you and believing in you are two very different things." I lifted an eyebrow. "Do I look like a curse breaker to you? You know best what to do when it comes to magic and the Fae... but I'm more than happy to provide moral support."

He laughed, his deep baritone ringing out over the canal. "Oh, so now we're talking about moral support?" He leaned in closer, his breath hot on my face. "Clever. Brilliant. Trying to lure me into revealing my secrets? Or maybe you are trying to soften me up?"

"A girl has to do something in her spare time, right? Besides," I said, taking his hands in mine and giving them a playful squeeze. "Maybe if you tell me your secrets, I'll share some of mine."

He shook his head slightly and took a step back, as if teasing me with something just out of reach. "I think I have something better in mind."

He led me away from the bridge and pulled me through the narrow alleyways and winding streets of the city.

He looked around cautiously, as if searching for something only he could see. What was he looking for?

Eventually, the houses and shops gave way to an open courtyard lined with fragrant trees.

A small pond glittered in the center, filled with colorful lilies that danced in the light of the lanterns strung up on either side.

A single white bird perched atop a branch above us, its wings spread wide as it sang its evening song.

We crossed another bridge, the golden light from the metalwork casting a shimmering haze around us.

He stopped, his eyes searching my face, before he pulled me into a hidden alcove beneath the bridge.

Blue roses and sunflowers lined the walls, swaying in the soft breeze.

"Do you trust me?"

I glanced up at him, studying the silhouette of his face in the moonlight.

He looked back at me, his expression serious yet gentle.

"That depends," I said, my heart racing. "What did you have in mind?"

He smiled and reached for my hands. He twirled me around the small alcove as if we were dancing, his eyes never leaving mine.

"I want to show you my world," he said. "The beauty and the darkness, so that you can understand why I do what I do."

He twirled me faster, the colors of the flowers blurring together until all I could see were his eyes. He halted, and I felt myself go still in his arms.

"Well?" He smiled, his hands still wrapped around my waist. "What do you say?"

twelve

THE CURSE OF DEFIANCE

I exhaled slowly, feeling the tension seep away from my body. I looked up at him, and despite all the uncertainty that lingered between us, I nodded.

He pressed a kiss to my forehead before releasing me.

Taking my hand, he led me further into the alcove, the walls decorated with inlaid patterns of stars and moons.

He whispered something under his breath, and the walls moved, slowly transforming into a long hallway.

He stepped forward, drawing me along with him until we reached the end of the corridor. He paused before a solid wooden door, holding up his hand to stop me from going any further.

"Welcome to my sanctuary." Opening the door, he stepped outside and gestured for me to follow.

The darkness swallowed us, and for a few moments, I felt disoriented.

Then my eyes adjusted to the lights, and I saw we were standing next to the river.

A small boat was tethered to the shore, its sails billowing in the night breeze.

He stepped into the shallow water and held out his hand. "Come, I want to show you something special."

I hesitated, but then I stepped forward and let him lead me further into the river.

The cool water enveloped us, and soon we were surrounded by colorful fish darting around us in an ever-changing kaleidoscope of light.

Water lilies floated on the surface, and there were flashes of iridescent scales everywhere.

Azair turned to me and smiled, his eyes aglow with the beauty of the moment. "This is my secret," he said softly. "The one I wanted to share with you. This is where I come when I need to find my peace. When the world outside becomes too chaotic, I come here and sink into the stillness of the water."

He led us to a large clump of rocks jutting out from the bottom of the river.

The rocks were glowing in hues of pink and purple, illuminated by rubies and sapphires embedded in the rocks.

He stepped back and waved his hand in a circular motion.

The rocks spun, and I watched as they formed a spiral pattern, slowly rising out of the water.

When the pattern was complete, a small island appeared.

The land was lush and green, with colorful wildflowers dotting the shoreline.

In the center, cushions embroidered with shimmering threads in all shades of blue and green were arranged around a small fire pit.

Azair stepped up onto the island, and I followed him. He gestured to the cushions, inviting me to sit down.

As soon as I did, fairy lights twinkled above us, and a soft melody filled the air.

"I had a place like this once," I said, my eyes never leaving the flames.

The fire in the pit grew brighter, its flames dancing in time with the music.

"Nothing as magical as this, of course," I added, smiling. "A small clearing in the woods, surrounded by trees and wildflowers. I used to go there whenever I needed to be alone and just think. It's the only place I ever felt truly at peace."

"Peace can be found in many places. What matters is that you recognize it when you find it."

"How did you find this place?" I asked, my gaze wandering to the trees and wildflowers around us.

"It found me," he whispered, his voice barely audible above the crackling of the fire. "The island is a manifestation of my innermost thoughts and desires. When I need to escape, this is the place I come to. Let me show you."

He took my hand and led me around the island, pointing out all of its hidden secrets: the trees that grow fruits in springtime, the waterfall that cascades over tall rocks, and the small grove of lush plants and herbs.

As we walked back to the fire pit, I realized I wasn't just being shown a secret place — I was being shown a part of Azair's soul. A part of him that few people ever got to see.

He let go of my hand and sat down on one of the cushions, his eyes never leaving mine. "Welcome to my sanctuary," he said again, and this time I knew he meant it.

I sat down beside him, and together we watched the flames as they danced their silent song in the night sky.

Azair was right — peace could be found in many places. And for that moment, peace had found us here on this secret island.

I raised an eyebrow as cups of tea and plates of sweet treats appeared before us, courtesy of an unseen force.

He smiled, his eyes twinkling in the firelight. "I told you it was a magical place."

I smiled and thanked him before taking a sip of tea.

The flavors of orange blossom and honey filled my mouth, the sweetness soothing away any lingering doubts I had about this place.

"So you've bared your soul," I said. "It's only fair that I return the favor."

He leaned back against the cushion, sprawled out in a way that made him look invincible. But I knew better. I'd seen the cracks in his armor, and underneath was a vulnerability that left me feeling breathless.

"Unburden yourself," he said. "I'm here to listen."

"Sometimes," I said, tracing patterns in the dirt with my finger. "When I had the chance... I snuck into high society events." I laughed, the sound of it echoing across the river. "Not to mingle with the elite or even steal anything. Just so I could feel what it was like to be a part of something, even if just for a night. To feel accepted and seen."

"It's okay to have those desires," he said. "We all want to be seen and appreciated."

I nodded, my eyes still focused on the patterns in the dirt.

It was strange how easy it felt to tell him these things, even though I'd never been able to bring myself to share them with anyone else before.

He reached out and covered my hand with his own. "You are seen," he said. His voice was gentle, and my heart fluttered in response. "You don't have to hide who you are, or what you want. Look around you. You're here, in this secret place, and you are seen. By me."

Around me, the fire crackled and the fairy lights glowed brighter.

On the river below, the boats bobbed in the moonlight as if they were dancing to the music of nature.

I felt seen, and accepted, for all that I was.

"My friend Marja used to tell me stories about the Fae realm." The words tumbled out of my mouth before I could stop them. "About how it was filled with magic and secrets beyond what we could imagine. I used to think these stories were make-believe, but now I know they weren't. The Otherworld, where no one goes hungry or uncared for and everyone is seen and treasured, exists. Right here."

"It's a tragedy how mortals so often limit beauty to only that which they can see with their eyes."

He gestured around us, at the shining river and all the wonders we had found here.

"Why must joy and tranquility be restricted to those who are deemed worthy? The world should be a place for all to find peace and contentment. Despite our brutal nature, the Fae know this."

"Greed and cruelty can be found everywhere," I said. "Maybe if more people had access to places like this, then maybe the world would be a different place."

"Do you know why I chose you as my wife?"

I raised an eyebrow. "I'd say that you must be a little bit mad to have chosen me as your wife, Azair. But maybe that's why I'm here? To bring a bit of sanity to your life."

My words surprised him, but then his eyes lit up with amusement.

"Ahh... so you think you can handle me, do you?" he murmured teasingly. "But no, I didn't choose you because of your sanity."

The water around us rippled and swirled, as if something was stirring beneath the surface. Then, out of the depths of the river, a group of black and white creatures glided into view.

Their sleek, curved bodies moved with a graceful elegance, while their gigantic eyes regarded us curiously.

They circled around us, as if assessing the situation, before swimming ever closer.

Azair held out his hand, and one creature came up to him.

He gently stroked his head before turning back to me. "Your defiance and rage," he said with a wild gleam in his eye. "The softness of your heart that you've so carefully hidden away. You remind me of myself, of who I used to be before the curse. Before I had to become a king."

Water splashed around us as the creatures swam away.

I laughed softly, but there was no mistaking the teasing glint in my eyes when I turned to him. "So that's why you chose me, is it? Out of all the women in the world, you chose me because I remind you of yourself? A peasant woman, a nobody?"

Hundreds of brides, each chosen from the kingdom's finest families, had been presented to him.

Young, innocent girls sheltered from the cruelty of the world and molded to become perfect wives.

"Is that hard to believe?" he said, amusement in his voice. "That a king could find beauty in someone so unrefined? Someone who challenges his ideas and refuses to kneel before him?" He grinned. "I chose you because of those very qualities. You were unlike anyone else I had ever met, and that was why you caught my eye. A wildfire, untamed by the world. Spiteful and daring. I knew you would bring something different to my court, something no one else could offer."

"Don't you dare," I said, my voice low and cutting. "Don't you dare to disgrace the sacrifice of the other brides. They were innocent, and you chose me because I was not. You demanded their sacrifice. Demanded that they put their lives on the line for you. Don't you dare to make light of their suffering."

His expression grew somber. "I demanded their sacrifice and I regret killing them," he said softly. "But I don't regret saving my people."

He paused, his voice heavy with emotion. The fire crackled and the fairy lights flickered in response.

"That fire in your soul," he said. "It was born from the same flames that threaten to consume me. That understanding made you my queen. The other brides were young, good, and innocent, but you were something else. You were strong, even in the face of despair. I can never tame you, and I wouldn't want to. But perhaps I can make you burn brighter."

He looked into my eyes, and a shiver ran down my spine. Here, in this hidden place, I was no longer just a ruined woman or an untamed fire. I was something else entirely. A queen.

"Burn brighter," I said the words back to him, letting them sink into my heart. "Make them pay for what they did to you. Burn them with the fire I know you have inside."

He pulled away from me, and the warmth that had filled his eyes only moments before was replaced by an icy rage.

"My realm cursed me," he spat the words out. "Not people, but the land itself. This land is alive, and it has a vengeance that can't be quenched."

Bright sparks flew around us, casting a warm glow in every direction. His magic spread throughout the entire area, igniting the night sky with its intensity.

"It seeks to take from me what I've earned with my blood, sweat, and tears. I will not let it succeed."

Something ancient and powerful stirred beneath my feet, and I realized that this was the land's response to Azair's words. It recognized his anger, and it was responding in kind.

I closed my eyes, and I could almost feel the land beneath me screaming out its rage. The song of a thousand dead souls, begging for vengeance and crying out for deliverance.

What had he unleashed? What kind of power had he tapped into, and would it be enough to break the curse?

I swallowed, unsure of what to say. "Your people seem so happy, content, and prosperous. How can you be sure the land wants to bring you harm?"

What cruelty had Azair inflicted on the land to warrant such a curse? What had he done that was so unforgivable?

His jaw clenched, and his eyes seemed to darken with every passing second.

"It was a story of betrayal," he finally said. "A woman I trusted, a woman who was supposed to be loyal and true. My future wife, my beloved. She betrayed me, and the land that I've sworn to protect."

He straightened his back, and the shadows around us seemed to grow darker.

The rage in his voice was palpable, and I could feel its intensity radiating from him.

This wasn't the same man who had been so kind to me moments before. This was a king, a ruler of an ancient kingdom, and one who would not be crossed.

My mouth went dry as I realized I had only scratched the surface of Azair's dark past, and I shivered as I wondered what other secrets he was hiding.

What other darkness lurked beneath the surface of this perfect kingdom?

A gust of wind blew past us, and though it was cold, I welcomed its chill. At least it would cool my heated skin and perhaps help to ease the dread that had settled in my heart.

"My realm doesn't take kindly to disavowal. Not of love, not of loyalty. The punishment for such a crime is a curse, one that will never be broken until the wrong has been righted."

A broken heart could be healed, but this curse seemed to go much deeper.

Fae magic, dark and powerful. The kind of magic that could tear worlds apart. That could bring an entire kingdom to its knees.

The tea in my cup had grown cold, and I took a sip. "Defiance and rage led to this, and only defiance and rage can break it. Don't be consumed by it, Azair. Your people depend on you, and the kingdom needs you. Don't let it take away your soul."

Bitter laughter filled the air. "My soul was taken a long time ago, my dearest dear. I am nothing but an empty vessel now, but I will see this through to the end."

"Fear and craving... They are one and the same, you know. The craving for something you fear. It's a never-ending cycle, one that I am all too familiar with."

"Afraid to trust, but still craving the warmth of love," he said.

The words cut through the air like a blade, and I wondered if he was thinking of his lost love.

"I know what it's like to want something and be scared to have it. To let yourself trust again." I bit my lip as memories of my pain threatened to overwhelm me. "Peace can only be found by letting go of the past and embracing what comes."

The hypocrisy of my words was not lost on me. I had been running from my own demons, refusing to let them go.

"Have you learned to let go after your husband abandoned you? Is it something that still haunts you?" A cruel glint appeared in his eyes, and I knew he was testing me.

Azair's question was unexpected and unwelcome. I had thought that he understood, that he would never ask me such a personal thing.

Icy fingers clutched at my heart as if they were trying to keep it from breaking. I knew I had to answer him, no matter how painful it was.

"Cruelty never leaves you, but I've learned to accept it instead of wallowing in my despair. Allowing him to win would mean allowing my pain to control me, and I refuse to let it do that. I won't be a victim anymore. He will not win."

"Spite is a powerful emotion, and it can be a source of strength if used correctly." He nodded, his expression now unreadable. "But it can also become a burden if you don't master it. Are you sure that you are strong enough to carry that burden?"

"The hurt that he inflicted upon me is still inside of me. I may still struggle with the pain of his betrayal, but I will not allow it to consume me. I will focus on loving and forgiving myself instead of hating him. That is the only way I can truly move on."

Azair gave me a long look, his gaze heavy and intense. "Little mouse," he said softly. "Do you know why I call you that?"

I looked up at him in confusion, unsure of what he was getting at.

"Because you think that you're better than me?" I ventured. "Mortals are small and insignificant compared to you."

A warm smile spread across his face. "People underestimate mice all the time. They are little creatures, but they can survive almost anything. You are like that. Small and wild, but strong enough to withstand the storms life throws at you. That's why I call you 'little mouse'. Mice will always survive, no matter what."

My inner walls of protection crashed down, and I felt more exposed than ever before.

It was a feeling that I had grown to loathe - the vulnerability that came with being known.

I wanted to flee from the intensity of his gaze, but I remained still and silent. I didn't enjoy being so exposed, yet this felt strangely comforting.

Pointed ears twitched, and my unease slowly dissipated.

I smiled kindly at him, grateful for his understanding and unwavering support.

"You may have come here intending to conquer me, to gain something that is beyond your reach. I respect that ambition. What will you do when you fail?"

"I will be dead," I said simply. I had accepted this long ago, and the thought of it no longer frightened me. "But I believe that the effort will be worth it. Even the most buried heart can be brought back to life, no matter how hopeless the situation may seem."

He cupped my chin with his thumb and forefinger, his gaze searching mine for any sign of malice.

Malice that wasn't there.

"Then let your ambition guide you, and may it bring me back to life." He released his grip on me, and the warmth of his touch lingered on my skin.

Was that a sign of approval? Or was he just humoring me before sending me off to my death?

Slowly, his lips curled into a smile, and he bowed his head in acknowledgment. "You are brave."

"Or stupid," I muttered.

"No, not stupid. Fearless. And that is a trait to be admired." His eyes darkened and his jaw seemed to clench as he added, "Do you think I'm heartless? Or are you just trying to give me hope?"

"I'm trying to give us both hope. I think, deep down, we all have goodness inside of us, and something worth fighting for."

He knew I was using him. Even so, he looked at me with warmth in his eyes. In fact, it seemed like he was daring me to break through the walls that surrounded his heart.

"You may be brave, but you're also cruel," he said, his voice low and dangerous. "Trying to conquer my heart like that. It could lead to something far more sinister than you'd ever imagined."

There was something dark and powerful in his eyes, something that made me both fearful and enthralled.

"There's a lot you don't know about me, husband." My dark hair tumbled around my shoulders as I whispered the words, daring him to challenge me. "Cruelty, kindness, love—these are my tools. I will use whatever means necessary to get what I want."

His eyes flashed with strange anticipation, and I knew I had him right where I wanted.

He wanted me to prove my strength, and I was more than willing to do so.

"You're dangerous."

The words were both an accusation and a compliment, and I smiled.

"Maybe," I said. "If you're willing to take the risk."

His skin shimmered and sparks flew around us as he unleashed the full force of his power.

"You have three full moons to prove yourself." His eyes burned with a fierce intensity, his gaze taking on a savage glint. "Convince me you are the one I need. The one who can break through my defenses and save me from my darkness."

My pulse quickened as I realized the implications of what he was saying.

He was finally putting his trust in me—granting me the chance to win, not just his heart, but his love. He was willing to open himself up to me, and I knew what it meant for a man like him.

The walls around his heart were crumbling down, one brick at a time, and I was the one who held the hammer.

"And if I fail?" I asked, my voice barely audible over the roaring wind.

Azair let out a ragged sigh. "Then the curse will consume our kingdom, and your hubris will be its undoing."

thirteen

CROWNS & CINDERBLOCKS

His attempts were so obvious, I almost felt sorry for him. Almost.

"Please," I drawled, leaning in closer. "A childhood crush is just a childhood crush. No need to embarrass her this way."

Inviting his closest friends to court was a bold move, but I knew it would be well-received. It showed he was committed to breaking the curse.

He wasn't just relying on me; he was making sure he had all the help he needed to succeed.

Elara's cheeks flushed a deep crimson.

Poor girl.

Clearly not accustomed to the games played in court. It was obvious she'd been sheltered from this kind of thing for most of her life.

My eyes crinkled at the corners as I tried to reassure her with my gaze.

Instead of cowering away, she stood her ground and met my gaze.

Azair's face darkened, but I didn't look away.

Three full moons. To an immortal, three months were nothing more than a few days, but to me, it felt like a lifetime.

It had to be enough.

Beautiful Fae ladies be damned.

Purple eyes met mine, a spark of understanding flickering in her depths. "You don't need to worry about me."

She sipped from a diamond flute adorned with rubies.

Her ink-stained fingers lingered against the cool glass as the lace of her sleeves slipped down her arm. "I can handle myself."

"His games won't cow you, will they?" I smiled as a streak of gold and orange raced across the room, pushing aside plates and utensils as it made its way toward us.

"No," she laughed softly. "I won't. Not anymore."

The animal came to a stop at Azair's feet, and he looked down at it with slight bemusement.

It was an animal I'd never seen before. A curious blend of fire and fur that seemed to be everywhere and nowhere at once.

I sipped from my goblet. "It gives me great pleasure to make his life difficult."

Elara grinned, and for a moment, I felt like I was looking at a completely different person. A person who was not afraid to take on any challenge.

How interesting.

Her mask had slipped for a moment, revealing the woman she truly was. Or at least, the woman she wanted to be.

I liked her already. Masks were suffocating, even if one wore them for protection.

"Then let's give him something to think about," she said.

I nodded in agreement and raised my glass, a silent toast to the future.

Azair's gaze shifted from me to Elara, and then back again.

His little plan of flaunting a potential love interest had failed.

Miserably.

I had seen the way his gaze lingered on her and the secret smile that he tried to hide. He was hoping, perhaps foolishly, that I would be jealous of Elara, and he was disappointed when that didn't happen.

His plan had been obvious and transparent, but I ignored it.

Instead, I made a mental note to keep an eye on the beautiful Fae woman, as she was clearly more than meets the eye.

I couldn't help but smirk as Elara's brother Casimir caught my eye. He had an impish grin on his face, and he winked at me when he noticed I studied them both.

It was obvious that he knew what was going on inside Azair's mind, but he was too much of a gentleman to say anything.

He just winked at me silently, as if to say "Good luck!"

I smiled back at him, thankful for his silent support.

In a strange way, the whole thing made me feel special. I vexed Azair. And that was something he wasn't used to.

Men like Azair were dangerous—they could break hearts and ruin lives. But now, I had the power to challenge him. To conquer his defenses and prove him wrong.

Azair looked at me like he saw something that made him pause and think twice before dismissing or disregarding me.

It gave me hope that maybe I wasn't just another faceless woman who would be easily forgotten. Easily discarded when my value had expired.

The animal stopped in front of me, fuzzy and warm. I reached out a hand and ran it through its fur, feeling the heat radiating off of it in waves.

How strange.

Smoldering, but it didn't burn.

With a graceful flick of its tail, the animal conjured a vast feast of vibrant fruits, spiced meats, and steaming platters of delectable dishes.

Dancing flames swirled around the platters, spinning and twirling before settling into soft embers.

As quickly as it had appeared, it slinked away, disappearing into the shadows. Gold and orange sparks sparkled in its wake.

Azair watched me, the smirk on his face turning into a frown as he observed my calculating gaze.

I had seen him attempt to make me jealous, and while I appreciated the gesture, it was nothing more than a distraction.

I had no time for such things, not when so much was at stake.

"I can feel your eyes on me, my darling husband. You'd think that after all this time, you'd be used to seeing my face by now." The cuffs of my dress twitched as I lounged gracefully in the chair, subtly shifting my gaze to meet his. "But I'm not complaining. You know you can look all night if it makes you happy."

He straightened, adjusting his ruby-studded crown. "It looks like we have our own little court jester now."

"One with better taste in jewelry," I quipped, gesturing to the golden bracelet on my wrist.

His engagement gift. A vulgar display of power, but one I accepted without hesitation.

Possessive, yes. But I'd be lying if I said that it didn't make my heart flutter a tiny bit when he slid it on my wrist before we arrived here.

Azair smiled a slow, appreciative smirk before reaching forward and taking my hand in his own.

His touch was electric, sending shivers up my spine as our fingers intertwined.

"A fashionable one, too," he said. "Pearls are always a pleasant touch."

The runes on the pearls glowed, sending a gentle warmth through my body.

Rage. Fear. Longing.

The meaning of our bond, carefully inscribed in each glittering bead. Runes he picked personally for me. Contradictory feelings and conflicting emotions that somehow made sense together.

"I have an excellent teacher," I said, as I leaned against him, my face tilted slightly to look up into his eyes. "But I'm sure you have a few more tricks up your sleeve."

He nodded, his gold eyes burning with a fire that had been smoldering since the day we met. "Oh, you have no idea..." He trailed off, his voice low and sultry as he let the words linger in the air.

The corners of my lips curled up into a smirk, daring him to prove it. "Well, I'm sure you can show me," I teased, unable to hide my own mischievousness.

Azair laughed, his deep voice sending shivers down my spine. "Oh, I'm sure I will."

Casimir and Elara glanced at each other.

A strange understanding passed between them I couldn't quite place, but it brought a fondness to the corners of their mouths.

The siblings were a strange pair, but they looked in sync. Like they had been dancing together all their lives.

It was a strange thing to witness, but beautiful nonetheless.

Smiling, I leaned closer to Azair, our arms brushing as we both reached for the same platter of roasted meats.

His gaze shifted to me, his gold eyes alight with a flash of irritation that made my lips curl in amusement.

"Are you going to win me over with food, too?" I asked, raising an eyebrow. "You'd do better if you used your words instead."

"If I used the right words, I could make this feast seem like mere scraps of food," he said, filling my plate with a flourish.

The corner of his mouth quirked up in an all too familiar smirk, and I shook my head at him.

"But if you need me to play server for you, I am more than happy to do so."

"Oh, I think I can handle it," I said. "But I appreciate the offer."

He pulled his hand away, and I felt a strange sense of disappointment. But whatever thoughts had been lingering in his mind vanished when Silyen addressed him.

I glanced around the room, taking in all the courtiers milling about.

Elara was deep in conversation with Casimir and a few other lords, her head bowed in concentration.

Maevar was speaking with a group of winged ladies, his arms crossed and an unreadable expression on his face. He winked at me when he noticed I was looking, and I smiled in response.

Azair cleared his throat, drawing my attention back to him. "Quite the gathering we have here." Amusement curled through his voice. "They all seem to believe that if they make enough noise, no one will notice the truth."

"A bride living a lie, a king in power, and a kingdom teetering on the edge of collapse," I said, picking at my plate. "It's quite the mess."

He sighed and ran his fingers through his hair. "It's a hopeless situation, isn't it? Their eyes may see, but their minds refuse to accept the truth."

I shrugged. "Maybe. But I like to think that it just takes a different perspective."

He turned to me, his eyes blazing. "You have faith in the impossible."

"Of course," I said, laughing softly. "Don't you?"

His lips pressed into a thin line as he looked into my eyes. "Hope is the only thing that keeps me going." He raised his glass, filling it with wine from the goblet nearby. "To you, my beautiful bride. May you never lose your thorns or your faith."

I clinked my glass against his and took a sip.

The sweetness of the wine lingered on my tongue like a promise.

Laughing wryly, I shook my head. "Am I breaking the record of the longest-living bride? Or are there others who have lasted longer than I?"

"Your record is unrivaled," he said, taking a sip of his wine before continuing. "Don't tempt fate. Bloodshed is a favorite pastime of Fae. So be careful what you wish for."

"How did the other brides die?" I asked delicately, unable to keep my curiosity in check.

I had wondered about this for a long time, but I could never bring myself to ask.

The answer could be far more gruesome than I wanted it to be.

Azair sighed, setting his glass down and turning to look at me. "The Fae Court is a living beast. It judges its Summer Queen like a wild animal would judge its prey—quickly, and without mercy." He shook his head sadly. "The previous brides have all died of unnatural causes. Some were poisoned, others cursed."

"Are you telling me you didn't kill any of the brides?" My glass wavered slightly in my hand as I tried to wrap my head around the facts.

His eyes darkened as he shook his head slowly. "I killed a few of them, yes. The ones who deserved it."

The shame in his voice was unmistakable, but he didn't shrink away from the truth.

"But most of them were taken care of by the land itself. The Fae Court lives and breathes, and it judges its Summer Queen with ruthless efficiency."

He paused for a moment, his gaze distant, as if he was lost in thought.

"It's a harsh world," he said finally. "But sometimes that's the only way to survive."

"What would you do without me?" I said, trying to lighten up the mood. "You need someone to keep you from getting too serious. It doesn't suit you."

Azair raised an eyebrow. "I don't know," he said, standing and slowly walking around the table to stand directly in front of me.

He leaned down until his face was inches from mine, his breath warm on my skin.

"But do you really want to find out?"

I shivered as his words caressed my lips.

Noticing the effect he had on me, he grinned and pulled away. "I'm glad you didn't take me up on that offer to dance," he said, taking a step back. "The wait is half the fun, after all."

"Fucking never solves anything," I said, breaking the spell. "Temptation, however..."

Azair's face lit up, and he let out a loud, carefree laugh. "Ah, the sweet and dangerous allure of temptation."

He sat back in his chair, one arm draped casually over the back of mine.

"A fruit best left uneaten, but sometimes too sweet to resist." His gaze burned into mine, intense and unhinged. "And I'm more than willing to take a bite."

The mood in the room shifted, and all around us, the conversations stopped.

Azair's words had that effect on people—the power of his voice commanded attention.

"Do you dare to taste it?" he asked, his breath hot against my skin as he leaned close. "Suck it off your fingertips and savor the flavor? Or will you wrinkle your nose and turn away?"

My eyes fluttered closed as I inhaled deeply.

His scent was intoxicating, a heady mixture of spices and something darker that made me ache with longing.

Gold eyes, a voice like thunder, and an intoxicating scent—Azair was a force of nature, untamable and wild.

This was a public affair—nobody wanted a scandal. I had to take control of the situation.

"Well, it seems like you've gone from wanting to kill me to wanting to bed me." I cleared my throat and pulled away from him. "Your moods change quickly, don't they?"

He grinned, his voice a low purr. "Should you choose to partake in this delicious temptation, I promise you will not regret it." He flashed me one of his signature smiles that left my knees weak. "But don't worry. I won't do anything you don't want me to. The rules of matrimony still apply, even in the Summer Court."

I remembered how it felt to be with Badis—the way his hands moved over me, never quite sure what to do next. His touch had been weak and uninspired, lacking in any kind of passion or desire.

I constantly sought out his gaze in the darkness, only to be met with a blank stare that seemed almost distant.

It was as if he simply didn't care—as if my pleasure meant nothing to him.

My body had felt numb and empty, my heart aching with emptiness.

But with Azair, I could feel the complete opposite—a spark of electricity that ran through me at his proximity.

I could tell he was experienced in pleasure, and his touch would be anything but mediocre.

Despite all of my doubts and fears, I wanted to sample what he was offering—to taste the temptation and discover what lay beneath.

But another part of me—the more practical one—realized that doing so would only wreck our agreement.

Men were so easily tempted, but once they got what they wanted, they quickly moved on.

The heat of the moment would fade, and all that would be left was regret.

He cleared his throat and flashed a charming smile that was more polite than genuine. "The Fae don't like rules, but they do like to make sure everyone follows them," he said, his tone light. "It keeps things running smoothly, after all."

"For such passionate people, the Fae sure are fond of rules," I said, still aching for something more. "Don't you ever tire of having to adhere to them?"

"Rules are necessary. They provide structure and stability in an otherwise chaotic world." He gestured around the room at the courtiers milling about. "Without them, things would be too unpredictable. Lethal, even."

"I think it's time we make our own rules."

Azair raised an eyebrow. "And what would those rules be?"

Biting my lip, I thought for a moment. "On Fridays, we'll always eat dessert first. No one may use the word 'should' more than twice a day, and never speak badly of anyone in front of others."

"Why the interest in rules all of a sudden?"

"Petty things can be so liberating," I said, shrugging. Petty things like this gave structure to life and a sense of order. It was something that I desperately craved after all the chaos of the past few weeks. "It's fun to make your own rules, and even more fun to break them."

Azair chuckled and shook his head.

He leaned back in his chair, the ballroom lights bouncing off the gold cufflinks at his wrists and reflecting in his eyes. "Once, I forced all of my courtiers to wear mismatched clothes for a day."

I raised an eyebrow, amused. "And why was that?"

"To see if they would obey a ridiculous order without question. Most of them did, though there were a few who refused."

"You certainly have a unique way of keeping order."

"Oh, come now," he said in a lighthearted tone. "Surely the courtiers should have known better than to introduce foreign influences into the Summer Court. We need to stay true to our roots and maintain our traditions, not succumb to outside pressures. But I suppose it is all part of the fun."

His words had a lighthearted edge, but they also carried an underlying warning to the courtiers present.

I smiled, appreciating both his subtle reminder and his playful sense of humor.

"Isn't that contradictory?" I asked. "To maintain order while also breaking the rules?"

He let out a low chuckle. "Well, I suppose it depends on your definition of order. If you know how to walk the line between what is expected and what is forbidden, you will find true freedom."

He gave me a meaningful look that sent shivers down my spine.

"There aren't many rules in the Summer Court, but those that exist must be followed."

He paused, and for a moment, the room was silent.

Then he raised his glass in a toast. "To maintaining our traditions," he said, his voice ringing out across the ballroom.

The courtiers echoed his words with a rousing cheer, their glasses held aloft in agreement.

I couldn't help but smile at the sight.

Casimir's eyes twinkled. "Well, isn't this interesting? It looks like your horrible habits are rubbing off on each other."

"Don't push it," he drawled. "It will take more than one meal to make us a happily married couple. Flirtation and frivolity are the keys to a harmonious relationship, after all."

A Fae courtier in the corner snickered, but Azair's gaze remained focused on me.

His intensity left me breathless, and my heart fluttered with anticipation.

Casimir chuckled, his gaze darting between the two of us. "Stranger things have happened, and a mortal like you could be just the thing to keep him in line."

Azair bristled at the implication, and I had to bite back a smile. "My husband knows how to behave. He just needs someone to remind him from time to time."

The courtiers exchanged glances. Was our ruse working, or did they think we were just putting on a show?

I couldn't tell, and so I simply smiled and held my glass aloft in a silent toast.

Azair set his glass down and looked around the room. "Now, if we are quite done measuring each other up, perhaps we can discuss our plans."

Casimir gave me an approving smile that seemed to linger for a few seconds longer than necessary. "Your presence gives this court a much needed spark," he said. "We found ourselves in a bit of a rut before you arrived. Boring, really."

Azair shifted in his seat and cleared his throat. "What can I say? This court needs a shake-up, someone who's not afraid to bend the rules and stir things up a bit. And that's exactly what I plan on doing." He uttered the last sentence with a hint of menace, his golden eyes flashing dangerously. "We won't be living in a boring world for much longer."

I shivered, feeling the intensity of his gaze as it swept around the room.

The courtiers sensed something was off too, because they all fell silent for a moment before bursting into frenzied conversation.

I glanced back at Azair and saw him smirking triumphantly, as if daring anyone to challenge him.

Theatrical as ever, I thought to myself. But then again, that's what made him so captivating.

I closed the gap between us, my breath tickling his ear. "Says the man who's afraid of love."

Azair stiffened, his body tensing against mine. He quickly regained his composure. "I'm not afraid of love," he said, his tone full of challenge. "I'm just cautious."

I couldn't help but wonder what Azair was really afraid of.

Was it the idea of trusting someone to love him despite his past, and being vulnerable enough to open up and let someone else in? Or was it the possibility that he could never break the curse despite his best efforts?

No matter what, I felt a strange tug toward him.

Was it because I wanted to be the one to free him from his curse? Or was I simply drawn to his enigmatic nature and the danger that came with it?

Either way, I wanted to unravel the secrets of his heart—to see if it was possible for a man cursed with a lifetime of solitude to finally find love.

I matched his gaze, my eyes daring him to keep going. "Cautiously optimistic, then?"

He blinked, then laughed. "You certainly know how to push your luck," he said, running a hand through his hair with a sigh of exasperation. "Mortals really have a way of keeping things interesting."

I grinned triumphantly. "It's a gift," I said, crossing my arms over my chest as if to punctuate the point. "Crying out for the Summer Court to take advantage of, if you ask me."

"As if I needed another reminder why I shouldn't fall in love," he muttered, half-joking and yet still deadly serious.

His words stirred something inside of me, but I pushed it away, dismissing it as nothing more than a silly game.

After all, that's what this was—a game of words, a storyteller's game. The best thing to do was to keep playing.

Azair rolled his eyes playfully and looked around the room, where several of the courtiers had stopped mid-conversation to watch us.

He gave them a pointed look, and they quickly scurried away, going back to their previous activities.

I leaned in close, my lips just inches away from his cheek. "Are you enjoying my company, then?"

He crossed his arms over his chest confidently, drawing attention to the broad expanse of his shoulders. "I'm starting to. Your wit and intelligence are rather refreshing." He flashed a devilish smirk. "But don't let it go to your head," he warned playfully. "I can replace you at any moment."

I pressed my lips against his cheek, savoring the moment for just a second before pulling back.

He tensed up, the muscles of his body locking into place like a statue of marble.

His breathing quickened, and I swear I heard a low growl escape his lips.

I grinned, hoping that my subtle display of affection would be enough to break through his defenses.

His golden eyes were like liquid fire, burning into me with an intensity that took my breath away.

He leaned forward. "You're bold," he said, his lips barely grazing my ear. "No matter how scared you might be, you always rise above it."

My heart raced in anticipation of what might come next. "I'm not afraid," I said, the words tumbling out before I could stop them. "Not when I'm with you."

He nodded slowly, his gaze never leaving mine.

He leaned back and my heart sank as the moment was broken.

But then he reached up and cupped my face in his hands, his touch both firm and gentle at the same time. "Look around you," he commanded. "You are the center of attention here. They all want to know what's going on between us."

"So let them wonder," I said, leaning into his touch. "Our plan is working, and that's all that matters."

Azair nodded solemnly, his expression mirroring mine. "That should keep them guessing," he said, his voice soft and satisfied. "Soft and gentle, but still passionate enough to make them know that things between us are... complicated."

I bit my lip and smiled up at him. "But always worth it."

He leaned in closer, pressing his forehead against mine. "You were always meant to shine."

A small girl with pointed ears, dressed in an exquisite gown of yellow silk and decorated with gold jewelry, stared at me from one of the tables. Her eyes widened as I caught her gaze, and a hint of a smile tugged at her lips.

I gave her a small wink, and she blushed before glancing away.

Azair let out a deep breath, his hands falling away from my face. "You have a way with people. The finer points of a game, that's your expertise."

I laughed, feeling suddenly lighter than air—as if I could float away with the slightest breeze. "And you have a way with words. Together, we make a good team."

Azair grinned, the intensity of his gaze fading back into a more playful expression. "You underestimate yourself. You have an energy, a spark that draws people in. I've seen it in the way you talk, the way you move. It's like a magnet, and even I can't help but be drawn to it. An actress worthy of any royal court."

I bit my lip, feeling a flush creep up my cheeks. "You flatter me too much."

No words seemed adequate to express the emotions swirling inside me—so instead I smiled, letting the silence speak for itself.

Azair returned the smile, his own eyes blazing with the intensity of a thousand fires. "No flattery intended," he said. "Just admiration. For you are my queen."

The corners of my mouth curled up in an impish grin before turning to Casimir and Elara. "I believe there is much to discuss."

Casimir looked at me approvingly, while Elara simply raised an eyebrow, unimpressed by our antics.

Azair gave me a sidelong glance, and the corner of his mouth twitched in what might have been amusement.

"If you want to truly get to know Azair," Elara said, her voice steady and sure, "I can help you. I know how his mind works and what he desires most."

Placing my fork down, I looked at Casimir and Elara. "Oh?"

"I know him better than anyone. All his secrets, all his quirks. If you want to figure him out and get the upper hand, then I'm the one you should talk to."

Azair groaned. "Elara, I don't think that's necessary."

She ignored him as her lips twitched. "I'm sure I can teach you a few things. It won't be so bad, I promise."

Casimir shot me a knowing glance. "She speaks the truth, Summer Queen. Elara is the one who knows Azair best."

I glanced at my husband skeptically, knowing that Elara's offer of help might prove useful.

It was clear she had her own agenda, and something about that captivated me even more.

She was already proving to be quite a handful, and I looked forward to it.

"Elara." I leaned forward as the courtiers surrounding us at the small tables stirred with curiosity. "I'll take your offer. How could I not?"

The silver circlet of diamonds around Elara's head glittered in the light. "A friendship between us would be quite interesting, I'm sure. I look forward to getting to know you better, Summer Queen."

I couldn't keep myself from grinning as the courtiers whispered to each other behind their fans.

Azair may have been trying to maintain his composure, but I could tell he was secretly pleased.

Casimir clapped him on his back. Strands of sun-kissed brown hair framed his strong jawline as he roared, "I have faith in you, you'll make it out alive. Just remember. When they team up against you, fight like it's your last battle. That's the only way to survive."

Leaning back, I let out a deep sigh. "Oh, don't worry. We'll enjoy it too."

Azair ran his tongue along the edge of his teeth as he watched me thoughtfully. "You just want to watch me struggle." He slowly licked his lips, a slow and languid motion that made my heart skip a beat. "But don't worry, I'm up for the challenge."

Casimir flexed his broad shoulders, his biceps bulging beneath the golden fabric of his shirt as he sipped his wine. "Maybe marriage won't be so bad for you after all," he said. "Summer Queen, have you ever hunted before?"

My arms crossed my chest as I shifted uneasily. "What are we hunting?"

A feral grin spread across his face. "The most elusive prey of all—the white stag."

fourteen

WEALTH & WANT

"I don't know the steps." My lavender dress swished as I shifted my weight from one foot to the other, nervously playing with a strand of my hair. "You bewitched me last time we danced. My lack of experience will only lead to us both being embarrassed."

I glanced around the room, taking in the ornate decorations and courtiers decked out in their finest finery. This was the last court event before we headed out to hunt for the elusive white stag.

All eyes were on us—we were the focus of attention.

Elara and Casimir watched us intently, their faces unreadable.

"Bewitched you?" Azair laughed, a deep and melodic sound that echoed in the still room. "My dear Summer Queen, I did no such thing."

"What did you call the music, the seasons fading, the portal of time?" I asked, my toes tapping to the rhythm of an unseen melody. "The only way to dance that pattern is with a spell."

He stepped closer, his robe sweeping across the marble floor. "It was a song of enchantment, designed to pull you into my world. And all I did was give you my hand." He paused, and his deep golden eyes met mine with an intensity that made me shiver. "And trust you to follow it. To bewitch you, Summer Queen, I need no spell."

The sound of drums echoed through my bones, vibrating with energy. It was a deep, primal sound that came from everywhere and nowhere at once.

Guttural voices followed, chanting a triumphant chorus.

"That's not what I mean," I said, my voice almost lost beneath the music. "I'm talking about leading. You may have the steps, but I still don't know how to follow them."

Azair moved around me in a slow circle, not touching, but still somehow keeping me in the center of his orbit.

"There's no reason for fear or embarrassment," he breathed, his voice a low murmur. "The rhythm of the music is in our veins. I am here to teach you, to guide you, and to make sure that by the end of the night, you ache for more."

His hand traced the dip of my spine, caging me in with his body.

My throat went dry, and I had to fight the urge to lean into his touch. "But I don't know—"

He smiled knowingly as he spun me around, arching his body around mine until my back was pressed against him.

He took my hand in his as his hips moved against mine in a slow, rhythmic motion.

The drums beat louder and faster, echoing through my veins and setting my body alight.

Mewling voices filled the air, hushed and urgent as couples moved in perfect synchronicity around us.

Their bodies draped like silk over one another, twining together in feverish passion. Wealthy fabrics of gold and scarlet clung to them like a second skin, highlighting every curve and dip.

Sharp cries pierced through the room, rising in pitch as their movements grew more frenzied. Bodies swayed, shifting with the melody of drums and strings that echoed around the walls.

It was a wild and chaotic dance, ancient in its roots, yet pagan in its effects.

One couple seemed to be particularly enraptured by each other's embrace, their hips undulating in a sensuous rhythm unique to them.

"Do you feel it?" Azair whispered, his breath hot against my ear.

He stepped closer, his body pressed against mine as we watched the others with a strange fascination.

"That pull, like a heat in your veins. Not knowing makes it more exciting."

I couldn't take my eyes off them, feeling a strange pull toward their intimate display of love and lust that seemed so utterly out-of-place amid this lavish court.

A heat ignited within me as I watched their movements, aching for something I couldn't quite put my finger on.

Azair stepped away, and in a single movement, he lifted me in his arms, spinning me around the room as my hair whipped behind us. "There are no steps, no rules. Just trust me and let go."

As if on cue, the drums grew louder and faster as dancers twirled around us.

Elara twirled by, a smile on her face as she clapped along with the music, her laughter filling the air.

His hips pressed against me as his lips brushed my ear. His tongue flicked out against my skin, sending a shiver down my spine. I could feel his breath, hot and urgent, against my neck as he whispered, "The secret is in the surrender."

Surrender.

Just the word made my heart flutter, and all of my inhibitions melted away in the heat of the moment.

My body grew lighter as Azair spun me around, his hands barely touching my skin.

My fingers dug into his back as he pulled me closer, his muscles tensing beneath my touch. I felt a thrill as he lifted me off the ground, his body arching to meet mine.

Sunflower petals fell from the ceiling, creating a soft carpet of yellow and orange beneath our feet. Gold roses and nightingale feathers filled the air, scenting it with a sweet aroma.

But the scent of Azair was stronger, and I leaned into him instinctively as my body moved in perfect harmony with his.

"You've been friends with Casimir and Elara for a long time," I said, my breathing coming out in shaky gasps. "Inviting them to a wild court dance seems so..."

Fae.

Azair laughed, the sound echoing around us. "Wild? You should see what they get up to in the privacy of their homes." His lips curved into a mischievous grin. "Their father is the epitome of impropriety."

My cheeks flushed as I realized the implications of his words, and I felt the heat rising in my veins. "I meant clever. They are your friends, and our ruse must be convincing."

His lips traced a path down my neck as he spun me around, our eyes never leaving each other as if our own movements mesmerized us.

"They're like family to me." He slowly traced a finger along my jawline, his eyes darkening. "We grew up together, and I can't imagine life without them."

My heart skipped a beat as his lips came dangerously close to mine and my hands reached for his shoulders. I wanted to look away, but something in his eyes was too captivating to resist.

"How did it all start?"

Gently brushing his thumb against my lips, he smiled. "We were all children once. We used to play in the courtyard and share stories about our dreams and adventures."

I felt a warmth spread through me at his words, and I fought the urge to bury my face in his chest. "And then what happened?"

His hand moved from my waist to the small of my back, pulling our bodies even closer. His lips brushed my neck. "A wager?"

"What kind of wager?"

He chuckled as his hand moved from my back to my waist, tracing patterns on the small of my back. "We grew up, and the stories changed. But some things never did. We were always competing, pushing each other to be better."

His voice trailed off as I waited in anticipation.

My gaze traveled from his eyes to the long, dark lashes that framed them. I had never noticed before how thick they were or how they curled up at the edges.

"And then one day... things changed." He slowly licked his lips, the corner of his mouth twitching. "The stakes were higher and so were the rewards."

My heart skipped a beat, and I froze, my breath coming out in shallow gasps.

Azair took a step back, his hand still around my waist. Circling around me like a cat, his hand moved from my waist to the nape of my neck, his fingers lightly tracing patterns on my skin.

"What rewards?" I asked, almost breathless.

His gaze remained focused on mine, and I felt myself slowly melting under its power. It was like a wild animal sizing up its prey, the power and intensity in his gaze radiating a heat that threatened to consume me.

"A gentleman never reveals his secrets."

"You, a gentleman?" The smile on my lips was weak, but the heat in his gaze never faded.

This wasn't real. He was just playing a role. This was a game, one that could save my life.

I had to remember that.

But as his eyes devoured mine, my resolve weakened.

He raised an eyebrow, his smirk growing wider. "You, my dearest dear, are far too difficult to be satisfied by a mere gentleman. You'd need something wilder, something more interesting." He leaned in closer until our noses were almost touching. "Something sure to tantalize your senses and make you surrender."

I took a step back, my eyes narrowing as I shook my head. "Temptation is something that's best avoided, Azair. I know what it looks like, and I'm not interested."

My heart raced as his hand moved from the nape of my neck to my hip, pulling me closer. "You may think you're immune to pleasure, little mouse. But I assure you, that's not the case."

I pulled back with a glare. "Maybe so," I snapped, trying to keep the anger from my voice. "But I'm not about to trust someone who calls it 'surrender'."

My stomach knotted with fear as I waited for his response.

His eyes were intense, searching mine for a sign of my intent. I felt like he could see right through me, and the thought of it made my skin prickle with dread.

He seemed to take my words as a challenge, and I held my breath as he stepped closer.

"I would surrender to you," he said softly, his gaze never leaving mine. "Feast on you until you beg me to stop."

My face flushed and stepped back again, steeling myself against the heat that was spreading through me.

I had been burned once by a man who'd promised me the world only to take it away when a prettier, more worthy woman had caught his eye.

I wouldn't make that mistake again.

I stared at him for a moment, unsure of what to say or do. We both knew that this was a game, and we'd both promised to play it until the end.

But something in his eyes challenged me, daring me to acknowledge the danger I felt when he looked at me.

So I did the only thing I could do: I smiled.

A weak, trembling smile I hoped would be enough to mask my fear.

He arched an eyebrow and smiled back, a serene smile that said he knew exactly what I was feeling. "Can I ask you a question? A serious one this time."

We swayed together in a slow, gentle dance, our bodies close but not too intimate. "Wha-what did you want to ask me?"

"Was there ever a time when you were allowed to be wild and free? Allowed to do whatever you wanted, without consequences?"

Wildness glittered in his eyes. The same wildness that had caught me off guard before.

I knew the answer to his question, but I didn't want to admit it.

As the oldest daughter in a traditional family, there were never any moments in my life where I could truly be wild and free. I had always been restrained by the expectations of others and my own fear of what might happen if I let go.

While others were running wild through fields, climbing trees, and chasing dreams, I had to keep things together at home.

But I nodded, slowly. "I remember a time when I could run and laugh without a care. I forgot how to do that for a while. But I think I'm learning to remember."

My grandmother allowed me to be myself in her garden, teaching me how to love the things that grew there. Olives and dates, pomegranates, and figs. She taught me to care for them all.

In that garden, I was free to be wild; there were no expectations, no consequences, just love.

"And him? Your ex-husband?" he asked gently.

I shook my head, a lump forming in my throat. "I thought he did. That he understood me, my dreams, and my desires. But he didn't. He wanted me to fit into a certain mold, one that I couldn't fill. We used to be happy together, but it changed. I felt like he stopped seeing me for who I was and started to see someone else instead. Not me."

I closed my eyes for a moment, letting the music wash over me. When I opened them again, he was watching me with an expression of understanding.

"But you don't have to live like that anymore," he said softly. "In the Summer Court, it's a virtue to explore yourself, your emotions and desires."

He paused for a moment, his gaze locking with mine.

"You can be whoever you want to be here. The only thing that matters is that you're happy."

"Responsibility and consequences are part of life," I said, my voice quivering. "I can't just forget that."

"You don't have to. Responsibility and consequences still exist, but they're softer here. You can make mistakes as long as you learn from them. It's about balance, not perfection."

My breath caught in my throat, and for a moment, I allowed myself to dream.

What would it be like to be wild and free in a place where I was accepted and loved?

To explore my own emotions and desires without fear of judgment or shame? To crave the things I wanted without hesitation? To kiss his lips and feel the fire that burned between us?

An involuntary shudder ran through me as my heart raced. I knew that this was going too far. That I was getting too close to something dangerous.

With a shaky breath, I stepped away from him and turned towards the crowd, desperately searching for another partner.

But Azair wouldn't let me go so easily. He grabbed my hand and spun me back around, pulling me against his chest as we resumed our dance.

"The wildest of nights can often come after a life of responsibility and hardship. We just have to know how to let go and enjoy the moment." His hips undulated against mine, his breath fanning my neck.

Hard muscles pressed against my body, my skin tensing as I tried to keep my movements in check.

Despite my mind wanting to find that sweet spot of relaxation, my body clearly hadn't gotten the memo. Every movement was a struggle, every step a battle between what I wanted and what I thought I should do.

"What responsibilities have you ever had to take on?" I spun around to face him, my words tumbling out before I could stop them. "What hardships have you been through?"

He stopped dancing and stepped away, a strange expression on his face. "Have you forgotten why we are here?" he breathed, but there was an edge to his voice that told me I'd hit a nerve.

"I'm sorry," I blurted, feeling my cheeks flush with embarrassment. "My anger got the better of me. Please forget I asked."

Azair's lips curled into a knowing smile, his gold eyes glinting in the light of the lanterns. "Your question is fair. I have been through a lot in the past few years, and it's made me realize what truly matters in life." He stepped closer, his hold tightening. "As a mortal, you don't understand what it's like to bear the weight of a kingdom..."

The music shifted to something softer and more intimate, and our dance changed with it.

His hands moved lower on my back, his fingers tracing circles on my skin as he pulled me closer to him.

I nodded in understanding, but I still couldn't help feeling a small stab of jealousy. "It must be nice to have so many choices and opportunities available to you. My responsibilities limited my choices, while yours are only limited by your own imagination."

"It is a privilege," he said, his voice low and husky. "But it can also be overwhelming. Having so many choices means that you sometimes have to make tough decisions, ones that weigh heavily on your conscience. It is important to remember that you cannot always have everything you want. Sometimes the best thing to do is accept what life has given you and make the most of it."

I nodded slowly, my heart pounding in my chest. There was a certain comfort I found in his words, especially since he was speaking from experience.

"And you think that's a privilege?" I asked, trying to keep the surprise out of my voice.

He smiled, a gentle expression that reached deep into his soul. "Being able to make hard choices and accept what life has given us is a privilege. Sanity and serenity come hand-in-hand, and it's important to remember that no matter how hard something seems, there is always a way through."

My breath caught in my throat as he finished speaking.

His words had struck a chord deep within me. A hurt that simmered just beneath the surface, one that I had been avoiding for far too long.

Only a wealthy man, one with an abundance of choices and opportunities, could understand how it felt to experience the privilege of living life on his own terms. To make hard decisions and accept what life had given him.

The ignorance of his comment was shocking, but strangely, I found comfort in it. He had not made me feel like I was wrong for wanting more, or that I should settle for less than what I truly deserved.

"No one is free." My lavender dress swished around my feet as he pulled me closer. "There's always something tying us down. The expectations of others, the fear of failure, the need to please. Not every burden is visible, but each one of us carries something."

My pulse quickened as I looked into his eyes. It was like looking into a mirror, seeing my pain reflected back at me. He understood the truth behind my words, and that understanding gave me strength.

"Suffering, responsibility, and consequences," he said. "These things are part of life, but the trick is to find the balance between them. To accept what we can't change and focus on what we can."

"That's easy for you to say," I whispered. "You have the luxury of choices. The luxury of falling back on your wealth and status."

"It's like you think I'm completely oblivious to what people go through every single day." He smiled, and a warmth spread through my body. "I'm a Fae king, but I also understand that life can be cruel and unfair. I'm just trying to show you that no matter how much life throws at us, it's possible to find a way through. To accept the pain and still be happy."

I nodded slowly, my eyes still trained on his face as he gently ran his thumb over my cheekbone.

It was possible to find happiness despite the pain and suffering. Life wasn't about having it all; it was about making the most of what we had.

"You may not understand the struggles of mortals, but you certainly know what it is to be Fae. You have your own burdens to bear, your own responsibilities. You may not suffer in the same way, but you understand suffering."

Twirling me around, he brought me back into his embrace.

His eyes darkened with intensity. "I do not understand the mortal experience. We may not suffer like mortals, but we can be just as affected by tragedy and heartache. We are not *immune* to pain."

"I never said you were," I said, a smile slowly spreading across my face. "I just wanted you to understand why I was so angry."

He chuckled softly. "And now I do." He dipped me down and then pulled me back upright, his hands never leaving mine. "It may be hard sometimes, but I believe it is possible to find happiness in the midst of tragedy."

"Your people are lucky to have you."

"And yet my wife still sees me as a spoiled, arrogant nobleman," he said with a rueful smile.

I chuckled, reaching up to brush my fingers against his cheek. "I think there's more to you than that. You care about your people and you will do whatever it takes to make sure that they have the best life possible. That's something I can respect."

He smiled down at me, his eyes twinkling with a mixture of gratitude and humility. "Thank you," he said softly. "There are so many moving parts, so many people who need help. It's difficult to be everywhere at once and make sure that everyone gets what they need."

"How do you manage it, then?"

He sighed. "It's a balancing act, really. I rely heavily on my advisors to help me make the best decisions for our people while remaining true to myself and what I believe in. In the end, I have to trust that everything will work out as it should."

"And if it doesn't?"

"Then I just have to pick myself up and try again. Again and again."

"That's easier said than done," I said, shaking my head. "It's hard to keep going when you feel like all your efforts are for naught."

He brushed his thumb lightly across my cheek. "Come now, little mouse." He twirled me around and flashed me a mischievous grin. "You mustn't be so hard on yourself. Take me as an example. I'm no good at seducing you, yet here I am still trying."

His cheekiness was infectious, and I laughed.

His laughter joined mine, and soon we were both lost in the moment.

"Poor husband, my heart still isn't swayed," I said as the laughter died down.

He sighed, his hands still gripping my waist as he leaned in close and brushed his lips against my ear.

"Maybe not. But I can't help but wonder what it would be like to keep you, just for a little while."

I allowed myself a few moments to imagine what it would be like if I surrendered to the temptation. If I let him into my life and we explored all that could be between us.

Soft smiles and tender kisses. Warm hugs that felt like home. The gentle caress of his fingers across my skin, as if he was trying to memorize every inch of me with his touch. The feel of his powerful arms around me as he whispered 'little mouse' in my ear.

The steady beat of his heart beneath my fingertips as I curled into him during those long nights when it felt like nothing else mattered but us. Knowing that he would never betray me, hold me back, or try to make me into something I'm not.

But the fantasy evaporated as quickly as it had come, leaving a pang of longing in its wake.

He was not mine to keep, no matter how hard I wished for it to be true.

For a man like Azair, I was merely a means to an end — a way to break his curse and escape the confines of his life as a king.

Once his goal was achieved, he would leave me behind, with only heartache and shattered dreams in my wake.

The realization brought a sharp pain to my chest, and I quickly stepped back out of his embrace.

No matter how I felt about him, it was clear that this relationship could never become anything more than what it was.

In the end, I could only offer him a sad smile. "Fickleness doesn't suit you, Azair."

He nodded, his expression unreadable. "Then I will just have to be content with your friendship." His lips twitched in a small, bittersweet smile. "After all, you can be just as fickle with your affections as I can. The smell of your desire lingers in the air like perfume."

I opened my mouth to protest, but he silenced me with a finger to my lips.

"You, my dear, are a contradiction. The Summer Queen in Winter's embrace. Walls of ice, yet still a flame within. I accept you, as you are."

I wanted to deny it, to tell him I was happy being the way I was.

But as I looked up at him, my mouth felt like it had been filled with cotton and my words died in my throat.

Because deep down, what he said made sense.

Had I been too scared to truly let someone in all these years? Was that why I constantly fell back on old habits? Because the idea of letting someone in was so foreign to me?

He chose someone who could never love him back, safe in the knowledge that I would never break his heart.

A Summer Queen, trapped in an icy prison of her own making.

fifteen

No Apples, Just Stones

Skeleton horses galloped across the sky, their manes and tails streaming in the wind. Howls echoed through the darkness, their haunting the only sound in the dead of night.

Azair and Elara exchanged eager glances, their eyes glittering in anticipation of the hunt.

My breath caught in my throat as I tried to keep calm.

This was madness, pure and utter insanity. Yet here we were.

This tradition had been passed down through generations of Fae, a ritual so ancient that no one knew how it began.

"Don't be afraid." Azair ran his finger over the thin scar on his eyebrow as if to remind me he was no stranger to danger. "Together, we will find this white stag, and together, we will conquer it."

"Overestimating my abilities won't do us any good." I tried to keep my voice steady as the horses circled us. "I know you're brave, but I'm just mortal."

"You have a habit of downplaying your abilities." He smiled, his eyes crinkling at the corners. "But I know you're more than capable of handling this. Just trust me, and we will make it through safely."

Azair would protect me. But could I really trust him? Could I put my life in his hands?

There was only one way to find out.

I nodded and took a deep breath. The time for doubt was over - it was time to hunt.

Casimir gave me a reassuring smile before striding off into the night, Elara close at his heels. Their pointed ears twitched, and their noses twitched as they searched for the stag's trail.

An ethereal horse of golden light appeared before us, its mane and tail crackling with fiery flames that burned hot enough to mimic the scorching heat of summer.

The horse reared up, its golden hooves pounding the ground, before it dropped back down and nudged Azair's hand.

I crossed my arms over my chest, narrowing my eyes at him with suspicion. "Are we really going to share one horse?"

He nodded, the corner of his mouth twitching into a smirk. "Have you ever ridden a horse before?"

I bit my lip, feeling slightly embarrassed. Only donkeys and camels. Nothing as majestic and powerful as this creature.

"No," I said reluctantly. "I've never been on a horse, let alone ride one."

His fingers trailed along the side of its neck, gently caressing it as he spoke soft words of encouragement.

The horse bent its forelegs and bowed to him.

Azair easily climbed onto the horse's back, settling himself in the saddle. He then held out his hand, offering me a way up.

I cautiously stepped forward, feeling awkward as I tried to figure out how to get on the horse.

"Just put your foot here," he said, pointing to a spot by the horse's shoulder. "And use my arm for balance."

I grabbed his hand, feeling the warmth of his fingers as I carefully lifted myself onto the horse. Except, instead of sitting primly in front of him like a proper lady should, I faced him with my legs straddling his.

His breath hitched, and his gaze darkened as he looked down at me, our faces mere inches apart. "So, this is your plan to seduce me? Sitting on my lap? Riding me into the night?"

"It appears you have some misconceptions about how one captures a heart." Flushed, I shifted in my seat, trying to find a comfortable position. "This is a flying horse, remember? We're here to catch a white stag. Not to...." My words drifted off, and I bit my lip in embarrassment as his eyes lingered on mine.

"Not to what?"

"Not to... Never mind." I tried to sound nonchalant, but my voice trembled ever so slightly.

"Not to capture mine?" His lips curved into a knowing smirk as his thumb brushed over my waist. "Are you telling me to hold back, Summer Queen?"

My cheeks flushed as I stared at his thumb, mesmerized by the slow circles it was tracing on my skin.

My lips parted ever so slightly, and my breathing became shallow as I was lost in the sensation.

Azair chuckled softly, but he continued tracing small circles on my skin, content to let me be. His other hand grasped mine tightly, reassuringly, letting me know he was there for me despite my hesitation.

"Has there been no one else since your husband? What kind of man would allow such an exquisite woman to remain unclaimed?"

His words caught me off guard, and I stiffened in his arms.

His eyes widened as if he immediately regretted speaking his thoughts out loud.

But as I looked into his eyes, I saw something deeper than just embarrassment.

He wanted to know. He wanted to understand me, as no one had bothered to before.

I exhaled slowly, my shoulders slumping with the weight of my secrets. "Why give away something that has no price? Why waste it on someone who doesn't appreciate it?"

His eyes darkened as understanding dawned on him. His lips pursed into a thin line, and he nodded his head solemnly. "The woman I told you about," he said, his voice harsh and bitter. "The one who used me and made me swear off love. She was beautiful.

Perfect in every way, or so I thought. But she was cruel. She wanted nothing more than power, and she knew I could give it to her."

His fingers stopped tracing circles on my skin as he spoke, his touch turning icy cold.

"She used me, and when I tried to break free of her, she destroyed my life. Sariya was her name. And I vowed never to let another woman have that kind of power over me again."

I was stunned.

Azair was so guarded, so closed off, that I had never imagined he would open up about such a personal part of his life.

Theatrics, no matter how convincing, were in his nature. But this... this was too real to be fake.

The flinching of his lips, the sad cast to his eyes... it was all too real.

He looked away from me, and I heard him take a deep breath. "Your pain has changed you, Zareena. You're more careful with your heart now. And I understand that, because I've been there too."

"What did she do to you?"

He closed his eyes and leaned into my touch, the icy chill of his skin slowly melting away under my fingertips.

He opened his eyes again, and I saw a flicker of pain in their depths before he smiled.

"She taught me that some things, like love, have no place in a Fae king's heart. That I should be content with power and prestige, without ever having to feel the warmth of love." He shook his head, a bitter smile playing on his lips. "But that doesn't mean I don't want it, Zareena. I still do. Crave it even."

Vulnerability.

He wasn't scared of love.

He feared being hurt again. Scared of being betrayed. Scared of feeling powerless.

"It hurts when someone we love doesn't feel the same," I murmured, tracing his cheekbone with my finger. "To realize that we were nothing more than a means to an end."

He nodded, his lips pressing into a thin line. "Yet we hunger for it all the same. We crave the warmth of another person's embrace. We long for the tenderness of a shared moment." His eyes met mine, and I saw a hint of vulnerability in them. "We want to be loved, even if it's only for a short while. Even if it hurts us in the end."

"Desire can be a powerful thing," I said. "It can make us do things we never thought we would and stay in situations we should have walked away from long ago."

He reached up and cupped my face with his hands, his thumb tracing the curve of my cheek.

His nostrils flared as he breathed in deeply, as if he were trying to imprint my scent on his memory.

My heart raced as I realized what he was doing. He wasn't trying to seduce me or push for something more. He was just... trying to remember how it felt to be loved.

"I used to think that I could control my emotions and keep them from spilling over," he said, as his fingertips traced my jawline and neck. "But when I am with you, I lose all sense of what is right and wrong. All I can feel is the heat of your skin and the pull of your heart."

I closed my eyes, savoring the feel of his touch. The warmth of his fingers on my skin, the gentle pressure as he caressed me.

Wet heat pooled between my legs as I pressed into his touch, wanting more.

"I fear that if I let myself feel this, it will consume me. But I find myself wanting to be consumed by you, Zareena."

He wanted me, and he was willing to risk everything for it. His pain, his hurt, even his pride... This wasn't love, but to a man like Azair, it was close enough.

I wanted to throw caution to the wind and let him consume me. To feel alive again, if only for a few seconds.

But my fear held me back, and I remained still, frozen in time. Fear of being hurt again. Fear of not being enough. But worst of all, fear that if I let myself go, he would be gone the next morning.

My heart raced and my head swam as I realized what I was doing.

I was so close to giving in, to letting Azair consume me and forgetting about the curse that had brought us together.

I was allowing myself to fall into his trap, losing my focus and the ultimate goal of breaking the curse.

In a sudden surge of clarity, I realized that this was not what I wanted. Not even close.

I wanted to go home to my family and friends - not here in this place with Azair. No matter how much he tempted me, no matter how much I felt about him, this was not what I wanted.

I had to remain focused. I had to remember my goal and stay strong.

I had to keep my heart guarded, even if it meant pushing away the man that I... I stopped myself from finishing that thought.

Azair pulled away slightly, his gaze searching mine. His lips were parted, but he said nothing as he tried to read my expression.

I could see the longing in his eyes, and I felt like if I made the wrong move, he would be gone forever.

But then he smiled, a slow smile that lit up his face and crinkled the corners of his eyes. "Someday you will be mine. Mine to claim. Mine to keep."

To keep, to submit, to surrender. Not to cherish or to protect - but to own and possess. The thought of it made my stomach churn.

If I allowed him to own me, I'd lose my independence completely. I'd lose myself to him. But if I kept running away from his embrace, I'd never know the warmth of it.

Temptation and fear danced in my head, vying for control.

I looked away from him, unable to decide. "Someday," I whispered, still unsure if it was a promise or a question. "Someday..."

He nodded, his eyes still searching mine. He seemed to understand my inner turmoil, and he softened the intensity of his gaze.

"Until then," he said, pressing a gentle kiss to my forehead. "We can take things slow." His arms wound around me protectively, as if he was guarding me from my own fears.

The horse beneath us stirred restlessly, eager for the hunt that was sure to come.

"Are you ready to catch that white stag? Or have you already forgotten why we are here?" I asked, surprised by the steadiness of my voice. The fact that my mind had shifted to a more immediate goal was comforting.

"Never. I could never forget. Especially when my wife is reminding me every few minutes."

His hand caught mine, and he pulled it up to his lips, pressing a soft kiss on my knuckles.

The tenderness of his gesture caught me off guard, and my heart soared.

"You are infuriatingly distracting." His voice held a hint of amusement. "But I suppose that's the point, isn't it?"

I grinned at him, a real smile this time. "If I'm too much trouble for you, then next time we hunt, perhaps I should stay behind and let you face the white stag alone."

He chuckled, his eyes sparkling with amusement. "No, I think I'd rather have you by my side. You keep me on my toes."

I reached into my pocket and pulled out the razor blade that I always carried with me.

Azair's eyebrows furrowed in confusion as he looked at it in my hand. "What is this for?" he asked, tilting his head to the side. "I thought our stabbing days were over."

I held it out to him, a small smile playing on my lips. "I want you to hold on to it for me," I said, my tone light but serious. "I'll need it back later."

His eyebrows shot up in surprise as he took the blade from me. "Why do you carry this around with you?" he asked, scrutinizing it. "This is the one you threatened me with before," he drawled, looking up at me. "Why are you giving it to me now?"

I shrugged, trying to play it off as a joke. "I worry that I'll hurt myself by accident," I teased, hoping my attempt at humor would cover up the real reason for my request.

That I trusted him enough now to let go of my need for protection through a weapon.

His face grew serious as he looked at me. "I'll return it to you later," he promised, his voice low and sincere. "But for now, I'll hold on to it for you."

I smiled at him gratefully, feeling a weight lift off my shoulders.

His acceptance of the razor blade was a symbol of how far we had come into our relationship. From enemies to partners to... whatever we were now.

He clicked his tongue against his teeth and urged the horse forward with a flick of the reins.

The stallion kicked off into a wild gallop toward the horizon, and I gasped as Azair wrapped an arm around my waist to keep me steady.

I shifted closer to him, pushing myself into his lap as I grabbed hold of his waist.

"You have nothing to fear. I will protect you."

My thighs tensed around his hips as I shifted back slightly, steadying myself against him.

The wind tugged at my hair, and I closed my eyes as the horse raced forward. I could feel the power of the animal beneath us, and the strength of Azair's embrace around me.

For once, it was safe to let go—and that was all I wanted.

Licking my lips, I smiled. "I know you will. I just wanted to give you a little reminder."

He laughed, low and throaty, and the horse galloped faster as we raced after our elusive target.

That was until we heard a distant bugle ringing in the night sky.

He stiffened and pulled away from me, his gaze now trained on the horizon. "It looks like Cas has found our prey."

He urged the horse forward, and we flew towards the sound of the bugle as I clung to him tightly.

Wisps of ethereal mist curled around us as we raced faster and faster. I held tight to him, as the horse flew down, down, and then plunged into the sea.

My eyes widened in terror as the icy cold of the water enveloped us.

We were going to drown! I thought frantically, as the horse's body struggled to stay afloat.

But just as I was about to panic, Azair's arm tightened around me. "Trust me."

The horse's legs morphed together and transformed into a tail, its mane becoming shimmering fins that glowed with a bright blue light.

The icy water engulfed us, gripping hold and crushing my lungs. The deeper we plunged, the darker it became, until the only light that remained was Azair's gold eyes.

But as suddenly as we had submerged beneath the waves, the horse changed direction and headed back up towards the surface.

I let out an almost hysterical gasp of relief as my head broke through the water, and I gulped in huge lungfuls of salty air.

I was alive.

Azair flicked the reins, urging the horse on.

The horse thundered faster and faster until it suddenly changed back into its original form, with four shining hooves pounding against the silvery ocean.

Every splash of cold saltwater against my face felt like a death sentence, but I clung to Azair for dear life.

He pulled on the reins, slowing the horse down to a steady canter.

He leaned down, his face inches away from my face. "Did you think I'd let anything happen to you?" he asked, his voice low and reassuring. "With our marriage, I granted you some of my powers — including the ability to breathe underwater. You are safe with me, always."

Safe? Until my presence was no longer necessary.

I stiffened, my heart hammering against my ribs. "What I think," I spat, narrowing my eyes at him in anger, "is that you're an arrogant, entitled bastard."

Colors swirled around us—blues, greens, and purples—and glowing fish darted around in the depths.

Azair chuckled softly. "Maybe," he said, his lips brushing against my ear. "But I'm still here, aren't I?

You wanted to see the real me. Well, this is it - beneath the surface of the sea, nothing to hide or shield you from." His fingers tightened around mine. "This is me."

"What was the point of all this? To impress me? Your friends? To show off your power?"

"You think this is me trying to show off? To seduce you?" He brushed a strand of hair from my face and ran his thumb along the delicate skin beneath my eye. "You're not the center of my universe, *my dearest dear*. This isn't about you. It's about something bigger. Something far more powerful."

Heat rose in my chest as I scrambled for something witty to say, anything that would help me save face.

"There is no shame in embracing your vulnerability. You don't need to carry the weight of the world on your shoulders. I'm here for that."

His words were gentle, but they cut deep.

I shifted in my seat, away from him, and took a deep breath.

I wanted words that would make him think twice. Words that were strong and unforgiving.

Instead, all I could do was swallow down my fear and hold on tighter.

His throat bobbed as he swallowed hard, and he tightened his arms around me. "White stags are magical creatures that roam the ley lines-"

Before he could finish his sentence, we were interrupted by the sound of a bugle ringing in the night sky.

Casimir and Elara, both on stallions that glowed with a milky white light, appeared on the horizon.

Elara's eyes lit up when she saw us, or more accurately, when she saw me. She cantered up to us, her face flushed with excitement.

"Don't listen to him," she said breathlessly, her gaze flicking between us. "He doesn't know what he's talking about. White stags are connected to the ley lines. They bring luck and fortune to anyone who finds them."

My eyebrows rose as I looked from Elara to Azair.

His expression was unreadable in the darkness, and he simply nodded in agreement with her words. "They are harbingers of change. And if we're lucky, the start of something new."

Casimir broke the silence with a hoot of laughter, and Azair shot him a glare.

"The shifts of the land are no laughing matter," he said sternly. He shook his head and turned back to me. "We should get going now."

At that, he kicked his heels into the horse's side, and we galloped off, with Elara and Casimir following behind us.

The white stag was a symbol of something bigger. Something greater than us both.

Azair had risked his life for a chance at it, but I still couldn't quite wrap my head around what that meant or why he would do something so reckless.

Unless it could break his curse... Could it be that Azair was actually looking for the white stag in an attempt to break his curse?

Did he believe it was possible to find a way out of his predicament without having to fall in love?

It sounded impossible, but I couldn't help but question it. Could the white stag really bring him the power to break free from his fate?

He had been so insistent on bringing me along. Not to fool his friends, but for something far more ambitious. A bold plan that he carefully orchestrated.

To do this, he needed a distraction - and as his wife, I was the perfect one.

He was willing to risk so much to be free, and if that meant sacrificing an innocent creature... Well, it was a sorrow I just couldn't comprehend.

Was there really no other way?

White antlers glimmered in the moonlight, and I realized with a start that it was the white stag.

It swam gracefully through the waves, its beautiful fur shimmering in the light.

For a moment, I forgot all about Azair and his mission.

The white stag looked so innocent and pure, like some of the horned horses I'd heard tales told by Marja. Myths about horses with the power of prophecy.

I could almost believe it was here to help us, to show us the way out of whatever danger we were in.

Reality struck. This creature was going to be sacrificed to break Azair's curse.

He was so desperate; he was willing to take a risk that would ruin him.

I leaned my head against his shoulder as I watched the white stag disappear into the night. "The white stag, you know a lot more than you let on."

He turned to look at me, his eyes glowing with a strange intensity. "It's an ancient creature." His nostrils flared, and he pulled back slightly, his gaze never leaving mine. "And it hides great secrets. Secrets that could free us all."

My teeth chattered as wet clothes clung to my body, but I refused to look away.

He had not seen this creature as a living being, but as an answer to his prayers. And that's why it didn't show itself to him - because he wasn't looking at it as a sentient being.

A faint shimmer of light illuminated from his hands, and a comforting warmth engulfed me.

In a flash, the warmth changed into a shimmering silver cloak, and I smiled with appreciation.

He draped it around my shoulders and over his own. Drying us both in an instant.

I nestled into his chest, his arms still around me. "Thank you."

Droplets of water still clung to his hair, and the glow of the moonlight gave him an ethereal look.

"We both know there's something that you're not saying, so why don't you just ask? What are you afraid of?"

My lashes fluttered, and I looked away.

His question was so simple, but the answer felt far more complicated than I thought it would be. Did I want to know the truth? Did I even have a choice anymore?

Cautiously, I met his gaze. "Don't you think it's wrong to kill something so pure and innocent?"

"Sometimes, it's necessary to do things that may seem wrong."

"Is this really what you want? Is your heart so full of hatred and bitterness that you'd sacrifice something so pure just to free yourself?"

Azair's gaze narrowed slightly. "What about the brides I killed? Weren't they also pure and innocent? What makes them different from this beautiful creature?"

My chest tightened, and my mouth went dry.

I had thought about this before, but it was still hard to hear those words out loud.

"Didn't you regret that?" I said slowly. "They were pawns in a game you had no control over. But this... This is different." The foul taste of guilt was rising in my throat, and I swallowed it down. "This is you. You're the one making this decision, not someone else. Not your lands or your fate. You."

Cocking his head, he looked down at me, his eyes blazing with intensity. "I thought you'd know better, little mouse. There was never anything good in me to begin with. I am the monster who killed those brides. I am the one who will do whatever it takes to get what he wants." His lips twisted in a wry smile. "This is my nature, and there's nothing that can change it. Not even you."

sixteen

BETRAYAL

"It's a pity that Azair and you aren't talking."

Elara rested a hand on my shoulder as if to console me, but I couldn't help feeling that the gesture was more about her own disappointment than mine.

"All this potential for something beautiful is lost because of... well, whatever happened between you two."

I stirred the stew a bit more vigorously than necessary, the clinking of my spoon against the pot echoing in the silence.

The air was thick with the smell of chicken and wood smoke as I tried to avoid her gaze.

Five days had passed since the white stag incident, but things between us were still strained. Five days of avoiding each other's eyes, five days of pretending that nothing had happened. Small talk was all we were capable of, and yet it felt like a dam about to burst.

I wanted to ask him why he had done what he did, but no matter how many times I teetered on the edge, I couldn't bring myself to actually utter the words.

I was afraid of what he would say; deep down, I didn't want to hear the truth.

"I don't know what you want me to do," I finally muttered, turning away from the pot. "He clearly doesn't want to talk about it, and I can't make him."

Elara sighed and squeezed my shoulder gently. "You have not approached him, so how would you know if he wants something to do with you or not? I cannot tell you what to do, but if there is any hope of salvaging something from this whole mess, then it might be worth the risk."

A man like Azair wasn't used to being vulnerable. He was always the one in control, the powerful Summer King who ran the show. The one who never had to ask for anything and always got what he wanted.

Why should I grovel for scraps when I don't have to? Why should I beg for something he couldn't even bring himself to offer?

Why did I even care what he thought of me? The curse was going to be broken, and I had nothing to prove.

Blood-soaked hands, haunted eyes. It was better to stay away from him.

But as much as I wanted to ignore my feelings, they were there, lingering in my heart like a persistent whisper.

"I will not beg him for a conversation. If he wants something from me, he can come to me and ask," I said firmly, my voice far more confident than I felt.

Azair was desperate to break his curse and willing to do anything for it. Even if it meant sacrificing something as precious as the white stag.

But there was something else at play here, something he wasn't willing to acknowledge or talk about.

As much as I wanted to be angry with him, I couldn't blame him for wanting freedom from his curse.

But I also couldn't deny that it had cost us something more than just our friendship - and if he was ever to break the curse, he'd have to face whatever it was he was avoiding.

If he wanted to make things right between us, then he was going to have to do it on my terms.

Elara's gaze was fixed on the flame beneath my stirring spoon, her attention so focused that it seemed as if she were lost in thought. "I thought you two had something special. Something that could last."

"What do you mean?"

"I can't say for sure, but there's something more to this than either of you will admit to. I can't help but notice the way he looks at you. Whenever you're together, he can't help but look at you. It's almost as if he doesn't control it."

"That look he gives me is not admiration or love." Chicken broth splashed onto the wet sand as I stirred. "It's raw anger and contempt."

And desire, affection, longing, admiration.

Fierce and silent, it was the kind of emotion that could only come from someone who had been denied something they desperately desired. The emotion that could only come from someone who was living in a prison of his own making.

"Maybe not, but it's still there. You just have to look for it. In his eyes, in his actions, even in his anger. There is something he doesn't want you to see, but it's there all the same."

I let out a breath and put my spoon down, finally turning to face her. "His heart? Is that what you're talking about?"

"He may not show it, but deep down, yes. His heart." She smiled sadly and took my hand in hers, squeezing it gently. "He has a heart, and it is beating with something that he cannot deny."

"It's in our nature to want to feel loved and accepted, even if it means being vulnerable," I said, the words tumbling out of my mouth before I could stop them.

Azair was so desperate to break his curse - because it allowed him to stay safe.

If he opened up to me, then his walls would come crashing down, and he'd be vulnerable.

But only by taking the risk could he actually break free of this curse - and maybe find something more than what he was looking for.

I blinked. "Loneliness is a powerful motivator. The void has a way of slowly consuming you if you don't confront it."

"As a king, that void can seem even bigger, especially when you're surrounded by those who want nothing more than to please you." Purple eyes looked back at me, understanding in her gaze. "His power and influence may have protected him in the past, but it's not enough to fill that void. For him to truly be free, he'll need something more. You fill a part of that void for him, Zareena. You have since the beginning."

Impossible.

I stared at the bubbling stew, at a loss for words. How could someone like Azair ever need me? It was impossible, and yet... I had seen him look at me with a kind of longing that couldn't be explained away.

He murdered every single bride he'd married, yet he had a hard time getting rid of me.

The prospect of Azair finally letting go of his loneliness and allowing himself to feel something more than just bitterness and animosity was too tempting to ignore.

I filled a void for him - one that he refused to acknowledge. Could I fill in the rest as well?

I clenched my fists and closed my eyes.

I had come this far to break the curse, but I could not deny how Azair had come to mean something more to me. That his presence filled a void inside of me I didn't even know existed.

He managed to sneak into the depths of my heart and take root - even if it blurred my goal of breaking his curse.

How could I ever untangle the mess of emotions that were making my heart beat faster and slower at the same time?

I opened my eyes, and Elara was still there, her gaze never leaving mine. "It's a risk, I know. But it might be worth taking."

Worth taking?

My shoulders slumped in defeat. "I can't see how. He's too stubborn to admit that he is mistaken, let alone that he needs me."

"He always kept an emotional wall up between Sariya and himself. But around you, he's vulnerable. He can't hide. He can't escape. It's like you have some kind of power over him."

"The one that broke his heart? The betrayer?" I asked bitterly.

"She didn't betray him. Not in the way that he thinks. But it doesn't matter now, does it? He was scared to get close to her too, but when he did... it changed him."

Not for the better, I thought to myself. Not how a lover should make you feel.

This Sariya had done more than break his heart. She had broken his trust, shattered his faith in love, and left him scarred for life.

The spoon in my hand snapped in two, and I dropped it into the fire.

The flames crackled and hissed with each gust of wind that blew through the camp.

"What did she do to him?"

Elara looked away, her gaze far away and distant. "She changed him in ways that only love can. The kind of love that hurts. Azair fears ever feeling that way again. To be used, to be abandoned, and to have his heart broken. He won't let anyone through that wall - not even you. Not until he is certain it's the right decision. It's a weakness of his."

"Don't speak about things you don't understand," I said, the anger in my voice clear. "You don't know the first thing about love or loss. Weakness is a choice. Not something that will consume you if you don't confront it. I know. I've lived it and fought for it as well."

"Fascinating. You still defend him. Despite all the pain and suffering that he's caused."

I bit my lip, torn between loyalty and betrayal.

He had hurt me too - in ways I could never admit aloud. But despite everything, part of me still wanted to help him. To make things right for once.

"Azair will bring nothing but destruction and chaos if he doesn't break his curse. A cycle of hatred and rejection will continue unless we do something about it. I can't let that happen."

"You think you can stop him? His choice should be respected." She met my gaze steadily, her voice cool.

My expression hardened. "Sacrificing something good and pure has never been the answer. You know this better than anyone as a scholar, a master of knowledge. You have seen what dark magic can do, how it can corrupt and destroy. So, tell me now, will his quest for vengeance bring him anything else other than sorrow and destruction?"

Silence hung between us as Elara considered my words. Then she sighed and shook her head slowly.

The heat of the fire seeped into my skin, and I closed my eyes, savoring the warmth. "The lands that cursed him are now the same ones that hide the white stag from his view."

The stag showed itself to me, but never to him. Never to Elara and Casimir either.

That was a sign in itself. No matter what I did, no matter how much I wanted to help him, he was doomed to continue his cycle of pain and suffering until he broke the curse himself.

"He must make a choice - to let go of his pain and take the risk of being hurt again or to stay in the darkness forever." A bitter laugh escaped my lips. "For all the years he's spent searching for power, he'll never find it until he conquers his own heart."

Elara's eyes flashed with anger.

Her skin glowed in the firelight, taking on a beautiful iridescence that was both captivating and frightening. Her hands clenched into fists, her fingernails turning into razor-sharp claws.

She looked like a beast, ready to tear me apart with a single swipe of her clawed hands.

For that brief moment, I saw a glimpse of her Fae heritage - the wild and powerful creature she could become in times of rage.

I gulped, suddenly finding myself intimidated by the dangerous creature standing before me.

Then, just as quickly as it had appeared, Elara's Fae features faded back into the darkness. Her skin returned to its usual milky white hue and the dangerous claws disappeared.

But her eyes still burned with a fierce intensity that I had never seen before.

"Are you trying to coerce him into breaking his own curse? Do you think forcing him to suffer will bring out the truth and make him realize that the white stag will not save him?" Elara asked, her voice cold and calculating. "You want to make him confront his own mistakes and suffer for them?"

Shivers ran down my spine as I considered her question.

If Azair wanted to break the curse, he had to make a choice - to let go of his pride and take a risk, or remain in the darkness forever.

"I don't want to see him suffer any longer," I said softly. "But he needs to confront his own emotions and make the right decision. He deserves a chance at freedom and joy - not chains and despair."

Elara watched me suspiciously for a few moments before she finally nodded.

"Good," she said simply, her voice still cold and distant.

Then she sighed and turned away, her shoulders slumping in defeat.

"Do you honestly think I want him to suffer?" I asked, a hint of desperation in my voice.

"No," she said quietly after a moment. "But if he doesn't confront his own demons, then the curse may never be broken. That would be much worse than any suffering he could endure now."

She sighed and stepped back towards the fire, her face illuminated by the orange-red flames.

I nodded slowly in agreement. "And no matter how much I want to change things, the only person who can fix this situation is Azair himself."

"When he finds out... When he realizes that the white stag will not save him," Elara said quietly. "Will you be there?"

Her voice was so full of hope that I wanted to cry.

She had seen enough heartache and betrayal in her life, and yet here she was, asking me to stay with him through the darkest moments.

"I can't save a man who doesn't want to be saved." My hands curled into fists. "I can talk to him until I'm blue in the face, but it won't make a difference if he doesn't want to listen. I can only do so much."

Elara nodded, her expression thoughtful. "You care for him, don't you?"

Did I care for Azair?

That was a tough question to answer. He had hurt me, and yet I still wanted to help him. I wanted to protect him from the darkness that threatened to consume him.

The truth was, I cared for Azair in a way I hadn't expected.

The shards of my broken heart still lay scattered on the floor, but somehow I had managed to piece them back together. Not perfectly, but enough to keep me going and to believe in a better future.

"Yes," I finally said, as much to Elara as to myself. "More than I should."

Elara smiled. "I don't think there is such a thing as caring too much."

"It is when you care and there is no reciprocation. That's when it hurts the most. His heart is too closed to love. No matter what I do, it won't be enough."

I looked away, ashamed of my foolishness.

She nodded deliberately, her gaze lingering on my face for a few moments longer before she looked away. The look in her eyes told me she understood my anguish.

We stayed like that for what felt like hours, neither of us speaking as we stared into the flames and thought of all the possibilities that lay ahead.

I turned to face her again. "Would he listen to you if you try?"

She sighed. "No one can reach him right now. He's too angry and hurt to listen to reason. He needs time, and he needs space."

"Time and space he won't get as long as the curse remains."

I watched as Elara bit her lip, stirring the logs in the fire with agonizing slowness. The heat faded away too quickly for my liking. Desperately, she tried to place another piece of wood into it, but it wouldn't fit.

My pot of stew would be ruined. The chicken would be tasteless and the broth would be cold. I frowned at the thought.

I stepped up behind her and placed my hands on top of hers, guiding them as she worked the wood into place.

Finally, with a satisfying snap, it fit perfectly, and the fire roared with new life.

She looked up at me, her braid brushing against my arm. "How did you learn to do that? The cooking, the fire, the camp life..."

"It's just something I picked up over the years. Whether it was working as a maid or whatever else I could find to make ends meet, I've learned to be resourceful with my skills." I smiled wryly. "If there's one thing I've realized, it's that having a good set of hands is worth its weight in gold."

She sighed, her gaze still fixed on the flickering flames. "I always wanted to travel. But I guess books will have to do for now. It's not the same, but it's something."

"You know, I used to dream of traveling far and wide, too. Not knowing what the future held for me, all the places I'd see." My expression softened as I met Elara's gaze again. "But now... Now I just want to be home with my family. You are lucky to have your brother and Azair. It must be comforting to know you have someone safe to return to, no matter what."

"I know that you'll find your way home one day, too."

I looked away again, the ache in my heart growing more intense. "Maybe. But until then..." I trailed off, unsure of how to finish the sentence.

Until then, I was still stuck in this world full of danger, with no one to rely on but myself.

"Thank you, Elara," I said finally.

Purple eyes met mine, and she smiled at me - a warmth and understanding that she had never shown before.

I returned the smile, feeling my heart expand with something close to hope for the future.

"They drive me crazy, but I love them. Their quirks, their idiosyncrasies. I'd be lost without them." A hint of longing filled her voice.

"I know the feeling. Family is the most important thing in life."

Firelight danced across her skin, and she looked away, her expression thoughtful. "You are family too," she said, her voice soft but certain. "In some ways, more than Azair and my brother."

I blinked in surprise. An unexpected sense of comfort filled me. A warmth that spread through my veins and chased away the chill of loneliness.

"Thank you," I said again quietly, meaning it more deeply this time, as I stepped back and grabbed my pot of stew, which was now bubbling away on the fire.

"Shall we eat?" I said, offering her a knowing smile and motioning to the makeshift table.

"Tell me more of your stories," she said, her voice suddenly light and playful.

We laughed as I filled our bellies with the warm stew, and as the night deepened, she listened to my stories of growing up in Almazigha - tales about the misadventures of my childhood friends, the hustle and bustle of everyday life, and all the little moments that made up my past.

For a few hours, I felt almost like myself again. Not just some wanderer lost in another world, but an

Almazighan citizen experiencing something new and wondrous.

seventeen

Torment

"What lies does my sister tell you?"

Strolling towards us, Casimir's face flushed red, sweat dripping from his forehead. He wore a bright blue jacket as if he'd just come in from the heat.

Elara rolled her eyes and groaned. "Oh, Casimir," she said with an exasperated laugh. "Didn't you take a bath?"

Casimir plopped down between us, his arm draped around Elara's shoulders. "What use is having a bath?"

I handed him a piece of cheese from the wheel next to the fire, my lips curving into a smile despite myself. "It might improve your chances with the ladies."

Casimir accepted the cheese with a wide grin and popped it into his mouth. "Maybe," he said with a shrug. "But I still think I have an advantage when it comes to finding the perfect wife."

I raised my eyebrows and crossed my arms in front of me. "Oh really? And what is that?"

He winked at me. "My charm, of course."

Elara and I both groaned in unison and Casimir let out an easy laugh.

"You never answered my question before. What lies does Elara tell you?"

He eyed me curiously, and I shook my head. "Your sister has only ever spoken the truth to me."

"Ah, so you two have been bonding? That's good to know. You know," he said, leaning in close and lowering his voice conspiratorially, "Azair has been taking long walks alone in the woods all night. Brooding, he calls it. Melodramatic, I call it. But who am I to judge?"

My heart fluttered in my chest at the mention of Azair, and I tried to keep a neutral expression on my face. "Am I vexing him? Or is he vexing himself?"

"A fool's question," he said with a smirk. "The answer is both. He's mad at the world, but more than that, he's mad at himself. He's too stubborn to admit it, though. I'm sure you know how that goes."

I nodded slowly. Why tell me this?

He leaned forward, his gaze intense. "Possessive and protective, that's who Azair is. He loves deeply and unconditionally, and I can see why he cares for you so much. But it takes courage to follow your heart, especially when the stakes are high. I hope he finds it soon." He paused, offering me a gentle smile. "Forgive me for intruding, but I think you could be just what he needs."

A hand grabbed my shoulder, nearly startling me out of my skin.

I spun around to see Azair there, his gaze alight with intensity and rage. His dark hair was wild around his face and his eyes smoldered.

Even in the darkness, I could make out a trace of blood on his cheekbone.

He grabbed my shoulder as if to steady himself.

He looked away again, but not before I saw it in his gaze: possessiveness, protectiveness, and a hint of longing.

"It is high time I reclaim some of your attention," he said, his words sharp but laced with desperation. "My wife."

He looked at me with a deep intensity. As if he wanted to say more, as if he had so much more to tell me. But in the end, all he could muster were those two simple words.

I wanted to reach out to him, to tell him I was here for him, but the words wouldn't come.

His tense shoulders and the guarded look in his eyes told me he wouldn't accept comfort or understanding from me.

The impenetrable wall between us had never felt so thick.

We stared at one another for a few long moments as the fire crackled and popped between us. Elara and Casimir had grown silent, their eyes cast downward.

Did I dare reach out to this man who was so full of longing and sorrow? Who had such a powerful presence, yet was so fragile all at once?

Finally, I stepped forward until we were only inches apart. Wordlessly, I reached up and brushed away the traces of blood from his cheekbone.

He closed his eyes as if savoring my touch, and for a split second, he relaxed in my presence. Then, without a word, he stepped back, his expression unreadable. His jaw clenched tightly, and he looked away.

And here I thought we were making progress. I sighed inwardly, feeling the familiar chill of loneliness again.

The moments of warmth I allowed myself to feel were quickly slipping away.

Perhaps this was hopeless, after all. He would never allow me close enough to heal the wounds from his past and offer him solace.

I stood up, brushing off my skirts. "Well then," I said slowly, my voice dripping with honeyed sweetness. "It appears I must bid you all farewell. The Summer King awaits. His glory will not be denied."

I flashed a bright smile at the three of them as Azair stepped aside, making way for me to pass.

Could I dare to reach out to him? To offer support and understanding?

I paused for a moment, mulling over the idea in my head.

It was a risk I had to take. After all, hadn't he just done the same for me? Coming here to reclaim some of my attention, and looking at me with that intense expression?

I inhaled deeply and turned towards him.

His face was a mask of stoic control, yet his eyes were full of emotion.

He seemed to expect some words from me, but what could I possibly say? No words would do justice to the intensity of his gaze.

I moved closer to Azair, my eyes never leaving his. Then I slowly offered him my hand. His touch was rough yet tender, and beneath his calloused skin, the warmth radiated through me.

He inhaled sharply and squeezed my hand in his own, but he still said nothing.

We stood together in that moment, the two of us locked in a silent embrace.

Then I raised my free hand and touched his cheek with my fingertips. The blood from his wound had dried, but I could still feel the sting of it.

Azair recoiled slightly but didn't pull away. Gold pulsed in his eyes as he looked at me, and at that moment, I knew he was fighting his own demons.

Elara's expression shifted to one of concern, but before she could speak, Azair's grip around my wrist tightened as he pulled me away from the beach campfire into the forest.

Thunder crashed above us, and the heat of his body pressed against mine.

We went deeper into the wild, darkness soon engulfing us until I could barely make out the shape of a tree.

He stopped and pushed me against one, his face dangerously close to mine.

His eyes were ablaze, and I could feel the intensity of his gaze as he stared at me, seeking an answer.

I didn't know what he wanted, but I knew whatever it was, it wouldn't be easy to give him.

"What do you want from me, Azair?" The desperation in my voice was unmistakable.

He didn't answer. Instead, he slammed his hands against the tree on either side of my head, effectively trapping me in place.

His chest heaved with the effort of his breathing, and I could feel the heat emanating from him.

I wasn't going anywhere. Not until he said what he needed to say.

My fingers curled around the bark of the tree, and I waited, watching the emotions play across his face.

Raindrops touched my skin, but I barely noticed them.

Muscles tense and breathing heavily, he growled. "I want to know why you keep coming back when I keep pushing you away."

The words were quiet, almost a whisper, but the intensity behind them shook me to my core.

He looked away from me then, as if he was ashamed of what he had just said. His hands dropped to his side, and I suddenly felt cold without him so close to me.

The storm raged around us. Even so, I stood there, not daring to move. Why did I care for him so much?

I had no answer, but the truth was that in spite of it all, Azair still held a piece of my heart. A bloody shard of it that refused to break free.

Blackened and jagged, I clung to it.

"Why did Elara and you not end up together?" I asked instead, my voice barely above a whisper.

He sighed heavily and ran a hand through his hair, which was now a wild tangle around his face. "What are you talking about?" His breath was hot against my skin as he grabbed my wrists, the fire in his eyes almost palpable. "What makes you think that Elara and I could ever be together?"

"She's beautiful and kind and she adores you. Why did you not end up together? Your curse—"

He cut me off with a sharp look. "She is beautiful and kind, yes. But she's not meant to be mine."

"But why?" I persisted. "Why not?"

"She's not you," he said simply.

I blinked, not expecting him to say that.

My throat tightened; my heart swelled with emotion. "Azair—"

He clenched his jaw, the rage in his eyes like an inferno. "She's not you," he snarled through gritted teeth. "You are the bane of my existence, the source of all my suffering and torment."

He grabbed me by the shoulders, crushing me against him as if to emphasize his point.

"You haunt my days and consume my nights with your cruel eyes. You are my damnation, and yet the only thing I want in this world."

His gaze seared through me, and his words were like a whip, lashing out at me.

There was pain in his voice but also something else, something deeper that he couldn't hide, an intense longing for something that he thought could never be.

It was like a physical force, radiating from him in waves and washing over me until I was breathless.

Fury and anguish swirled within him, a tempest of emotion that seemed ready to consume us both.

I could feel the heat of his anger, but also the bitter touch of desperation as he held me in place with nothing more than his gaze.

A hiss of pain escaped my lips as he released me. Instinctively, I rubbed my arms where his fingers had been.

This was useless. How dare he? How dare he torment me like this when his heart was aching for something he thought he could never have?

"Kill me then," I said, my voice shaking. "If that's what you really want, if I'm the source of your pain, then why don't you just kill me?"

He stepped back as if he'd been struck.

He opened his mouth as if to say something, but nothing came out except a strangled noise.

Why did he look so hurt? How dare he look so hurt when it was me who should be hurting?

His eyes widened in disbelief, his mouth now a thin, white line of anger. "Kill you? Do you think I want to kill you?" he snarled. "You do not know what this curse is doing to me! You don't know the agony it causes every day!"

"Kill me," I repeated, my voice unwavering. "You know why I'm here. You know the time is running out - just twenty-five days remain until your curse is fulfilled and you can be free of me."

He lunged forward, his hands closed into fists as if he wanted to strangle me right then and there. But he stopped short, his face contorted with rage and despair.

"There are twenty-five days, nine hours, and forty-three minutes until the curse is fulfilled," he spat out. "When it is, my court will be plunged into an eternity of darkness and despair. Summer will be nothing but winter, and joy will become sadness. None of us will escape the consequences of this curse."

"End it," I insisted, my voice breaking. "End it now, before it's too late."

Azair stared at me for a long moment, the fire in his eyes slowly dying out until there was nothing but hollow emptiness in their depths.

He stepped away from me, and what little warmth he had provided was gone.

"You mean it?" he asked in a quiet voice.

Fire rose within me, threatening to consume me.

How dare he make me feel this way? How dare he make me want something I could never have?

"Why are you torturing me like this?" I spat, taking a step back. He didn't move, but his eyes followed me, dark and intense. "Do you want to drive me away? Is that what you want?"

"Torture you?" he repeated, his voice distant. "You think I'm trying to torture you?"

"You want to possess me like some kind of thing, but you will never give yourself to me completely. You play this game with me, a back-and-forth between us that will never be resolved."

I saw the truth in his eyes - he would never be free from whatever kept him trapped in this cycle.

Only then did his expression falter, a flicker of pain dancing across his face.

The silence stretched on until I thought my heart would burst from the agony of it all.

"Don't play innocent with me," he said in a low, heated voice. "You knew what I was the moment we planned this ruse. Yet here we are, both of us bound by this cruel fate."

He stepped back, his gaze still burning through me. The fire in his eyes died down, but there was still a hint of smoldering anger beneath the surface.

"You choose to help me, to keep me from complete damnation. Your weak attempt at compassion, and yet my heart clings to it like a lifeline. Damned by my own desires. I cannot help but want more from you."

I drew myself up to my full height and glared at him, feeling betrayed by the truth of his words.

I knew what he was, but I had still allowed myself to be drawn in by him.

This Fae was cursed, and still, I let myself be ensnared by him.

The king of the damned, a creature of fate and magic. Beauty and splendor, darkness and despair.

The balloon of emotions bursting inside me deflated, my anger turning to sorrow.

I reached out and touched his cheek, feeling the warmth of his skin beneath my fingertips. "Your feelings are not real. They're a product of your own arrogance and pride. Your own sense of entitlement."

He closed his eyes and leaned into my touch, a shudder rippling through him.

The rain came down harder, drenching us both, but neither of us moved.

"You will never be able to love someone tormented by your own demons," I said. "You will never find the peace or happiness you so desperately seek."

He opened his eyes again and looked at me with a heartbreaking sadness I had never seen before. "That doesn't make the ache in my heart any less real."

I stepped away from him.

Despite the raging storm around us, all I could feel was an intense longing for something that we both knew couldn't be.

Tears threatened to spill down my cheeks, but I held them back, knowing that if I started crying, I would never stop.

The bloodied shards of my heart lay scattered on the wet ground, and a wave of despair washed over me.

"It consumes me. I cannot escape it." He swayed on his feet before shaking himself back to reality. "But I still come back for more. I don't know why or how, but I still come back to you." He turned away, his back stiff and unbending, and walked away. "I'm doomed no matter what I do, it seems."

eighteen

THE ANIMALISTIC PANGS OF POSSESSION

"Prove it! If this is real, if you care, prove it."

He stopped and slowly turned to look at me.

Running up to him, I grabbed his arm and looked up into his eyes. "Prove it to me!"

His expression shifted, his eyes smoldering with a heat that rivaled the raging storm around us.

With startling intensity, he pulled me close against him, holding me so tight I thought we'd become one.

"What would you have me do?" he growled, his lips mere inches from mine. "Tell me. Tell me how I can prove it to you."

I shivered at the warmth of his breath against my skin, and, for a moment, I was tempted to succumb to his unspoken demands.

But I resisted, knowing that if I gave in now, then it would be too easy.

"Don't hunt the stag. Don't shoot the arrow."

Please, give me a chance to help you. Your curse is a tragedy, but it doesn't have to be the end of your story. Your lands can be saved if you just let go of your anger and your hate.

The stag was only a symbol of the things that he had lost and would never get back. It was not the stag that needed to be sacrificed, but his pain and suffering.

The thoughts raced through my mind, but I couldn't seem to find the words to express them.

Instead, I just looked up at him with pleading eyes, hoping that he would understand my silent message. "Don't do it."

Azair's grip around me tightened, and he let out a shuddering breath. "Wretched woman, you would condemn my soul to an eternity of suffering?"

Rage and something else swept through me as I pushed him away from me. "I would condemn your soul for what it deserves," I spat, my voice shaking. "If you truly care for me, if any of what you feel is real, then you will prove it and forsake your arrow."

He stepped back, frozen in place.

Black clouds swirled above, the storm raging like it meant to consume us.

"Do not ask me for something that I cannot do."

But I was undeterred. If he wanted redemption, he would have to earn it. Earn it for himself, and for the people he was supposed to protect.

I stepped closer and looked into his eyes. "You will prove it, or I will never forgive you."

Grabbing my face in his hands, Azair leaned in and kissed me.

At first, it was gentle and hesitant, but then his lips met mine with a fervor that I never knew existed.

He kissed me hungrily, passionately, like he wanted to consume every last bit of my soul. My breathing quickened and my heart beat faster as his tongue explored my mouth.

His hands roamed up and down my body, leaving a trail of fire in their wake.

He pulled away, leaving me breathless and trembling. "Undo me as you wish, for I accept your hold over me," he whispered against my lips, his breath hot and his grip around me so tight that it almost hurt. "Tell me you hate me, that you will never forgive me. But if I have any hope of being saved from my fate, it is only through you."

"I hate you," I gasped, my heart thudding wildly against my ribcage. "I hate you so much."

His kiss became more urgent and desperate as he moved his lips down to my neck, leaving a trail of burning kisses.

This wasn't love. It was something else entirely, something primal and raw and powerful.

It was dangerous, and it scared me. But I couldn't help but respond to his touch, to the heat of his body against mine.

I wanted him, even knowing that he was cursed. Even knowing that he could never be mine.

"I hate you so much that I can't bear to be away from you." His fingers curled around the back of my neck as he kissed me, as if he was trying to draw out every ounce of emotion from me. "I hate -"

I weaved my fingers through his hair and pulled him closer, desperate for more.

His desperation was contagious, and I felt a deep ache in my chest that crept up to my throat.

"Loathsome creature, I hate you," I breathed against his lips. "Haunting my every thought, you invade my dreams and make me yearn for something impossible. You are the bane of my existence, yet I long for your touch all the same."

He pulled away and looked at me, his eyes blazing with a fire that was both beautiful and terrifying. "I want to own every inch of you," he growled in a low voice.

His hands moved lower and cupped my buttocks, lifting me up as his lips crashed down on mine.

My thighs trembled around him, the heat between us almost unbearable.

"I want to drive you wild with pleasure," he purred, sending a shiver down my spine. "Make you forget that pathetic ex-husband of yours and replace him with my touch."

His hands moved up my waist, one hand trailing higher and higher until his fingers brushed against the underside of my breast.

"I want to make you moan with pleasure, and submit to my every whim," he murmured as his lips found the sensitive spot on my neck. "Tear away all your walls and own you completely."

My breath hitched in my throat as he bit my skin softly, his tongue tracing circles around the spot.

My nipples strained against the rough fabric of my dress as his hands kept moving higher, exploring my body as if he owned it.

My knees shook, and I clung to him, almost afraid that this was all a dream. But the heat of his body against mine and the smoldering look in his eyes were too real to be imagined.

"Your scent intoxicates me," he whispered, his lips now trailing down my throat. "Your touch consumes me. And I will never be able to escape it."

His hands moved down to my hips, and he pulled me closer, pushing his growing arousal against me.

Thick curls of desire twisted and coiled within me as he shifted his hips, and I gasped as his thick cock pressed against me.

It was almost intimidating in size, but a deep heat coiled through me at the thought of being filled by him.

Badis never made me feel this way. Badis never made me feel anything but cold at the end.

Azair's breathing was ragged as he reached up and cupped my face, his fingers exploring my skin gently. "Tell me you want me," he whispered, his lips so close to mine that I could feel the warmth of his breath on them. "Let me own your pleasure."

I hesitated for a moment, my mind trying to make sense of the chaotic emotions coursing through me.

"If you tell me to stop, I will." His fingers brushed against mine and I let out a shuddering breath. "I will do anything you want. Command me."

A jolt of electricity shot through me.

This was what I wanted - not Badis' coldness, but Azair's burning passion.

"Yes," I whispered, my voice barely audible. Yes, I wanted him.

His mouth moved hungrily down my neck as he pressed himself against me, and I felt his tongue flicking over the sensitive skin. His hands moved up to my breasts, and I let out a moan as he roughly cupped them through the material of my dress.

The rough fabric scratched against my nipples as they hardened in response to his touch as raindrops plastered our skin.

His mouth moved lower, and his tongue licked a path down my chest as he explored me hungrily.

He sucked the sensitive skin of my nipples through the material, making me moan out loud as pleasure rippled through my body.

His hands held tight to my hips as he ground himself against me. "You are mine," he growled against my skin as I clung to him, overwhelmed by the sensations coursing through me. "My beautiful, wild creature. My doom. My salvation. Mine."

His lips found mine again, and I melted against him as the rain pounded down on us, our skin slick with moisture.

He moved his hands lower, slipping them beneath the fabric of my skirt and skimming in between my thighs. His fingers trailed up the inside of my thigh before finding their target, a soft moan escaping from me as he touched me there.

Rubbing circles around my clit, he coaxed another moan from me, and I leaned back further into him.

His other hand reached up and tightly gripped my hip as a second, thick finger pushed into me. "You are so beautiful," he hissed as I gasped, my body trembling against him.

His fingers moved faster now, sending wave after wave of pleasure through me that made my whole body quiver.

"So pretty, so perfect. Mine."

"My husband," I breathed between gasps, his hands driving me wild with pleasure. "My Azair..."

He growled, his eyes blazing with a feral heat. "Say it again," he demanded as he pushed deeper into me, his fingers now thrusting hard and fast.

I gasped as pleasure surged through me - pleasure that only came from him.

I clung to him with one hand and used the other to hold on to my skirt, pushing against him as he thrust into me.

"Azair," I moaned, my voice raw with desire. "My Azair..."

His fingers stilled for a moment before he moved them again, faster and harder.

"Say it again," he commanded, his voice a low growl.

"Azair," I screamed as my body shook with pleasure and I writhed against him.

His thumb circled faster over my clit and the waves of pure bliss crashed through me, making me tremble in his arms.

"My Azair," I whispered as he released my hip and I slumped against him, my body limp with pleasure.

He kissed me deeply and then pulled back, a satisfied smirk on his lips. Then, he slowly and teasingly licked one of his fingers clean, sucking hard on it before letting out a deep moan.

His eyes were closed and his breathing ragged as he savored the taste of me, pleasure radiating from him.

I felt a little embarrassed and a bit scandalized as I watched him, thinking that it was wrong for him to taste me like this.

But as he let out another moan of pleasure, I felt my body responding in kind - warmth pooling between my legs and an undeniable desire building within me once more.

No matter how much I may have thought it was wrong, I couldn't deny that I wanted it.

That I needed more.

Azair opened his eyes and grinned, knowing exactly what he was doing to me. He pulled me back into him, his hands pressing hard against my hips as his lips met mine once more.

And at that moment, all thoughts of right or wrong vanished - the only thing that mattered was that he wanted me.

His tongue explored my mouth hungrily, the tangy taste of me still lingering on his lips.

And as his fingers teased my clit again, I gasped against him. No longer unsure or embarrassed, but free and unrestrained in the depths of our pleasure.

He pressed me against the tree, his face so close to mine. Flowers and plants brushed against my legs, their sweet scent intoxicating me.

"Azair," I whispered, the word barely more than a breath.

He grinned and moved his lips to my ear, his voice low and husky with desire. "Yes?" he asked, making me shiver in anticipation.

My eyes fluttered closed as I leaned against him. "This is all I ever wanted."

He released a low laugh and pulled away from me, his eyes never leaving mine as he brushed a strand of hair out of my face. "And it's all mine," he said, his voice low and possessive. "You are allowed to feel pleasure, little mouse. You are allowed to be wild and free. As long as you remember that it all belongs to me."

He leaned in and kissed me again, his lips gentle yet demanding. His hands moved possessively up and down my body, claiming me with each touch as my tongue explored his.

"You are mine," he growled against my lips, the words sending a shiver of pleasure through me.

I smiled and grasped his wrists tightly in mine, pulling them around me as I arched into him.

I wanted to savor this moment, even if it was fleeting. Even if it was doomed from the start. He felt like home, like a place I could stay forever.

A petal drifted down from the tree above us, landing on my cheek and making me gasp. The white petal scratched against my skin as it slowly slid down my face.

My nose tingled and my eyes watered. I gasped, trying to control my breathing as a thin layer of sweat gathered on my skin.

Blinking rapidly, I saw Azair reach out and grab my arm, pulling me away from the tree.

Hundreds of small white petals cascaded down like snowflakes on a winter night.

How beautiful.

Almost like the jasmine flowers my siblings and I used to pick for our mother. Crowns of yellow and white, woven with love. We'd pick and pluck, our hands sticky with nectar.

Then we'd run home to see the look on my mother's face when she saw our gift. That wild, happy laughter filled the room when she saw what we made.

How I'd long to hear it again.

Then the pain started. My throat felt like it had been set on fire and my skin itched and burned.

I tried to push away from Azair, but he held me tightly.

I couldn't breathe. I couldn't think. I just wanted it to stop.

Strong arms pulled me close, cradling me against a broad chest.

I looked up and saw Azair's blurry face, his eyes wide. There were two Azairs, and they both looked so worried, before I saw only one again.

His mouth moved, but the words were too thick and heavy for me to understand. The panic in his voice was unmistakable, and I wished it had been me who felt the fear instead of him.

"I think I'm starting to like the pain, Azair." My eyes felt heavy, and I couldn't seem to focus. I reached out to him, and he grabbed my hands.

The last thing I heard was the sound of his heart pounding in my ear.

nineteen

THE DISEASE OF LONGING

The gods had cursed me; I was sure of it.

Pain lanced through my throat, searing like a brushfire, while my skin prickled with icy sweat. I groaned and opened my eyes, only to find myself in my bed.

My room, usually my sanctuary, now felt like a funeral with heavy ornate furniture and flickering candles casting eerie shadows across the deep blues and purples of the velvet curtains.

I could swear I heard a low rumble like thunder in the distance, but when I listened carefully, there was nothing.

Azair sat in a chair at the edge of the bed, still in his hunting gear. The black leather and fur of his garments soaked up the dim light, while the silver buckles shimmered softly.

His face looked gaunt and drained of color, uncharacteristic of the golden king of the Summer Fae I had come to know.

His gold eyes were smudged and hollow as he stared into the candlelight, his hands clenched so tight that his knuckles turned white.

Slow fire licked through my veins as I looked at the broken facade he wore.

My throat burned as I croaked, "What happened?"

He didn't respond right away, focused on something beyond me. Then he slowly turned and looked at me, the intensity of his gaze almost enough to spark a fire.

His lips silently mouthed the words, "You are safe now."

I swallowed hard, my throat burning with the effort. "What happened?" I asked again.

"I annihilated every single flower." His voice was hoarse, and his fingers were tight and cold as he grasped my hand in his. "I should have seen it coming. I should have known that the flower was poisonous to mortals."

He let out a ragged sigh and squeezed my hand.

"The effects were overwhelming, little mouse. I almost lost you."

He shook his head slowly, as if he could not believe what he had done.

"What did you do?" I asked, dreading the answer.

He took a deep breath, and the air around us thickened with magic. A moment later, flames engulfed the walls of my bedroom, licking up towards the ceiling.

I gasped as terror threatened to overwhelm me, but he held me close and whispered calming words in my ear.

The fire slowly receded until all that remained was a charred reminder of the destruction he had unleashed.

He released me and gestured towards the walls. "I destroyed every single tree within a five-mile radius, just to make sure none of them harmed you."

He paused, and the weight of his words hung heavy in the air.

"The Summer Trees are sacred, but I could not bear the thought of any more harm coming to you."

In my mind's eye, I saw the blue fruit that glowed with an unearthly light. The taste of that fruit still lingered on my tongue.

It was the same fruit I had eaten when I first arrived in this realm, and it had sealed our marriage.

The Summer Tree was sacred to the Fae, and with it came a power unlike any other.

His lands and people depended on the natural balance he kept, yet here he was, destroying it for me.

Destroying it to save me.

My throat burned, and my vision blurred with tears. I reached out to take his hand, but he pulled away.

He didn't look angry, just exhausted.

He closed his eyes and seemed to become one with the shadows of the room.

"Azair," I said quietly. "Thank you."

His jaw clenched as he looked away. "You were poisoned. I had to do something." His fingers entwined with mine and he brought our hands to his lips, just like my mother used to do when I was younger.

The tenderness in the gesture was almost too much to bear, and I had to look away.

He brushed his lips against my forehead, and I closed my eyes.

"You are safe now," he breathed, his voice barely audible. "I will let no one hurt you again."

It was a sight I never thought I'd see - Azair, the King of the Summer Fae, broken but unbowed in his commitment to protect me.

The strength he exuded, even in his moment of vulnerability, was awe-inspiring. But behind it all, I saw the pain he was struggling to keep hidden.

He had destroyed his own kingdom, with no thought to the consequences, just to save my life.

Before I knew it, I pulled him into a tight hug.

His body stiffened at first, but then he slowly melted against me, wrapping his arms around my waist as if to draw strength from me.

We stayed like that for what felt like an eternity until eventually his breathing became even and his body relaxed.

"All thi -" I stopped, not wanting to add more burden on his already heavy shoulders.

He let out a deep breath and pulled away, his eyes still troubled, but the tightness in his face a bit less.

"Shh," he soothed, his lips brushing against my skin. "It's over now. You're safe."

He carefully helped me sit up in bed, the smell of smoke and fire radiating from him.

He brushed my hair away from my face and stood up, heading over to the bedside table. He grabbed a crystal glass and a crystal decanter, pouring a deep red liquid into the glass.

He propped up my pillows behind me before placing the glass of deep red liquid into my hands, its warmth drawing some of the chill out of my bones.

He sat down on the edge of the bed next to me and smiled softly as I took a sip of the liquid. It was sweet and tangy, warming my throat as it went down.

"It will help," he said gently, his hands still hovering near me in case I needed support. "It will soothe your throat and help you rest."

I smiled weakly, grateful for his kindness. I took another sip of the liquid and added, "Thank you for everything."

"Of course," he said simply.

Exhaustion overwhelmed me, and my eyes slowly drifted closed. All I wanted was to close my eyes and forget this nightmare ever happened.

When I opened my eyes again, he was still there, watching me in the dim light. His fingers lightly traced circles on my arm, and he leaned forward so his forehead touched mine.

"My mother used to comfort me like this when I was little," I said, my eyes still half closed. "Sometimes it feels like she's here with me."

Azair's hand stilled for a second before continuing its gentle caress.

"You called for her in your sleep. You called for her. Your father. Your siblings. And even for me."

My eyes snapped open, and I looked up at him, my throat dry. "I did?"

He nodded, his expression unreadable. "You called for all of us. I never expected that you'd call for me. Not after I..."

He trailed off, his eyes searching mine.

A weak smile appeared on my face. "You are my husband."

He leaned away, the intensity of his stare replaced with a faraway look that seemed to take him somewhere else. "I manipulated you into this fake courting arrangement," he said, his voice sharp. "I used you as a distraction for my court so I could break the curse that was put on me." He looked down, his words tinged with guilt. "But I never wanted to hurt you. Never wanted you to get hurt because of me."

"Azair," I said softly, wrapping my hand around his wrist and squeezing gently. "You warned me from the beginning. You were honest with me."

I paused, letting my words sink in.

"It was my choice to be your pretend beloved, to be your wife, and I have no regrets. You saved me. From a dark fate, from hurtful words, from the poison in my veins."

"I was so selfish," he hissed. "So manipulative and desperate to be rid of the curse that I didn't think about the consequences for you. And then..." He trailed off, his fingers gripping my arm tightly. "I do not deserve your forgiveness."

I tilted my head up and looked him straight in the eye, a fire burning inside me that was almost overwhelming.

"Don't belittle me," I said. "I chose to help you, and I'm not sorry for it. We both wanted this... for different reasons perhaps, but we both agreed to it. Neither of us are innocent. We both knew what was at stake... Our families, our people. We both did what we had to do to protect them."

He exhaled heavily, his shoulders slumping in relief. He looked back at me, a faint smile touching his lips. "You are more Fae than I ever expected you to be."

More Fae than he ever expected me to be.

To have him recognize me as such sent warmth coursing through my veins.

To him, I was more than just a mortal in his court. I was somebody who belonged - a Fae among Fae.

My skin tingled under his touch as he moved his thumb over my cheekbone.

"Manipulation is a virtue, especially when it comes to saving those you love," I said.

"Not to mortals," he tsked, his lips twitching in amusement. "But to us, it is an art form, and here you are wielding it like a master."

"Have you slept at all?" I asked, already knowing the answer.

He tucked the heavy blankets around me and shook his head. "How could I, when you were in such pain?"

He reached over to my bedside table and grabbed a small bowl filled with a thick, green liquid. Adding a few drops of a dark brown powder, he stirred the concoction until it was smooth.

"It's an herbal remedy." He placed his hands on my head and slowly rubbed circles around my temples with his fingertips. "It will help you heal."

"Heal from what?" I asked, not quite understanding.

"It will prevent any scarring."

He gently scooped up some of the herbal remedy with his fingers and spread it across my cheeks and forehead. The warmth of his hands and the coolness of the remedy were a pleasant contrast to my skin.

"Did your mother used to do this for you?"

"My father did. He was a great healer. A great man." He smiled, his expression nostalgic. "He would always make sure I was well taken care of."

"You've never mentioned your parents before. What are they like?"

He moved his hands away from my face and sighed. "My mother is fierce and loving, a true leader among the Fae. She was always there for me when I needed her most. My father is more gentle, but he has a wisdom and strength that few possess."

Biting my lip, I watched his expression carefully. "They are still alive?"

"Yes, thankfully. They are in the forest." He smiled wryly. "I'm sure they have heard about my 'marriage' by now."

I glanced away, not wanting to pry into his past. "How did you become the Summer King if they are still alive?" I asked cautiously.

He let out a long breath and looked away. "The Fae are not like mortals," he said softly, his voice wistful. "We feel the life of the land in our very bones. It's part of us; it's who we are. The Summer King is chosen by the land itself, and when it chooses one of us, we must accept it. My mother was tired of always playing the same game, so she stepped aside and allowed me to take her place."

"That must have been difficult."

He nodded, his mouth set in a firm line. "I was surprised and overwhelmed, but I couldn't refuse the call. It was my responsibility to protect our lands and our people, so I accepted it with humility." He smiled sadly. "It has been a great honor to serve as king, but

I can never forget the reason I'm here. The land chose me to be its guardian, and so long as I live, I must honor that."

"Have you told them about your curse?" I asked, curious why he hadn't gone to them for help in the first place. "Surely your parents would have been able to lift the curse, right? Your mother was a leader, after all."

"I didn't want them to get involved in this mess I created. They are aware of the situation, but they disagree with my decisions," he said, his brow furrowing. "My mother believes I could have found another way."

That must be hard for him.

She was right. There were other options available to him, ones with less bloodshed. But he had chosen the path he had, and in doing so, bound me to him.

He slowly drew circles around my temples with his fingertips, working in small circular motions all over my forehead and cheeks until he reached my chin.

He kept going until I was relaxed, and the throbbing in my head had lessened.

My fingers lightly caressed the mosaic tile necklace around my neck, its cool texture providing comfort. "What scarring?"

He glanced down at it, his lips curving into a faint smile as he wiped away the last of the remedy. "It was a gift from your sister." His fingers tenderly trailed over the tiles. "She wanted you to have something special. Something that would always remind you of home."

My mind raced back to the day we married, and I remembered seeing bright gold eyes in the shadows.

I shivered, my fingers tightening around his. "You were there," I whispered, realizing now that he had been watching me the whole time. "Watching me."

Observing his new bride, unsure if she would accept him or reject him. Unsure of what kind of husband he was about to become. Another dead bride or a successful one?

Azair nodded, gently rubbing my back in reassuring circles. "I could not take my eyes off of you. Even when you smiled at someone else, it felt like I was the one who was blessed with your attention."

"I-it was as if you saw something no one else could," I said slowly, lifting my gaze to meet his. "What did you see?"

A hungry look crossed over his face as he stared at me.

The memory of his fingers filling me lingered in my mind, and I blushed at the thought.

The gasps of pleasure that I had let loose, the sweet ache in my chest as I reached the peak of pleasure...

"A bitter beauty," he said, his voice low and deep. "A woman who was trapped in the shadows but refused to be broken by them."

He brushed a strand of hair away from my face, his eyes never leaving mine.

"You were strong even when no one else could see it. Sharp wit that cut and healed at the same time. I knew then that you were something special."

He reached up to trace my lips with his thumb, and I shuddered at the touch.

"That's what I saw, Zareena," he said softly. "A beautiful soul that was waiting for someone to see it. But all I bring you is ruin and danger. Unworthy of the gift I was given."

I couldn't help but burst out into laughter. Laughing, and laughing, and laughing until tears were streaming down my eyes.

He froze, unsure of what to make of my reaction.

"It's almost like one of those silly fairy tales," I said between giggles. "The kind I've heard my mother tell when I was younger."

He stared at me incredulously, his eyebrows furrowed in confusion. "I'm not sure I follow."

"You think so little of yourself," I said, wiping away my tears. "If it were not for our foolishness, I would have never experienced the world without working my hands to the bone. You have done the opposite of ruining me. You have opened my eyes to things I never thought possible."

Disbelief flashed across his face before it softened into something that was almost peaceful. "I'm not sure whether to be grateful or ashamed. I stole you away from your home, and yet you thank me."

"My home was never really mine." My hands trembled as I gripped the blanket. "My divorce shredded the fragile thread binding me to the life that once was. I left home almost ten years ago, and it's been nothing more than a beacon of what could never be."

Gold eyes regarded me thoughtfully. "You have the power to remake your home. The power to create something new from the ruins of your past, if you so choose."

"Maybe I will," I said, slowly untangling my fingers from the sheet. "But for now, I am happy where I am."

He smiled, a glint of something akin to relief flashing in his eyes.

"My family suffered in my absence, so I worked to make up for that. I wanted them to look at me with pride again, even if it meant tarnishing my reputation," I said with a hint of bitterness.

"You paid the price for their happiness, and you did it without hesitation. What parent wouldn't be proud of their child for that?"

The divorce had taken a toll on my parents, and I could only imagine the strain of financial difficulties that followed in its wake.

A tension that had been relieved only after I sent back some of my earnings, money that should have gone to my own needs rather than theirs.

"You must understand they never asked me to do that," I said quietly, guilt weighing heavily on my heart. "I chose the path myself. They supported me in everything, but that was my decision."

Azair shook his head. "Yes, but you still put their needs before your own. That is a sign of extraordinary love. A love that speaks to what kind of person you are." He paused for a second, studying me intently. "What happened in your previous marriage?"

My hands trembled as I clenched them into fists, my breath coming out in short bursts.

The memories of my ex-husband's malicious cruelty still haunted me, and I could feel the tears prickling at the corners of my eyes.

"Why do you want to know?"

He sighed and brushed away an angry tear that had escaped down my cheek. "I want to make sure you experience nothing like that again."

"Badis left me because of his ambition," I said slowly. "He grew up in my neighborhood. The son of a baker, he had dreams of being something greater. We... He worked hard and eventually found success as a merchant, becoming wealthy beyond our wildest dreams. He wanted a wife who could reflect that new status, someone who was smarter, richer, and more widely accepted than me. So he left me for someone else."

His jaw clenched as if he was about to say something, but then changed his mind.

Instead, he reached for my necklace once again and ran the tips of his fingers over the mosaic tiles. "He was an idiot," he said simply, but the conviction in his voice made me smile in spite of myself.

"We were childhood sweethearts," I said, remembering how we used to kiss and whisper secrets under the stars. "Two naïve children who thought they could conquer the world together. But then the dream turned into a nightmare. What Badis did to me was beyond cruel. He betrayed my faith in him, shattering my trust and leaving me feeling broken and alone."

His eyes darkened, and anger flashed across his face. "And so you were cast aside like a piece of garbage," he said, his voice tight with emotion.

"A ruined woman, and a fool." A bittersweet smile crept on my face. "That's what I became."

He grabbed my face with his hands, making me look directly at him. "You are not ruined," he said fiercely. "And you never were a fool. Your husband was the fool for ever thinking that money and power are worth more than love and loyalty. But that's his loss, not yours."

"A woman sent back to her parents' house to be hidden away from the world. To be shamed. It ruined my family; it ruined my reputation. How do you even escape something like that?" I asked in a hoarse whisper. "I'm not sure if I can."

"Yes, you can." He dropped his hands and stepped back from me, the anger slowly fading from his face. "One day I will make everyone who made you feel worthless regret it. They should pray that your kindness will be enough to restrain me from taking the revenge that I want to give them. Flay them just as they flayed your reputation and life."

I stared at him in shock. "Azair, I…"

"It's time you remembered who you are, little mouse. You are strong and brave. You are a fighter who will never give up, no matter what life throws at her." A sly smile crept onto his face. "It's time you stood up for yourself and stopped letting other people define your worth."

My throat tightened as his words echoed around us, almost as if they were a promise of something better.

The vulnerability of the moment felt alien, as if I had stepped out of my skin and into someone else's.

He reached out to take my hands in his, and a sense of peace washed over me. "You will always have a place in my world. No one will ever take it away from you."

"What scarring?" I asked hesitantly, as his fingers stilled on my skin.

His words had been meant to reassure me, but instead, they had left me with more confusion than before.

"You never answered my question."

His golden complexion paled, and the warmth that had been radiating off his skin moments ago dissipated. His eyes were distant and haunted, almost as if he was looking into the past rather than at me.

twenty

THE RIPPLE EFFECT OF EMOTIONAL HAIRCARE

I hesitantly touched my face, my fingertips brushing lightly against the delicate skin.

The tacky residue of the herbal remedy was all over my face, but beneath it, I felt patches of bumps and roughness.

Smooth skin suddenly interrupted by a patch of roughness — like a flower garden with its roses and thorns.

I gasped as Azair grabbed my hand and pulled it away from my face.

The Fae valued beauty above all things, and wounds that I couldn't hide marred my face. But if the Fae valued beauty so much, why had Azair looked at me with such gentleness?

"The paste will heal the scars," he said gently, as if he knew what I was thinking. "And you will be as beautiful and flawless as ever."

A warmth spread through my veins, and a slow tingle climbed up my spine like a vine winding its way around a tree.

His words were sweet honey on my soul, and I slowly relaxed.

Beautiful and flawless. No man had ever said that to me before. At least, not with such genuine sincerity. As if I deserved such a compliment.

His fingers were gentle, and he was so careful with each touch that it almost felt like love, as if he wanted to make sure no part of me would be hurt or damaged in any way.

I leaned forward and kissed him lightly on the cheek, my lips lingering longer than necessary on his warm skin.

He cupped my chin with his hand, tipping it gently upward. "You missed a spot," he said, his voice low and husky.

I smiled as I looked up into his eyes, my heart pounding in my chest. "Where?" I asked breathlessly.

His fingers slowly traced my lips before his mouth met mine. Pointy teeth scraped against my bottom lip and an involuntary moan slipped out from my throat.

His kiss was gentle but desperate, as if he wanted to consume me.

My hands threaded through his hair, my fingers tugging gently at the dark locks.

This man was my undoing, and I didn't want to let him go. He kissed me like he meant it - like I was the only thing that mattered at this moment.

Nibbling gently, he finally pulled away and stepped back. "There," he said with a satisfied smile.

I stared into his eyes, still feeling the warmth of his lips against mine. Somehow I felt better, healed even, as if that single kiss had swept away all my worries.

"That's better," I whispered in agreement, a smile spreading across my face.

His gaze softened as he ran his thumb along my cheekbone, the gesture almost reverent. I felt beautiful in his presence, not despite the scars, but because of them.

"It's time to wash your hair," he whispered. "The water will help heal your wounds."

Chuckles escaped my lips before I could stop them, and he smiled in response. "Do I smell that bad?" I asked, raising an eyebrow. "It's been days since I took a proper bath."

"Worse," he teased, his eyes twinkling with amusement. He stepped back and lightly tapped my nose. "The sooner we get you clean, the sooner you can be done with this nightmare."

Steadying myself, I slowly stood up and attempted to take a few steps. But as soon as I moved, a dizzying wave of disorientation swept through me, and I grabbed onto the bedpost for support.

Azair stepped forward to assist me with a gentle arm around my waist.

"Take it slow. You've been ill for some time now."

I nodded and allowed him to guide me back to the bed. Laying down, an overwhelming wave of exhaustion washed over me.

"I don't think I can do this," I said quietly, my voice sounding tiny in the room.

He kneeled down beside me and brushed away the hair that was stuck to my forehead. "I can carry you," he said, his voice gentle yet firm. "You don't have to do this alone."

I opened my mouth to protest, but no words came out.

To not be the one responsible for everything was a foreign concept to me. Even as a child, my parents were hardly around because of their busy lives, and I took care of myself and my siblings.

As an adult, that responsibility had only increased. I was always the one in charge of taking care of things.

He seemed to understand my hesitation and nodded in acknowledgment. "It's okay. Let me take care of you now, wife."

To be a burden was something I had never wanted to be, but here, in this moment, with him at my side, I felt like it was okay to be taken care of for once.

There was something comforting about letting him take the lead. Trusting that he would do what needed to be done.

"Okay,"

Carefully scooping me into his arms, he slowly carried me out of the room and towards the bathroom.

My head rested against his chest as I listened to the comforting thumping of his heart. Arms clenched around his neck, I breathed in his familiar scent.

His eyes crinkled with the slightest hint of amusement. "It's time to get you cleaned up."

Gently, he placed me down on the soft, glimmersilk rug that was laid out in front of the tub.

Clawed feet of a bronze lion stood on either side of it, their eyes made of a vibrant turquoise that glimmered in the candlelight. On each side of the tap stood large glass jars filled with different colored salts and herbs.

On the far wall stood a large mirror framed with twining ivy. A single sunflower was carved into the bottom right corner of it, its petals reaching out to meet the vines.

In the reflection, I saw myself lying on the blue rug, my eyes wide with wonder. Dark circles hung beneath my eyes, and my skin was yellowish. Patches of redness spread across my face, and I could see the outline of several scabs that had yet to heal.

He kneeled beside me and smiled lovingly as he filled the tub with hot water, slowly adding a handful of herbs to the mix.

I watched as he stirred it with his hand, creating a gentle whirlpool of sudsy bubbles.

A sweet aroma filled the room, lifting my spirits instantly.

Orange blossoms, jasmine, roses, and lavender. All of it deliciously blended together to create a scent that was both calming and invigorating.

The scent reminded me of my perfume, a light floral blend that was subtle yet unmistakable.

I closed my eyes and breathed in deeply, allowing the calming fragrance to envelop me.

As he stepped back and gestured for me to get in the bath, I realized that I'd have to undress in front of him. No man had seen me naked since Badis.

The steam rising from the surface of the tub fogged up my vision, and for a moment, I was unsure of what to do.

With Azair looking at me intently, a calm settled over me that had been absent since Badis left me for her. I was safe with him, and strangely, I welcomed his gaze.

Wanted him to see me. All of me. Not just the broken, mangled parts, but also the beautiful ones.

With trembling hands, I slowly untied my dress and stepped out of it, allowing the fabric to pool at my feet.

He averted his eyes respectfully as I stepped into the hot water, but they wandered back to me the moment I was submerged.

The scalding heat stung at first, but soon I was enveloped in a gentle warmth that permeated every inch of my body.

Closing my eyes and resting my head against the edge of the tub, a soft moan of pleasure escaped my lips.

"I will not look." He kneeled beside me and gently poured water from a copper pot over my head. "I will keep my eyes on your face and nowhere else."

I closed my eyes and let out a deep sigh, feeling the tension in my body slowly ebb away. "I trust you," I said, my words echoing in the candle-lit bathroom. "I trust you."

Trusted him to take care of me, even if it was just in this one moment. Trusted him to cherish me like I was precious. Trust.

His hands were gentle as he lathered up the soap and ran it through my long hair.

Fingertips massaged my scalp in slow, soothing circles that seemed to cleanse my soul as much as they cleansed my body.

He took his time, focusing on each strand of hair and untangling any knots he found.

I sighed in pleasure as his fingertips trailed down the nape of my neck, sending shivers down my spine.

"Tell me about your life before you became king." I leaned back against the edge of the tub, my eyes locked on his as he rinsed my hair. "What was it like?"

His fingers stilled in my hair. "It was simpler," he said, his voice wistful. "I was a warrior, and I spent my days training and honing my skills in combat. It was all I ever wanted to do. Protect this kingdom and its people."

"It must have been difficult when you became king." I watched as his hands lowered to my shoulders, kneading the muscles gently. "The transition can't have been easy."

"It was," he said, his voice fading away into a distant memory. "But it has been worth it."

Knots of tension melted beneath his touch, and my body relaxed.

"I'm proud of what our kingdom has become under my rule. The people are happy and healthy, and our laws are just and fair. It's been an honor to serve this land."

He'd moved so close that his chest pressed lightly against my shoulder. A wet lock of his hair brushed against my chin, sending a shiver through me.

I watched as he shifted in the candlelight, the otherworldly glow highlighting his golden eyes and full lips. He was a vision of beauty, from the dark, sensuous swirls of his hair to the thin scar on his right eyebrow.

"Kiss me," I said.

My voice was barely a whisper, yet it seemed to reverberate around us like a command.

His lips met mine in a passionate embrace, and soon his hands were everywhere - in my hair, on my face, tracing my body with gentle reverence.

He kissed me deeply, exploring my mouth like a long-forgotten treasure. His heart raced against mine as he pressed himself closer, and I opened to him willingly, tasting honey and spice on his tongue.

The sensation was overwhelming, yet it felt so right. As if this is where I belonged. In his arms, in his embrace.

He pulled away, a satisfied smile on his lips. "I aim to please," he said, pressing a tender kiss against my forehead.

I smiled up at him, feeling as if I had come home. "You certainly do."

He ran a hand through my hair and looked deep into my eyes. "And what about you?" He bit his lip, his gaze never leaving mine. "What did you do before all of this?"

I took a deep breath, gathering my thoughts. "It was... difficult," I said. "My days were filled with endless chores and tasks that never seemed to end. I had no time for myself. Barely enough hours in the day to finish all of my duties."

Lavender-scented bubbles floated around me as his hands lowered to my waist, his fingers brushing lightly against my skin.

I closed my eyes and let out a deep sigh, feeling my body relax beneath his touch.

"There were good days too," I sighed, my thoughts turning fondly to the past. "I saw wonders that most people will never know and tasted flavors foreign to my tongue. I experienced a life far from the one I grew up in, and it opened my eyes to a different world. But nothing compares to Almazigha, the blue city that raised me and shaped me into the person I am today."

"What do you miss most about Almazigha?" he asked, his voice soft and curious.

I opened my eyes and looked at him, a small smile tugging at the corners of my lips. "The vibrant colors," I said without hesitation. "The hustle and bustle of the markets, the smell of spices wafting through the air. The sound of music and laughter echoing through the streets. Almazigha is a city that never sleeps, and I miss its energy."

My breath hitched in my throat as his fingers lightly grazed against my nipples, my legs parting slightly in response.

I opened my eyes and saw the intensity of his gaze, and knew that he could feel the desire coursing through me.

"Make me forget," I said softly, my voice barely above a whisper. "Make me forget everything else in the world. Just for this moment, make me feel alive."

He moved closer, his lips brushing against mine as he spoke. "You are strong," he whispered, his breath caressing my cheek. "Stronger than you think.

Forgetting is below you; living your life to the fullest is what will set you free."

"What makes you say that?" I leaned my head back, feeling my chest flush as he moved lower, trailing kisses down my neck and onto my shoulder.

Nibbling softly, his lips moved lower until they reached the peak of my breasts. "Because you never gave up." He licked my nipple, sending waves of pleasure coursing through me. "You faced your struggles head-on and emerged victorious. That is the strength of a true warrior."

I gasped in surprise as he slipped a finger inside me, my body quivering in pleasure.

His fingertips teased me, tracing circles around the edges of my folds before dipping in and out of my wetness.

"Oh..." I gasped, my back arching as his fingers moved deeper.

Two fingers, three fingers, then four as he explored my depths with an expert touch.

"Yes..." I whimpered, unable to control the pleasure that was coursing through me.

He twisted and turned his digits inside of me, finding the right angle that sent pleasure radiating out from my core.

His thumb found its way to my clit, rubbing lightly on it before pressing down in a rhythmic circle that had me moaning louder and louder.

"You're amazing," he murmured, his mouth coming close to my ear. His breath was hot against my skin, sending shivers down my spine. "Beautiful, needy, and so responsive to my touch. I can feel how much you want me."

I gasped in pleasure as his lips found their way down to my neck, tasting the exposed skin before returning to my ear.

"What do you want?" he asked, his breath tickling my neck.

"You," I murmured, my head spinning from the sensations that had taken over my body. "I just want you."

My walls quivered around his fingers as he brought me closer and closer to the edge of bliss, his other hand supporting my back.

I was panting now, my hands gripping the sides of the tub as I felt myself on the brink of orgasm.

Just before I tipped over into oblivion, he pulled away from me.

He stared at me with a hunger in his eyes, and I smiled back. "Don't you dare stop now," I said breathlessly. "I'm so close."

He grinned and slowly moved back up my body, pressing a gentle kiss against each of my breasts before returning to my lips.

His tongue explored mine eagerly as he thrust his fingers inside me again, sending waves of pleasure radiating through me.

"Let go," he commanded. "Give in to it."

And I did.

The world around me blurred and spun, and all that remained was Azair and the fire inside him that had been unleashed.

"You deserve to be savored, little mouse. And I'm going to savor you until there's nothing left."

And with those words, I let go and felt myself tumbling into an endless abyss of pleasure.

My head was spinning, my skin buzzing with electricity as the orgasm rocked through me like a wave.

I floated back to reality slowly, my body still quivering from the intensity of it all. Azair held me in his arms as I came back down to earth, his lips trailing kisses against my forehead.

"I never want you to forget this," he said softly, a satisfied grin on his lips.

As I looked into his eyes, it hit me like a thunderbolt. I was in love with him. I had no doubts; nothing could make me question the truth of it.

Suddenly, everything made sense — why he made me feel safe and alive, why bonding with him felt so natural.

I was in love with a man who disavowed love, and yet I was sure of my feelings.

"I won't," I whispered back, leaning into him.

He reached down and lifted me out of the tub, carrying my dripping body to the soft rug in front of the fireplace.

He dried my body with a fluffy towel, his hands lingering on my skin as he drew it across my curves. Then he put me down and moved to lie beside me on the rug, pulling me close before letting out a deep sigh.

"It's nice to just be here," he said, his hand tracing circles on my back. "Just the two of us, with no obligations to fulfill."

His fingers stroked my face, pushing a few stray strands of hair away from my eyes.

His heart beat beneath my ear, and a contented smile settled on my face.

He leaned down and kissed the top of my head before getting up to add another log to the fire.

As he stoked the flames, I looked up to see him undress. The silver buckles clinked softly as he unfastened them one by one, revealing the gold skin beneath.

Toned and tanned, I could not take my eyes off of him. His muscular frame was sculpted to perfection, his broad shoulders tapering down into a slender waist.

His butt was firm and round, begging for my touch as he bent down to slide his pants off.

Bite into his hips and feel the warmth of his skin against my lips. Lick my way up his stomach and taste the saltiness of his sweat.

He would enjoy it, I knew. Just as much as I would.

My lips parted slightly, and I sucked in a deep breath as I could feel the wetness between my legs growing with each passing second.

Turning around, his cock was long and thick, the head glistening with his arousal as he stood before me.

My heart flipped in my chest as I watched him, unable to move or speak.

My toes curled, my breath coming out in shaky bursts as his cock twitched ever so slightly.

It wouldn't fit, I thought to myself. It was too big, and I was too small. Too small for the pleasure it promised.

Stop staring at him, I thought to myself.

I forced my gaze away from his body and back up at his face.

Stop thinking about it.

It's been 10 years since I've been with someone, I thought to myself. Our time in the forest was magical, but this... this was real.

This was what I'd been missing for years. The warmth of another body, the scent of skin, the feeling of being fully alive and in the moment with someone else.

Ten long years of being alone and unsatisfied.

But not anymore. Not tonight. A man whose body was a feast of muscles and curves, whose body was just begging to be touched, whose voice alone could bring me to the edge of pleasure.

Tonight, I would no longer have to deny myself satisfaction.

Tonight, I would finally allow myself to be enraptured by a man who wanted nothing more than to pleasure me. A man who was ready and willing to savor each and every inch of my body.

Tonight, I will finally be fulfilled.

Azair smiled at me knowingly. "Are you ready?"

I nodded, unable to speak as his gaze held mine in its spell.

He lifted me into his arms, his grip tight and possessive.

His cock pressed against my stomach as he leaned forward, our lips a hair's breadth away from each other.

Hunger - raw and unbridled - consumed me, my body trembling in anticipation.

"Sit down," he commanded softly as he lowered me onto the chair.

I sat down slowly, my skin still tingling from the touch of his hands. His voice was low and sensual as he spoke, sending shivers up my spine.

He bent down and trailed kisses along my neck, his teeth gently grazing my skin, before he stepped away. "What do you want, little mouse?"

My body trembled with anticipation as I looked up at him and answered truthfully, "I want to feel all of you."

He turned away from me, a smirk playing on his lips as he stepped into the tub.

That fucking smirk. That smirk that made me want him, that smirk that said he knew exactly what he was doing.

His butt flexed as he moved, his muscles rippling beneath the water's surface.

My nipples tingled as he moved, and it took all my willpower not to jump into the tub after him.

But I knew that wasn't what he wanted. His smirk had said so much more than words ever could. He wanted to tease me, make me ache for him until I begged for his touch.

And I would do just that.

He sunk down into the hot water, the suds lapping against his skin.

I watched as he closed his eyes and sighed in pleasure, my fingers itching to join him in the tub.

But I waited. Waited for him to give me the signal that he wanted me. That he wanted my touch as much as I wanted his.

twenty-one

WEDDING REJOICING AND REVEALING SECRETS

Water cascaded over his body, lavishing him in its warmth.

Azair tilted his head back, eyes closed as he savored the sensation of the soapy water against his skin.

His hands moved slowly and languidly over his chest and down to his waist, each stroke teasing out a shudder from deep within him.

The suds clung to every inch of his body, accentuating the carved lines of muscle and curves.

I could feel my heart pounding at the sight of him, my mouth going dry as I watched and waited.

A gasp escaped my lips as his fingers brushed against the head of his cock while he washed himself.

"To think that such perfection belongs to me," he said in a low rasp, his gold eyes smoldering as they met mine. "You are exquisite, Zareena. I could look at you for days and never tire of the sight."

My breasts heaved as my desire for him grew. A wave of heat spread through my body and settled in between my legs.

"You crave my touch, don't you? You want to feel me inside of you, filling you with pleasure that only I can give."

His hands moved lower and began slowly stroking his length, his breathing growing heavier with each pass.

"You want to feel my hands on your body," he purred. "Let me be your guide as you experience pleasure like you've never felt before."

His fingers quickened their pace, and I could see his eyes roll back in bliss. His hips thrust forward involuntarily as he breathed out a moan of delight.

"Come to me, little mouse," he said huskily, his voice thick with desire. "Let me show you what it feels like when I make love to you."

My knees trembled at his words, and without thought, I stepped forward and into the tub.

Azair smiled as I joined him in the water, wrapping a strong, wet arm around my waist and pulling me close.

His mouth descended on mine hungrily, his tongue exploring the depths of my mouth as he kissed me with a passion that made my head spin.

He pulled back slightly to look at me, his eyes blazing with desire and need. "You never have to deny yourself pleasure again," he drawled. "Tonight is all about giving in to what we both want."

I reached out and wrapped my hand around his cock, feeling the hard heat of him in my palm. My finger traced circles around the head, tracing along the ridges of his veins until I heard a soft moan escape from his lips.

His skin was so smooth and soft, a contrast to the rigid hardness beneath it.

"Do you like that?" I asked, my voice low and throaty.

Azair's eyes closed in pleasure as he nodded his head, his hips bucking slightly against my grip.

His breathing was heavy and ragged now, the intensity of his arousal clear to see.

"You do not know how long I've wanted this," he said in a strained voice. "Just keep going."

I wrapped both hands around him and began pumping slowly, my fingers gliding along his length in perfect rhythm.

Licking my lips, I increased the pressure and speed of my strokes, reveling in feeling his body respond to each one.

He released a deep groan as he grabbed my hands, preventing me from moving them any further. "Good girl," he said, his voice thick with pleasure. "You're doing wonderfully."

Good girl.

The words echoed in my mind and a wave of warmth spread over me.

My entire body flushed with pleasure, my heart racing as the intensity of his desire for me filled the air.

His gaze was hungry, possessive – and it made me feel wanted and cherished in ways I had never experienced before. I felt like the only woman alive who mattered to him.

He slid his hands up my body, leaving a trail of fire in their wake. He moved his hand to my ass and gave it a sharp slap, the sound reverberating through the room.

He grinned as I gasped in surprise, my skin tingling with pleasure at the sudden contact.

"It trembles so sweetly," he murmured in awe, as he ran his palm over my ass again. "Will it tremble when I touch you in other places, too? If I fucked you, would it tremble then?"

My cheeks burned at his words, my breath coming in jagged gasps as I imagined what it would feel like. Him pounding into me as I trembled beneath him, my skin slick with sweat and pleasure.

"Yes," I breathed, the word barely audible.

Azair growled in triumph and yanked me forward. "Your body is telling me something," he growled, his voice low and hungry. "It's saying you're ready for me, that you want me to take what I want."

His hands moved down to cup my hips, pulling me closer against him. His cock was hard against my stomach, thick and pulsing.

"And I'm going to take it, Zareena. I'm going to make you feel so good. So good that you'll never want me to stop."

My skin tingled at his words, desire pooling between my legs.

I had no doubt that he could make me feel good – very good – and I wanted to find out just how far he could take it.

He moved his hands to my waist and lifted me up, cradling me against him as he stepped out of the tub.

His eyes never left mine, burning with an intensity that made my heart beat faster.

He carried me across the room and laid me down on the bed, hovering over me as he looked deep into my eyes.

"I can feel your heat through the bond we have," he murmured, pressing a gentle kiss against my cheek. "Your body is calling for me, begging me to make you mine. Begging me to take what I want."

His hands slid up my legs, his fingertips teasingly tracing circles on my inner thighs.

"Tell me what you want, Zareena. Tell me what I can do to make it even better."

My breasts heaved at his words, and I closed my eyes, letting out a soft moan of pleasure.

"Touch me. Please touch me."

His lips curved into a satisfied smirk as he heard my words, and his hands moved to cup my face.

His thumbs brushed against my cheeks in gentle circles, teasingly brushing back and forth.

"Is this what you want?" he asked, the low rumble of his voice sending shivers down my spine. He leaned in closer, his lips inches away from my own. "Tell me what you want, Zareena."

I reached up and grabbed his face, pushing him down.

His eyes widened in surprise, but he didn't resist as I guided him down to my most intimate parts.

"Make use of that clever tongue of yours," I said, a flush creeping up my cheeks. "Show me what you can do."

A sinful grin spread across Azair's face as he settled between my legs.

His tongue flicked out, teasingly tracing circles around my clit before delving deeper.

My hips bucked in pleasure as he worked his magic, exploring and tasting every inch of me.

His tongue slid up and down my slick folds, licking and sucking on my most sensitive parts.

He lapped and feasted on me like I was a feast worthy of a king. Worthy of pleasure, of delight.

Lick after lick, his tongue explored me, teasing out the most exquisite sensations from my body.

I moaned and writhed beneath him, my whole being consumed by the pleasure that he was giving me.

"You taste so good," he murmured, a smile spreading across his face.

His voice was low and sensual, like the devil himself had come to take me away.

"If I could stay here forever, I would. What man would ever give up such a feast, such a gift of pleasure?"

His tongue flicked out once more, sending a wave of pleasure crashing over me. His hands moved to my hips, holding me in place as he continued to lick and suck.

I gasped, every inch of my body alive with desire and want.

"Azair," I moaned, my voice shaking. "Please don't stop."

He looked up at me with a smirk and his fingers dug into my hips as he increased the pace of his licking.

I listened to my own cries - loud, unrestrained, and uncontrollable - as his tongue explored me.

His hands moved to my breasts, kneading and massaging them as he tasted me. "Do you like that?" he asked, his voice thick with desire.

"Yes," I gasped, my eyes rolling back in pleasure. "Don't stop."

He let out a delighted laugh and increased the intensity of his movements, licking and sucking until I could barely take it anymore.

Dark hair brushed against my thighs, tickling the sensitive skin as he moved. "Come for me," he whispered against my skin.

And I did - I came so hard that it felt like a tide of pleasure washing over me, every muscle in my body tensing before finally relaxing.

I lay beneath him, panting and trembling as he smiled and licked the last traces of my orgasm from his lips.

He grinned at me and said, "Well, now it's time for my reward." His eyes sparkled with mischief as he brushed a strand of hair out of my face.

I couldn't help but smile back. "You feasted on me already," I teased, arching an eyebrow. "What else could I possibly give you?"

Azair leaned up and wrapped his arms around me, pulling me up on top of him. His gaze was intense as he looked into my eyes, a deep hunger burning in his own.

"Take your pleasure from me," he said, his voice low and commanding. "Take what you need, Zareena. Ride me until there is not a single drop left."

His hips bucked beneath me, his cock thick and ready.

I leaned forward and put my hands on his chest, pushing myself onto him.

It was incredible, the feeling of being so full and complete overwhelming me.

Inch by inch, he moved further and further inside until I was completely filled with him.

He growled in pleasure as he moved inside me, his hands still caressing my hips. His thrusts were slow and steady at first, but soon he was pounding harder and faster.

Every nerve in my body was alive with pleasure, and I clung to him as the heat of our passion rose.

This was not like any other time. This was pure, unbounded pleasure that I'd never experienced before.

He moved inside me like a beast unleashed, his body shaking with passion and need.

How could I ever have known that being taken care of would feel this good? That letting go would be so pleasurable?

He moved to put me on my back, lifting my legs over his shoulders as he continued thrusting.

This new angle gave him even deeper access, and I gasped in pleasure at the sensation of every inch of him inside me.

I moaned and writhed beneath him, desperate for more of what he was offering.

I needed all of him, every thrust and movement. I wanted to be taken over the edge.

Was this why women craved men? Was this what people meant when they talked about passion and chemistry?

That sweet, dizzying feeling of being taken by someone you trust and desire. Someone you loved.

"You feel so fucking good," he murmured, his voice raw with desire. "So tight and wet, you're driving me wild. You were made for this."

"Only you." The pillow muffled my cries as he moved faster, his fingers finding my clit and teasing it in time with his thrusts. "Only you make me feel this way."

"Open the bond between us," he gasped, his body shaking with pleasure and the effort of holding back. "Let me feel what I do to you."

"How?" I moaned, my body trembling with pleasure.

"Just let go," he murmured. "Focus on my cock, on the pleasure it's giving you. Just let go and let the pleasure take you away. Open the bond between us, Zareena."

I nodded against the pillow, my breath coming in ragged gasps as I let myself go. A wave of pleasure rushed over me, sending shockwaves through my body in its wake.

I could feel the pleasure he was experiencing with each thrust.

It was almost like I could feel him inside of me. The intensity and depth of his pleasure overwhelmed me, making my head spin and my heart race.

The shape of my ass against his hips, my tightness around his cock - it was all too much for me to bear.

Sharp teeth bit into my shoulder as an animalistic growl escaped his lips. The sensation sent me over the edge.

I cried out, my whole body shaking as wave after wave of pleasure coursed through me.

He tensed and, with one last thrust, joined me in bliss.

For a moment, there was no sound but our heavy breathing and my heartbeat in my ears. Just the two of us, connected on a level I didn't know existed.

His seed trickled out of me as he slowly withdrew, and I smiled in contentment.

"You are mine," he murmured against my neck, sending shivers down my spine. "My beautiful wife."

"Is it always like this?" I asked, my voice quiet but trembling with emotion. "This intensity, this feeling of being one with you?"

"When you let open the bond between us," he said softly, gathering me into his arms. "Yes, it is always like this."

I settled down in his embrace and let out a contented sigh as he stroked my hair.

He stared at me, a satisfied smile on his face. We lay together for a few blissful moments before his cock stirred again.

The hunger in his eyes was unmistakable, and I couldn't help but laugh.

"Again?" I teased him, my laughter turning into a moan as he leaned down to kiss me.

"How could I resist?" He grinned against my lips as he crawled over me. "A beautiful woman like you? Not a chance."

"My darling husband," I murmured, my eyes searching his. "I could get used to this kind of treatment."

"Good, because I plan on fucking you like this every single night."

Our bedroom door flew open, and we jumped.

"Ahem," Lady Catriona said, looking amused. "Am I interrupting something?"

My cheeks flushed as we scrambled to cover ourselves, but she just laughed.

"Don't let me stop you," she said. "I was actually coming to check on my daughter-in-law and make sure she was being treated properly."

"What do you want, Mother?" Azair said, glancing at me.

Mother? His mother?

I remembered how she had approached me that night at the Summer Court. The night I had to prove myself or die trying. The night of the bridal dance.

She had looked into my eyes and told me the truth behind the curse. The story of how Azair would be cursed unless I won his heart.

She had given me the key to surviving, and I took it.

My heart raced as she stood there in the doorway, watching us with a knowing smile.

I could feel her expectation and apprehension - she wanted me to win her son's heart, but she had no way of knowing if I would be successful.

But here we were, four months later, tangled in each other's arms in our bedroom. The curse wasn't broken yet, but Azair and I were closer than ever.

I pulled the blanket tighter around me, trying to hide my body. My mother-in-law had seen enough.

Catriona smiled, seemingly unbothered by our state of undress.

"I'm glad to see that you two are making use of your time together," she said, her voice dripping with amusement. "Azair, you've always been an attentive lover, and I'm sure Zareena is grateful for that."

"Mother!" Azair said, his cheeks red. "Must you always embarrass me like this?"

"It's a pleasure seeing you again, Zareena," she said warmly. "You took my advice to heart, I see. Marriage suits you well."

It was as if she were giving me her unspoken blessing. I couldn't help but smile in return, grateful for her acceptance.

"Thank you," I murmured, my cheeks flushing as I glanced up at Azair.

He seemed embarrassed, but undeniably pleased.

"Don't let me keep you two from your... activities." She shot her son a pointed look. "But there is something I would like to talk to you about, Summer King."

His chest heaved as he sighed. "What is it? Can it wait?"

Lady Catriona's gaze shifted back and forth between us, her expression unreadable. "No," she said finally. "It cannot." Her voice was formal, and I felt awkward under her scrutiny.

He nodded, resigned to his fate. "Very well," he said curtly as he rose to his feet and grabbed a blanket from the bed, wrapping it around himself. "Zareena, I'd like to have your input on this matter."

Her gaze shifted between the two of us, her expression unreadable.

I noticed a hint of surprise in her eyes as she looked at me, and then a subtle understanding seemed to pass between us.

Her gaze lingered on Azair's features - his gold eyes and aristocratic features so similar to hers- before she finally nodded and said, "Very well."

Lady Catriona gracefully lowered herself onto the plush chair next to my bed.

She watched his movements with a hint of amusement, her gaze eventually finding mine. "You two make quite a pair," she said with a knowing smile. "You have my blessing, Zareena. Love him well."

"Mother," Azair said warningly, but she waved her hand dismissively.

"You have my blessing," she repeated, staring at me. "Do not forget it."

I nodded, feeling suddenly overwhelmed by the situation.

I had only met Lady Catriona once, and never in such an intimate setting. She was so powerful, so regal - it was hard not to be intimidated.

But her gaze was kind, and the warmth I had seen in her words had to be genuine.

I nodded, my voice stuck in my throat. "Thank you," I murmured, and she nodded before turning her attention to her son.

"Azair," she said sternly. "You have a duty to the Summer Court, but foremost, you have a duty to yourself." She rose to her feet and touched his arm gently. "Don't forget that."

He froze, staring at his mother in surprise before nodding slowly. "Yes, Mother," he said, his voice full of emotion. "How could I forget?"

"A messenger arrived from one of our spies in the nearby kingdom," she said, her face serious for a moment before returning to its usual serene expression. "A mysterious curse plagues the Autumn King."

She shook her head, her lips pressed into a thin line.

"Our people are panicking, and I'm afraid it's only a matter of time before the other kingdoms find out about your curse as well."

He was pacing around the room, his hands rubbing his temples in frustration. I could feel the tension radiating off of him and wanted nothing more than to help him.

"What do you need us to do, Lady Catriona?" I asked, my voice shaking slightly.

She turned her gaze to me, and I could see a hint of approval in her eyes. "My son must break the curse," she said. "It's the only way to restore peace and stability to your kingdom."

She gave him a meaningful look as he nodded in understanding.

"Don't forget Zareena can help you with this endeavor."

Two Fae kings cursed by a mysterious force, I thought to myself, feeling a chill go up my spine.

That couldn't be a coincidence, could it? What was the connection between these two forces?

I glanced at Azair, who was staring off into the distance with a distant look in his eyes.

The white stag.

Would he hunt the stag down to break his curse? A creature of such beauty and power... I shook my head, feeling a pang of fear in my chest.

"We must be prepared for whatever comes our way." Lady Catriona's voice broke through my thoughts, and I looked up to see her looking at us kindly. "Our people are counting on you two."

He nodded, his jaw set with determination. "We will be victorious," he said, squeezing my hand in assurance. "I'll do whatever it takes to protect my kingdom. But first, I have a wedding to attend to."

Lady Catriona arched an eyebrow. "Is that so?"

He nodded, his lips curling into a smile as he looked at me. "My sister-in-law is getting married, and we are both expected at the celebration."

twenty-two

WELCOME HOME

"This isn't my home," I whispered to Azair as we stepped through the door of the grand palace. "It's too big, too beautiful."

The blue marble walls were inlaid with intricate white and gold designs, the sunlight streaming through the stained-glass windows casting rainbows onto the gleaming floor.

I reached out to touch it, feeling a strange sensation of familiarity and nostalgia.

My father's work, I thought.

He was the one who designed and built this palace. The mosaic tiles were his legacy, as were the lush gardens and flowing fountains. An artisan's eye with the handiwork of a master craftsman.

"It's breathtaking," he drawled, his voice a low whisper as he stepped closer to me. "Your father put a lot of love and care into this place."

"Did you pay for this?" I asked, feeling a sudden surge of guilt. There was no way I could ever repay him for such a grand gesture.

"No, it's your bride's price." He gestured to the grandeur of the palace. "I might have had a few coins to spare. It's a small price to pay to honor my wife's family in such a way." He smiled, his golden eyes twinkling with amusement. "Just don't tell my mother I said that."

"I won't," I promised, a rush of affection for him welling up inside me.

He had gone above and beyond to show his appreciation for my family.

How proud my father must have been, I thought, a lump forming in my throat. To create something so majestic and beautiful to house his family. A son-in-law, who would go out of his way to honor them like this.

Palm trees swayed gently in the breeze as we made our way across the garden. The sun was setting, and the air was sweet with the scent of jasmine.

The path through the garden led us to a large wooden door at the entrance of the palace, guarded by two Fae soldiers in golden armor. Spears crossed, they stepped aside as we approached, allowing us to enter.

Tall double doors of dark, ancient wood opened into a courtyard with white marble floors. A fountain in the center of the room spewed water high into the air, creating sparkling rainbows that shimmered in the afternoon light.

My father was in the garden, tending to a bush of fragrant roses.

He was older.

The lines in his face had deepened and his hair had grayed, but he still looked just as I remembered him. Curly, dark locks framed his face and deep-set eyes, while a thick beard covered his chin.

He looked up when he heard the doors open, and his eyes widened as they locked onto mine. He slowly stood, his hands gripping the spade tightly.

"Zareena, my daughter, is that you?" he asked, his voice trembling slightly. "Is that really you?"

"Baba," I murmured, my eyes wide.

He opened his arms, and I stepped forward, wrapping my body in his embrace.

"I'm sorry I stayed away for so long. The last few years have been hard."

He smelled like earth and sweat, and I breathed deeply, trying to savor the moment. "It's alright, my Zareena."

His chest shuddered as he inhaled deeply, and tears spilled from his eyes.

I had never seen my father cry before. Never heard his voice crack like that.

"I missed you, my child," he said, his arms never letting go of me. "It's been 11 and a half years since I've last seen you. I was afraid you would never come back. Stay. Stay as long as you want."

As I hugged my father, the realization hit me it had been just over 10 years since I had last been home.

But in the Fae world, time ran differently, and for me, it had only been a mere four months.

My heart ached at the thought of all the time I had missed with my family and how much they must have worried about me. Yet, here they were, welcoming me back with open arms as if I had never left.

A lump formed in my throat as I tried to hold back tears.

My father pulled away from our embrace, his hands on my shoulders as he looked at me with a mix of love and concern. "You've been gone for so long, my child. What happened?"

Azair cleared his throat behind us, and I realized he was still there. He stepped forward hesitantly and bowed to my father, hand on his heart. "My lord," he said. "I am Azair, husband to your daughter. I thank you for accepting us into your home and family."

My father's eyes widened in shock as he looked at Azair, then back at me. His mouth opened and closed a few times as if trying to form words, but none came out.

He finally found his voice, his tone laced with hope and disbelief. "You're married?" he asked, his brows furrowed in confusion.

I nodded, smiling back at him. "Yes, Baba."

He stood there for a moment, processing the information before finally pulling Azair into a hug. "Welcome to our family, son," he said, his voice filled with emotion. "It's an honor to have you in our home."

My father's gaze lingered on me for a moment longer, his eyes conveying unspoken questions and concerns. It was clear that he wanted to have a private conversation with me about my marriage to Azair, but not before our guest.

He gave me a small nod, silently acknowledging that we would discuss this later.

Azair smiled, looking a little embarrassed but humbled by my father's gesture of acceptance.

He bowed his head as if he received the greatest gift of all, and I could see the pride in his chest swell despite himself. "Thank you," he said again, reaching out to grip my father's hand tightly.

"My son!" my father exclaimed, his voice full of joy. He pulled away and looked at me, his eyes twinkling with happiness. "Where's your mother? Louisa will be so happy to hear this news. Louisa!"

I heard my mother's voice echoing from somewhere in the house. It sounded like a distant song, growing more and more clear with each passing moment.

My father grabbed our hands, tugging us along as he rushed to the door. "Louisa!" he shouted gleefully, opening the door and leaning out into the night. "Come! Come quickly! Our daughter has returned home!"

A moment later, my mother appeared in the doorway, her long braid trailing behind her like a banner.

"Don't lie to me!" she said, her voice full of joy and surprise. "Mehdi, tell me the truth - is this really my daughter?" Her eyes met mine and her face lit up with a beautiful smile. "Zareena, is it really you?!"

"Yes, Mama," I said, my smile growing wider. "It's me."

She rushed forward, gathering me in her embrace. Tears spilled from her eyes as she kissed my forehead and held me close. "Oh, thank the Gods you're safe," she said, rocking me back and forth. "My baby is back."

Behind her, my six siblings trailed in, their eyes wide and mouths agape.

My brother Maaz was the first to reach us.

His normally stoic face split into a wide grin as he swept me into a bear hug. "It's good to have you home," he said, his voice thick with emotion. "The Gods have truly blessed us this day!"

The others crowded around us then - my sisters Salma, Yasmina, and Dana, and little Jamil, my youngest brother. Their voices blended together into a chaotic chorus of joy and welcome.

It was as if no time had passed since I had left this place - as if the years living abroad had been nothing more than a dream.

They were older now, but their faces held the same warmth, the same love that had been in my heart since I was a child.

This was home.

Salma crushed me in a tight hug, her laughter ringing out like a sweet melody. "Sister," she said, her voice choking with emotion. "I missed you so much. I was so worried when you didn't..."

"I know," I said, my eyes filling with tears. "But I'm home now."

My mother stepped forward and grasped Azair's hands in hers. "Welcome," she said warmly. "Welcome to our family."

"It's an honor to be here."

We followed her through the door, my siblings circling us like a protective cocoon.

I glanced up at Azair, who was watching me with a tender smile. "Welcome home," he whispered as we passed into the hall together.

My father grabbed my hand and pulled me away from the group, while my siblings dragged Azair inside, eager to show him every corner of our new home.

We stopped in a quiet hallway, and my father looked down at me with an unreadable expression on his face. "You look like your mother," he said slowly. "But with my eyes."

I couldn't help but smile. "It's good to be home, Baba," I said, squeezing his arm.

He nodded and took a deep breath. "Come," he said, gesturing for me to follow him down the hallway.

Blue mosaic tiles lined the walls, creating intricate patterns of flowers and stars. Bergamot and rosemary wafted through the air, and flowers of every color cascaded from baskets and vases.

We stopped at a large door carved with geometric shapes. My father pushed it open, revealing a room full of light and color. A round table in the center was draped with a thick purple cloth and surrounded by low cushions.

On the walls, my mother's tapestries hung in beautiful contrast against the deep blue tiles, while soft, wooly carpets lined the floor. The ones I remembered from childhood, full of swirling shapes and vibrant colors.

In the center of the room, over the round table, hung a faded yellow blanket I had woven years ago. Frayed threads hung loose at the edges, yet the loom pattern was still visible in the center.

Sunlight streamed through the window, bathing the blanket in a soft, golden light. The little red and blue flowers I had embroidered in the corners glimmered in the sun.

My father glanced at me with a knowing smile. "I visit this room often," he said. "Your mother and I come here to talk, to remember."

"You kept my tapestry." I touched the edge of it gently.

He settled onto a cushion across from me and cleared his throat. "I remember when you made this," he said, his voice soft and full of emotion. "Badis just left and you were so sad, so angry at the world."

He paused and reached out to brush his fingers along the edge of the blanket. The frayed edges looked like they were on the verge of unraveling.

"We missed you," he said finally. "All of us - your mother, your siblings, even the animals in the barn. When you left, it broke our hearts."

"There was nothing for me here," I said, my voice low. "No future."

He shook his head. "I failed you," he said, and I heard the regret in his voice. "As a man, I was raised to take care of my own, and I failed you. When that man left you, I wanted to go after him - punish him for what he did."

I reached out and touched his arm. "Baba, it wasn't your fault. I made my own decisions, and I did what was best for me."

"Do you not think I saw you hurting?" he asked, his voice strained. "Do you not think I wanted to help you? Do you not think I felt your pain, too?"

My eyes filled with tears. "I never wanted to disappoint you."

My father sighed, his face softening. "You were never a disappointment." He reached out and brushed away the tear that had trickled down my cheek. "I was never mad or upset with you, Zareena. I was angry at the world for what it did to you. For taking away your future before you even had a chance to make one."

"You don't have to worry about me anymore," I said, taking his hand in mine. "I'm happy. Azair, he makes me happy."

My father nodded and clasped my hand on his own. "That's what I wanted for you all along." Calluses lined his fingertips, evidence of a life spent working hard and providing for us. "To be happy. And I'm sorry I could not give this to you."

"You gave me everything," I said, my voice thick with emotion. "A home, a family, and your love. That's all I ever needed."

He shook his head. "I gave you a home," he said. "But I never really spoke to you. Not about what was happening, not about how I felt. It hurt to see my daughter so broken, and I didn't know how to fix it. So instead of talking with you, I pushed you away."

He paused and looked away for a moment. The lines of his face became deeper, more creased.

He took a deep breath and looked back at me. "But I want you to know," he said, his voice low but full of emotion. "That my heart was with you the entire time."

My eyes filled with tears, and I hugged him tightly. It felt so good to be held by my father again - something that I had not experienced since I was a child.

Not a burden. I was not a burden.

I was loved and accepted and wanted.

I had come home again, and this time, it felt a lot different.

Not a ruined bride, not a stranger, but as me - Zareena. My father's daughter.

As I hugged my father, I finally felt the warmth of his love and acceptance that had always been there for me, no matter where life had taken me. The warmth I hadn't been able to feel until I was ready to come home.

"Does he treat you right?" My father's voice broke through my thoughts, pulling me back into the present.

I looked up at him, a small smile on my lips. "He treats me like a queen," I said. "And I couldn't be happier."

My father nodded, a small smile of his own forming. "That's all I ever wanted for you," he said. "To be happy, to be loved."

"I am," I said, squeezing his hand. "And it's all thanks to you and Mama for raising me with love and strength."

As my father's eyes searched mine, I could almost see the hesitation in his words. "Is he... is he some sort of Djinn?" he asked, his tone careful and hesitant. "A being from another world?"

Did he bewitch you? I could hear the unspoken question in his words, and I couldn't help but laugh.

"Baba," I said. "He's just a man. A wonderful, loving, supportive, and kind man. A Fae, yes, but still a man."

My father let out a sigh of relief, his eyes softening with understanding. "I apologize for my ignorance," he said. "It's just... you have changed so much since we last saw you. And Azair is unlike anyone we have ever met before. Those ears, those eyes... they are not of this world."

I nodded, understanding my father's concerns. "He's from a different culture and background," I said. "But he loves me and treats me with kindness and respect. He has never used his powers or magic to control me. He accepts me for who I am, flaws and all."

My father's expression softened even more, and he let out a small smile. "I am glad to hear that," he said. "It is important for a man to treat his wife with love and respect, no matter what their differences may be."

I couldn't stop the tears from falling then. Tears of happiness, tears of relief, tears of love for my father.

"Thank you, Baba," I said, hugging him again. "For accepting me and my choices."

My father hugged me back, his embrace warm and strong. "My daughter has found a partner who loves her for who she is. That is all that matters to me," he said, his voice choked with emotion. "You will always have a home here, Zareena. But right now, your mother will kill us if we don't join the family for dinner."

twenty-three

ALMAZIGHA

"What are you doing here?" I asked as the basket of goods in my hands grew heavier.

"I came to see this place with my own eyes." Azair took a few slow steps forward, his gaze sweeping across the blue-tiled rooftops that surrounded us. "You grew up here, didn't you? In the marketplaces and alleyways of this city?"

His simple white robe contrasted beautifully against the blue walls of his surroundings, making him look almost serene.

His dark hair was pulled back in a simple knot, displaying his sharp cheekbones and piercing gaze.

Clutching the handle of my basket, I nodded. "Yes... it's a place that will always be home to me."

He reached over and gently grabbed the handle of my basket.

His eyes slowly drifted across the market stalls before settling on a group of children playing together in the street.

Without warning, he pulled out two large bread loaves from my basket and handed them to the kids.

The children's eyes widened in surprise as they took the bread from his hands. "Thank you," I heard them murmur before they rushed away with their prized possessions.

He smiled as he watched them go.

"That was nice of you," I said, as he turned back towards me.

"It's nothing," he replied, before taking the basket off my hands. "Let me carry this for you."

We strolled through the marketplace together, stopping every now and again to admire a trinket or watch a street performer.

Every once in a while, he would give away a few of our goods to the children that we passed, his kind gesture bringing a smile to their faces.

People parted for him naturally, their heads turning in admiration as he passed.

The Fae were an unfamiliar sight for most of them, yet here he was, strolling through the streets as if this was his home too.

The city itself was painted in shades of blue, from deep navy to pale turquoise. The houses were made of terracotta bricks, each one more ornate than the last, and were topped with domed rooftops and intricate mosaics.

And then there was the sea, stretching out for miles, its deep blue waters reflecting the sunlight.

Azair stopped for a moment to take it all in, his face illuminated by the sun's rays. "If I close my eyes," he said softly, "I can almost imagine you running barefoot through this city, a dark-eyed girl with a light step and unbridled joy."

A wave of nostalgia washed over me, and I laughed. "That was a long time ago. The pigtails have been traded for plaits and instead of running through the streets, I now walk them."

He smiled. "But you still carry the same joy in your step. It's beautiful to see." He reached out his hand and grabbed mine, his fingers twining around my own. "It's ironic, isn't it? This is where the rules of our society are formed and maintained. "

I tilted my head, confused. What did he mean?

"It's in these marketplaces, alleyways, and rooftops that people come to trade gossip, secrets, and stories. And yet, it's also here that they come to make connections, create relationships, and form their own little communities." His eyes scanned my face as he spoke. "Here in this city, you were molded into who you are today. And now, its daughter shapes the future."

"Why the poetic speech?" I asked, raising an eyebrow. "Weren't we just talking about food and trinkets?"

He chuckled. "My pretty wife, one thing I've learned in all my years is that sometimes it pays to be a bit of a dreamer. To look at the world through different lenses and see what lies beyond it." He brushed his finger along my cheek, making my heart flutter. "And you, my dearest dear, are the perfect one to do it."

I grabbed his hand, eager to show him the city as I knew it. "Come on," I said, tugging him along with a smile. "To really understand this city, you have to see it with your own eyes."

We strolled through the streets, passing vendors of all kinds. Kaftans and jewelry, perfumes, and spices, handcrafted instruments, and traditional dishes.

Everywhere we went, people welcomed us warmly, their eyes twinkling with curiosity as they asked us questions.

It all enthralled Azair. He asked me questions about the culture, the customs, and even the architecture.

I answered each one with enthusiasm, eager to share my knowledge with him.

As we watched a street performer weave stories with her music and words, he looked at me in awe. "It's like you have a special bond with this city. Like you understand it, in ways I never could."

I laughed. "That's because it is my home," I replied, squeezing his hand gently. "It's been a teacher, a mentor, and even a source of inspiration."

"And it will be for many more," he added with a grin. "Pigtailed girl, dark-eyed beauty, wise woman of the city streets... you are one of a kind."

"Fae king, wise wanderer, beloved husband... you are one of a kind."

Arching an eyebrow, he looked at me in surprise. "Little mouse, you know how to find the right words."

"I'm just speaking from my heart." I smiled, leaning into him.

"Do you want to see the house I grew up in? It's not far from here and it holds a lot of memories."

He nodded, his eyes glimmering with excitement. Taking him by the hand, I led him through the busy streets, pointing out landmarks and telling stories as we went.

We made our way through winding alleyways and cramped streets until we reached the poorer side of town.

The buildings were made from cobblestones and the rooftops were adorned with strings of dried fruits, herbs, and flowers.

A few children ran around in ragged clothes, playing tag while their mothers chattered with each other nearby.

"It's beautiful," Azair said as he took in the sights. "I can see why you love this place so much."

I pointed to a small house tucked away in the corner of the alleyway. "That's where I grew up," I said, nostalgia thick in my voice.

Blue paint was flaking off from the walls and the roof needed a few repairs, but it still held its charm. It was a humble home, far from luxurious, but it still had stories to tell.

He ran his fingers along the walls, as if trying to connect with its essence. "Your roots run deep here." He looked at me and squeezed my hand gently. "And it is an honor to be part of them."

The iron gate that led to the garden was still standing, and I could almost picture my mother hanging up her aprons on the back porch.

The herb garden was still full of fragrant herbs and the fruit trees were still bearing ripe fruits.

"When I was young," I said, "I used to play in this garden with my siblings. We'd race around the trees and hide behind the old stone walls. It was our own little world."

Entering the house, we came upon my old bedroom. The same wooden bed I used to sleep in was still there, but the sheets were faded and worn from time.

I pointed to the corner where my needlework was still hung up, the same one I used to spend hours on during my childhood.

Making him laugh, I told him about the time when my younger siblings and I used to make up stories of dragons living in our garden.

Leaning against the windowsill, he chuckled. "It's amazing how much you can remember," he said. "I think this place will always be special to me, too. The way you see this city, your home, it's like falling in love all over again."

"Falling in love with what?" I asked, my heart pounding.

He smiled and reached out to touch my cheek. "Falling in love with life," he drawled, as his fingers grazed my skin. "And all it has to offer."

His smile faded, and he looked at me with a seriousness that made my heart stop.

"Do you have your blade with you?" he asked in a low voice.

The small razor blade I used to carry for protection had been a part of me since I was young. But I didn't carry it anymore.

Not in the Summer Court. Not when I was with him.

"No," I mumbled, feeling a little embarrassed. "I don't need it anymore."

He nodded, as if he had expected this answer. Then, silently, he reached out and handed me a small box from the pocket of his robe.

Inside was a delicate silver dagger. The blade shimmered purple in the light and was decorated with intricate carvings of mice and dragons along the hilt.

Glowing on the handle was a small symbol of what I recognized to be the crest of the Summer Court. A sunflower in bloom.

"Why are you giving this to me?" I asked in disbelief, turning the blade over in my hands.

The craftsmanship was exquisite, and I could feel a strange warmth radiating from the metal.

Fae Iron. Only Fae Iron could have such an effect.

He lifted my chin so that our eyes met. Darkness filled Azair's eyes, and a sad smile graced his lips. "When I tell you to run, run. When I tell you to fight, fight."

My palms were sweaty, and my heart was pounding as I looked out of the window. The streets were eerily quiet. I could hear only the occasional outburst of laughter or snatch of conversation.

Children in simple kaftans were playing tag in the alleyways, and I didn't have to use my imagination to know that mothers were nearby, watching over them.

Nothing seemed out of the ordinary. Nothing seemed dangerous.

But I knew better.

Slipping the blade into the pocket of my dress, I turned to Azair.

"Just promise me one thing," I said, looking up at him.

There was something he wasn't telling me, and I wanted answers.

His gold eyes gleamed in the dim light as he nodded slowly. "What is it?"

"Promise me you'll come back," I said, my voice trembling. "Promise me you won't leave without saying goodbye."

He reached out and touched my cheek, his thumb tracing the curve of my jaw. "I promise." His nostrils flared and his eyes grew dark. "I will always come back for you. Are you not going to ask me why I gave you the blade?"

"I trust you."

A wicked smile spread across his face, and he laughed softly. Wild and untamed, just like the wind. Then he kissed me - hard and fast, as if he would never let go.

"Good," he said when he finally pulled away. "Stabbing enemies is much more fun when you have a supportive wife."

He winked and stepped back, letting his fingers graze my hand one last time before he faded into the shadows.

The door slammed open, and a group of men barged inside, their voices loud and menacing. Dark masks covered their faces, and they seemed to be looking for something.

Instinctively, I jumped back, my hand reaching for the silver blade in my pocket.

My heart was pounding, but I remained still, not wanting to draw attention to myself.

"Run," a voice hissed in my ear.

My heart raced, and I spun around, expecting to see Azair standing behind me. But he wasn't there.

Instead, a tiny figure was crouching beside me - an orange pixie with powerful wings and glittering eyes.

"Run," she said again, gesturing for me to jump out of the window.

I hesitated, not wanting to leave without knowing what was happening. But then I heard shouting and the sound of wood breaking from inside the house.

Without another word, I leaped out the window and landed in a pile of leaves outside. I scrambled to my feet, and I took off running.

The pixie flew beside me, her wings beating against the wind.

We ran through back alleys and narrow streets.

I did not know what was going on - all I knew was that someone was after us, and that I had to get away as fast as I could.

Women and children scattered as I ran past, and I heard the distant screams of guards behind us.

I glanced over my shoulder, expecting to see the men from before chasing after us. But there was nothing except an empty street and a few cats scavenging for scraps.

Fear clawed at my throat, but I pushed it down and kept running.

A hand grabbed my braid, and I felt a sharp tug on my head. I whirled around, ready to fight - until I saw who it was.

Red hair. A familiar face.

"Well, well," he said mockingly. "If it isn't my petty thief." He smiled, but it didn't reach his eyes.

It was the lord from before - the one I had scammed.

Lord Ralston.

Pushing him away, I tried to scramble back onto my feet.

But he was too fast. He grabbed me by the shoulders and pulled me up, his fingers digging into my skin.

A groan escaped my lips as I struggled to break free, but he just tightened his grip.

The pixie disappeared, and I was left alone with Lord Ralston.

"You think you can run from me?" He sneered, his face inches away from mine. "Think again."

My gaze darted around the street, my heart pounding in my chest as I searched for any sign of help, but there was nothing.

Desperate, I whispered a prayer to the Gods.

Pressing a blade against my throat, his fingers tightened around my wrists. "Just let me go," I said, my voice trembling. "Please."

Hot breath tickled my cheek as he leaned in close, his eyes blazing. "Why should I?" His hands moved to my neck, choking me. "My daughter owes you her life, and I'm going to make sure that debt is paid. Tell me her name. Now."

I was too shocked to answer. I couldn't even remember the girl's name. All I could do was stand there, frozen in fear.

His face twisted into a mask of rage, and he backhanded me so hard that I stumbled backwards.

My face stung, but I didn't try to fight him off. Instead, all I could do was stare at him, terror gripping me in its icy claws.

"You can't even remember her name?" he growled, his face inches away from mine.

Guilt and remorse surged through me, making my stomach twist.

I had been so focused on the dangers around me - the threats, the curse, the schemes - that I had completely forgotten about her.

She had been taken from this world too soon, and yet here I was, standing before her father without even knowing her name.

"My daughter was a bright and kind girl, and you dare to forget her name? I found her corpse in her bed with dead mice in her mouth and blood written on the wall that said 'Zareena sends her regards'. Does that sound familiar to you?"

The words hit me like a punch in the gut.

I opened my mouth, but no sound came out.

For a moment, we just stayed like that - his hand gripping my neck as he glared down at me with barely contained rage.

Azair, you fucking theatrical bastard. You'd better show up soon, or this is going to be the end of me.

"The Summer King, he's..." I trailed off, my voice barely a whisper. "He's coming for you. I didn't hurt her... I didn't hurt your daughter. The Summer King did, and he's coming back for you."

"Elunid. Her name was Elunid." He snorted in disbelief. "What's he going to do? I'm not afraid of him." He laughed, as if it was all a giant joke. "Do you really think that I'm afraid of the Summer King?"

But then the laughter died on his lips, and his eyes grew wide.

A flash of light lit up the sky, followed by thunderous roars that shook the cobblestones beneath our feet.

Howls and screams echoed through the night air, as if something dark and terrible was coming.

His grip loosened as he looked away, just enough for me to twist free.

It was now or never. I had no choice.

Taking a deep breath, I spun around and lunged forward, slashing my blade across his chest.

Blood splattered across the cobblestones as he stumbled backward, shock written across his face. His tunic was stained, and he was breathing erratically.

He lurched forward, a scream of wild rage tearing from his throat.

His fingers dug into my arms, pinning me to the ground. A burning sensation coursed through my body, and I tried to scream, but no sound would come out.

The ground beneath us shook, and the air filled with an eerie humming noise.

I screamed and struggled to break free, but he was too strong. Too strong for me to fight against.

He wrenched me around, lifting me from the ground like a rag doll.

My back pressed against his chest, and he snarled into my ear. "I will make you suffer," he spat, pressing my blade to my throat. "You are going to pay for what you've done."

The blade was cold against my skin as he pressed it harder against my throat.

I closed my eyes, waiting for the inevitable pain that was sure to come. "I never wanted your daughter to be in danger. I didn't want any of this. Elunid, she was..."

He laughed, a cold and cruel sound. "You should have thought of that before you meddled in my affairs."

"My, my, my," a voice echoed through the night air. "What do we have here?"

Landing lightly on the cobblestones, Azair's feet ignited with a bright flame. It raced up his body, consuming him in a brilliant gold light.

Gold eyes stared out from beneath the flames, and a wicked smirk curved his lips. "I believe," he said calmly, "that is my wife you are trying to harm."

Lord Ralston's throat bobbed as he swallowed. "S-she's not your wife," he stammered. "She's a thief, a criminal. Even her husband abandoned her because she's worthless gutter trash."

Azair shrugged, a dangerous glint in his eye. "She is mine," he said, the flames around him flickering brightly.

He stepped closer to Lord Ralston, his eyes glowing with a fierce intensity.

"Don't touch my wife or..." His voice trailed off as he looked away, and when his gaze returned, it was dark and deadly. "I will rip your intestines out with my bare hands and feed them to your hounds."

Bow down, a voice in my head commanded. *Bow down and beg for mercy.*

"You don't scare me!" Lord Ralston spat as he brandished his blade at Azair. "I will not bow down before you!"

He just laughed. A cold laugh that sent a chill down my spine.

"Very well," he said, his voice low and menacing. He raised his arm, pointing a finger at Lord Ralston. "Then I will show you what fear is."

A surge of power filled the air as Azair's eyes glowed with a brilliant blue light. The cobblestones beneath our feet shook, and a fierce wind whipped around us.

Lord Ralston's blade clattered to the ground as he stumbled backward.

"I thought you said you weren't afraid of me?" Azair asked, his voice laced with amusement. "It appears that was a lie."

Lord Ralston reached into his cloak and pulled out a small glass bottle, holding it up to the light. A blue liquid swirled inside. Sunfyre, a powerful and illegal substance.

It would burn through anything in its way.

"Do you think I'm a fool?" he sneered, his voice dripping with venom. "I promised my daughter that I would bring her justice, no matter the cost. Even if it means using Sunfyre against you."

Azair's smirk widened. "Sunfyre? How original." He raised an eyebrow, unimpressed by Lord Ralston's theatrics. "But do you really think that will work on someone like me?"

My heart raced as I stared at the bottle.

A single drop of Sunfyre would reduce us all to a pile of ash. I had never seen it before, but all I knew was that it would kill.

Kill everyone and everything.

The city would burn to ashes.

I glanced at Azair, and my stomach twisted in fear.

"Fae iron, mixed with Sunfyre," Lord Ralston. said, the heavy weight of his words sinking in. "Even you cannot withstand its power."

I could see the glint in his eyes as he held up the bottle, relishing in his own twisted victory.

This was it. We were going to die.

My mind raced as I stared at Azair. This would be my last chance to tell him how I truly felt, and I had to make it count. He had to survive this, no matter what.

"Azair," I said softly, my voice trembling with emotion. "Please don't die here. You mean so much to me."

A flicker of surprise crossed his face, but he didn't respond.

Lord Ralston's hand tightened around the bottle as he stepped forward, and Azair stepped back.

"Zareena," he said calmly. "Don't worry. We'll be fine. I can handle this."

"Husband," I said, my voice trembling. "Run. You must survive, no matter what happens to me. I -"

My mouth was dry, and my heart raced. I had to say it before I lost my chance.

Closing my eyes, I forced myself to speak the words. "I love you. Run," I repeated, desperation in my voice. "Save yourself. That is my last request. My final boon."

I opened my eyes and saw a look of shock on his face that was quickly replaced by something else. Regret? I couldn't tell. All I knew was that he had to leave, no matter the cost.

"Goodbye, Zareena."

Gold eyes stared out from beneath a curtain of flames, and a painful scream echoed in my ears as Lord Ralston launched the bottle of Sunfyre.

Suddenly, I stood in my home, a strange warmth surrounding me.

My father's face drained of color as I appeared before him, and he stumbled back, shock written across his features.

Azair.

twenty-four

THE WEDDING

My hand trembled as I buttoned up my sister's wedding dress, securing the last of the pearl buttons. I could feel her gaze on me, watching my every movement.

Salma had always been so in tune with my emotions. She had felt my pain, and at this moment, she knew how much I wanted Azair to be here with me.

It had been a week since Lord Ralston had launched the bottle, and I hadn't seen him since.

"He'll come back," she said softly, as if reading my thoughts. "I know it."

I nodded in agreement but didn't speak. I couldn't let myself hope too much - not after all that we'd been through.

But I knew that if he was out there, alive and well, then we would find each other. No matter what.

He promised me, I thought fiercely, trying to push away the doubts that crept into my mind.He promised he would never leave me without saying goodbye.

But why hadn't he come back? Why hadn't he given me any word or sign that he was alive? Was it because he didn't want me anymore? Did he regret choosing me as his wife?

He said goodbye, a voice whispered in my mind. Right before I disappeared. But it didn't feel like a proper goodbye. It felt like he was leaving me behind, with no explanation or closure.

The toxic thoughts swirled in my mind, causing my heart to ache.

I shouldn't allow myself to spiral into negativity, but it was hard to not question everything when someone you loved disappeared without a trace.

But just as quickly as the doubts had crept in, a fierce determination replaced them.

He wouldn't have promised to come back if he didn't intend to keep it. And I wouldn't give up hope until I knew for sure that he was gone.

For now, I had to focus on the present. Salma's wedding was in a few minutes, and I couldn't let my worries overshadow her special day.

She deserved all the happiness in the world, and it was my duty as her sister to make sure everything went smoothly.

I took a deep breath, straightening out the skirt of her dress before turning to face her with a reassuring smile. "You look beautiful," I said sincerely, tears pricking at the corners of my eyes.

I had dreamed of this day since we were children - Salma twirling around in a beautiful wedding dress, finally ready to be wed.

She had grown up so quickly over the years, becoming not only my sister but also a daughter to me.

"I can only hope to look half as beautiful as you did on your wedding day."

I laughed, remembering my wedding day. "Oh, believe me. I looked far from beautiful on my wedding day. I stank of pig shit and my skirts were muddied." I gestured to the dress she was wearing, so very different from my own. "But you look absolutely gorgeous in yours."

Dark eyes lined with kohl and a daring red lip - yes, she looked stunning. But more importantly, she looked happy.

Her dark hair was swept up in an elegant updo at the back of her head, adorned with pearls and gold chains.

A full skirt of teal silk swirled around her ankles as she walked, decorated with intricate beading in golden thread.

As she spun around, I could almost see the form of Azair behind her - his tall frame and broad shoulders standing protectively by her side.

"Did you ever think," she said softly, "that this would be our lives?"

I looked around the room, at the gilded furniture and soaring ceilings, and thought of all that we had been through together. And yet here we were, still standing.

"I thought it was impossible," I said, and Salma smiled.

"That's what makes it even more special," she replied, taking my arm as we walked out of the room. "Nothing is ever truly impossible."

No matter how many obstacles life throws our way, no matter how much heartache we endure, nothing is ever impossible. We just have to keep believing and never give up hope.

"Your Azair will be here soon," she said, squeezing my arm. "And when he does, you two can finally start the life that you both deserve."

"Aeric will lose his mind when he sees you. As for my husband, he'd better make it back in time or else I'm going to kill him."

Her eyes twinkled. "I'm sure he will," she said. "Do you think Aeric will like the dress?"

I nodded. "He's going to love it," I said. I could already see him, his face lighting up with delight when he saw Salma in her beautiful wedding finery.

"How could he not? It would impress even the Sultana."

"Do you think Azair will be there to see it?" she asked, her voice tentative.

She had been asking about him constantly since his disappearance, her eyes bright with hope.

"Don't think about him," I said sadly, though a glimmer of hope lingered in my heart. "Today is your day and yours alone. We will worry about him later."

I enveloped her in a hug, and she hugged me back tightly.

I could feel the tears prickling my eyes, but I held them back - for today was not a day of sorrow. Today was a day of hope and happiness, and I wanted to savor every moment.

"Zareena, stop being so strong all the time. It's okay to cry. It's okay to be scared. You don't have to pretend, not with me."

"If I do, I'm afraid I'll never stop," I said, my voice trembling with emotion. "And I can't do that. Not today."

"You sacrificed so much for me. For us. You don't have to do it alone."

Salma's voice was full of love and understanding, and I couldn't help but cry.

"But it was worth it. To see you happy."

All of it was worth it. The pain, the loss, the fear. It was all worth it to see Salma grow up into a beautiful young woman, ready to start her own life and family.

I smiled through my tears, thinking of Azair. Even the pain of being a mad Fae king's bride, thrust into a life I had never imagined for myself, was worth it - because in the end, it led me to him. To love and friendship like I'd never known before.

What would have happened if we hadn't met? Would I still be living a lonely and isolated existence, never experiencing the joy of finding someone who truly understood me?

Even if he didn't love me.

I shivered, glad for once that I scammed a nobleman. Otherwise, who knows where I'd be right now?

Salma's warm brown eyes filled with tears, and she gave me a watery smile. "We made it, Zareena. You and I. We are survivors."

"Don't you ruin your makeup," I joked, wiping away the tears. "You've got a wedding to attend, and you look absolutely beautiful."

She nodded, but her eyes still glimmered with tears. I took her hand in mine and squeezed it tightly.

Drums started thumping outside, and I grabbed her hand, smiling.

Women sang in the distance, and I knew it was time.

Glancing out of the window, I saw a procession walking towards us, colorful flags waving in the wind. Gold coins were thrown, and the sound of laughter filled the air.

Aeric's red hair was clear even from a distance, and my heart jumped with joy.

"He's here," Salma said, her voice trembling with excitement. "It's time."

Dressed in a deep blue velvet tunic, Aeric walked into our house, trailed by a line of guests.

Walking down the stairs, I saw a vast banquet hall filled with servers carrying platters of food and trays of drinks.

People dressed in vibrant kaftans were milling around, chatting and laughing as they prepared for the ceremony.

A small crowd had gathered near the doorway leading out to the gardens, their faces turning towards me in surprise.

My ex-in-laws had come as well, their faces a mixture of shock and admiration. What had they expected of me? Did they think I could never do this? That I would hide?

Aeric's face lit up when he saw me, and I felt my own lips turning up into a smile.

He ran to me, and I put my arms around him in a tight embrace. "You're finally here," he said, his voice breaking. "I thought you were dead."

"Not quite." I stepped back and looked into his eyes. "We made it, Aeric. Welcome to the family."

He smiled and kissed my forehead, and then he stepped back as the crowd gasped.

Salma descended the stairs in a flourish, her face glowing with joy. My father held her hand and smiled, his eyes twinkling with pride. Around them, a chorus of women sang in celebration, their voices rising and falling in harmony.

Her dress of teal silk swirled around her ankles, and the pearls adorning her hair glinted in the soft light. Her lavender eyeshadow shimmered as she cast a glance at Aeric, who stood at the foot of the stairs, waiting for her to arrive.

Aeric's eyes widened when he saw her, and I could almost hear him think: My wife is the most beautiful woman here.

My stomach filled with warmth as I looked around me at my family and friends - all here to witness this special moment.

Salma had found her happily ever after, and Aeric had found his bride.

She smiled softly as Aeric raised his hand to her face, gently caressing her cheek. "You are the most beautiful thing I have ever seen," he whispered, his eyes full of love and admiration. "And I am the luckiest man in the world to have you as my wife."

He was right.

Salma blushed and her lips curved up in a small smile as she looked at him. The veil slipped from her face, and she took a step towards him.

As he leaned forward to kiss her, I coughed and cleared my throat, reminding him to be mindful of the audience gathered around us.

He glanced at me, his face flushing.

Grabbing her hand, he led her to the middle of the room, where they stood facing each other.

Baba began reciting a prayer for their union and the crowd bowed their heads in reverence.

"Today, we are gathered here to witness the holy union of my daughter Salma and Aeric," he said. "May their love be as strong as a mountain and last until the stars fade away from the sky."

"That is a beautiful sentiment," a familiar voice drawled behind me. "Don't you agree, little mouse?"

I spun around, hoping that my ears weren't deceiving me. But sure enough, Azair was standing behind me with a mischievous glint in his eyes.

Not a scratch on him to show that he had been through any sort of ordeal.

Grabbing my waist, he pulled me closer and rested his chin on my shoulder.

"Salma is your sister," he said, his voice low and gentle. "Watch her wedding and be happy."

Baba sprinkled rose petals on their joined hands as a sign of good fortune and protection, and the crowd erupted into applause once more.

"Where have you been?" I whispered, my heart racing.

He gently kissed my neck, before biting down on my earlobe and sending a shiver down my spine.

"Taking care of some business," he said, his breath tickling my skin. "And just in time, too. I wouldn't miss my little mouse's sister's wedding."

"That's not an answer," I said, stubbornly. "I was worried sick about you."

He turned me around to face him and his smile softened as he wiped away a lone tear that had escaped my eye.

"Lord Ralston is a clever man who knows how to play his cards well. I had to undo all of his plans before he could harm anyone else. But don't worry, little mouse, everything is under control now," he said reassuringly, as he twirled me to face the newlyweds. "Now let's focus on celebrating this joyous occasion."

Aeric stepped forward and kissed Salma's hand, and the crowd's cheers rose to a crescendo, echoing through the hall.

Gold coins were thrown in the air, and the laughter of children mingled with their parents' joyous shouts.

Drums beat, and couples started taking their places on the dance floor.

I watched as Salma and Aeric danced in each other's arms, my heart brimming with happiness for them.

Azair reached for my hand and pulled me close.

Then, he bowed down before me and placed a delicate golden crown on my head.

The gemstones sparkled in the light as I looked up at him in surprise.

"The Summer Queen should wear her crown," he said softly, his eyes twinkling with mischief. "It's time to show off my pretty wife. I don't think you will allow me to kill the wedding guests?"

"Don't you dare."

He wrapped his arm around me, and we made our way onto the dance floor.

We laughed and spun around, a whirlwind of colors and sounds, while the guests looked on in confusion.

The musicians increased the tempo, and I felt my body move to the beat, as if it was in perfect sync with Azair's.

We glided across the room, his gaze never leaving mine.

"Did you know you are the most beautiful creature in this world?" he asked with a grin.

"I'm not," I said, my face turning red as I looked away.

He laughed and pulled me closer, his lips brushing against my neck. "You are to me," he murmured in a low voice.

"Why did you bring me home?" I asked, my heart beating faster. "Did you know he would be here? Is that why you brought me here?"

Did he save my family and me? Did he do all of this just to protect us?

He stopped dancing and looked at me, his eyes serious. "I brought you here because your place is by my side," he said, his voice carrying an uncharacteristic edge. "And I will always protect what is mine."

"Yours?" I asked, feeling a flutter in my chest.

"Yes," he said firmly. "You are mine."

His hands tightened around me as they drifted lower down my waist.

"I can assure you, my dearest dear," he said, his voice laced with a hint of amusement. "That mortal pest was the least of your worries. Do you think I would let anyone harm my family or miss out on such a beautiful event?"

I smiled, the tension in my body melting away. "No," I said softly. "You are too protective."

Twirling me around, he smiled and kissed my forehead. "Do you honestly not know why I brought you here?"

I shook my head, a little bewildered.

He gazed at me with a seriousness that I had never seen before. "I made a vow that the day I would break my curse I would bring you here to see your family," he said, his voice steady and sure. "Have I not kept my promise?"

He promised me he would bring me home when he broke his curse.

The curse that he had been burdened with, the one that meant he needed to fall in love, because he had disavowed it. I always wondered how he would break the curse - whether he would find true love or if there was another way to break the curse.

And here we were, dancing in the midst of my family and friends, with his arms wrapped around me as if he never wanted to let go.

My breath caught in my throat. "Impossible. Don't tell me..."

It dawned on me that this was more than just a promise kept. This was a declaration of love, a testament to the fact that he found love in me.

He had broken his curse, and in doing so, he had broken down all the walls around my heart.

He grinned and gave me a gentle squeeze. "You underestimate me, dear," he drawled. "Nothing is impossible for the likes of me."

I stopped dancing and stepped back, my heart thumping wildly in my chest. "Do not lie to me," I said, my voice shaking. "Not about this."

He raised an eyebrow and stepped closer, cupping my face in his hands. "I don't lie."

He kissed me with a hunger that was impossible to ignore.

"From the moment I saw you, a brave mortal woman, I knew that something was different. It was like a puzzle piece that had been missing from my life suddenly clicked into place."

He twirled me around once more and then dipped me low, his mouth hovering over mine.

"When your fever wouldn't break and you slipped away for those few hours, it felt like someone had ripped out my heart. The thought of living a life without you was unbearable," he said, his voice soft and passionate. "So I promised myself that if you were granted a second chance at life, I would make sure to never take it for granted. That I would love you with every breath, would rip apart the world if that's what it takes to keep you safe."

"Azair..." I breathed, tears streaming down my cheeks. "Is this really happening?"

"Do you not see what's been standing between us since the very beginning?" he said, his voice fierce and desperate. "It wasn't a curse that kept me from loving you. It was my refusal to accept that I felt something more than friendship for you."

He lifted me back up and kissed away my tears, his tongue tracing the path they left.

"But now... now I realize just how much I need you in my life. Zareena, you are the only one with whom I can be myself - a vengeful, selfish Fae. And I love you for it."

"I love you too," I said, pressing my lips against his. "More than you'll ever know. When I thought I had lost you forever, it felt like part of me was gone, too. You are everything to me."

He smiled, and his lips brushed softly against mine.

"I knew it," he said in a low voice. "From the moment I saw you, I knew that falling in love with me was inevitable." A mischievous glint shone in his eyes as he added, "I just hoped you would be brave enough to admit it."

"I tried so hard to deny it," I said, my voice barely above a whisper. "But you were always there, like some kind of magical force that drew me to you. Even when I told myself that loving you was foolish, my heart refused to listen. I was terrified that you lifting the curse would be the end of us. That you would no longer need me, and I would lose you forever."

He pulled me into a tight embrace, his arms warm and strong around me. "I will always need you," he said earnestly. "Just as you need me. We complete each other."

"Promise me you will never leave me," I whispered, my voice breaking with emotion.

"I promise," he said, his voice firm and unwavering. "I will always be by your side, through every challenge and triumph. Together, we can face anything. And tonight, I'll show you off to the world. A ruined bride has become the Summer Queen."

My mother's voice broke the spell. "Zareena! Azair! Please remember that people are watching you," she said in a gentle but firm voice. "Make sure to behave accordingly and not give them any reason for gossip."

I blushed and laughed, realizing that my mother was still the same overbearing but loving mom she had always been.

"Yes, Mother," I said, teasingly rolling my eyes at Azair.

He chuckled and pulled me even closer, his lips brushing against my ear as he whispered, "Don't worry, dear. I'll keep you out of trouble."

"Mama, you have nothing to worry about," I said, reassuringly placing a hand on her arm. "We'll behave ourselves, I promise."

Her eyes softened as she looked between us, a knowing smile on her face. "Newlyweds," she muttered, shaking her head in mock exasperation.

Azair chuckled and kissed my forehead. "Forgive our rudeness," he said to my mother with a smile. "We seem to have forgotten that we are not the only ones here. My beautiful wife certainly deserves admiration."

My mother nodded, her lips twitching in amusement. "I don't doubt that."

She raised an eyebrow at us and then shook her head with a smile before turning to greet some of our guests.

We continued dancing, and soon enough, I realized that many of our guests were staring at us with interest.

I avoided glancing at them, feeling my cheeks heat up as we twirled around the room.

But when I caught sight of a familiar face standing in the shadows, something inside me shifted. It was Badis - my ex-husband - and for a moment, my heart skipped a beat.

He was watching us with an unreadable expression on his face, and I couldn't help but wonder what he was thinking.

As soon as our eyes met, he looked away, clenching his jaw tight.

I noticed a beautiful woman standing next to Badis, her arm linked with his. Tall and slender, with long dark hair cascading down her back, she had an air of elegance and confidence about her.

I recognized her as the daughter of the vizier, a woman who had been praised for her beauty and intelligence.

Instead of feeling jealous or sad, I simply felt a sense of relief.

For the first time, I realized that Badis and I were truly over. We had both moved on with our lives and found happiness in our own ways.

Azair noticed my expression and pulled me closer, his gaze following Badis' retreating figure. "He can't hurt you," he whispered in my ear. "Do you still love him?"

I felt nothing, not even a hint of regret or sadness.

All I felt was an immense sense of relief that my life had taken a different path. One that led to Azair and me being together.

I shook my head and smiled. "I thought I would feel rage, or a broken heart, but I'm not. I'm grateful for everything that has happened because it led me to you," I said, looking into his eyes. "Badis taught me what love is not, and you have shown me what love truly is."

He smiled and brushed a strand of hair away from my face. "They will sing songs about us one day, my love. The Summer King and the mortal girl who conquered his heart."

"Does the Summer Court know the curse is broken?" I asked, suddenly remembering an important detail. "Does your mother know?"

He shook his head and smiled ruefully. "I've been waiting for the perfect moment to make the announcement."

Chuckling, I stood on my toes and kissed him softly. "You want to wait until the last act of our story." I grinned. "When the curse dooms your court, then you can save the day and tell them it's all been a misunderstanding."

He laughed and held me close, spinning around the dance floor with me in his arms. "I was thinking of something more... dramatic," he said. "Flames and trumpets, banners of victory, that sort of thing. But I guess we can always improvise. Our kingdom is built on stories, and I am no exception."

He paused and looked down at me with a soft smile, his eyes shining with love.

"My story, our story, begins and ends with you. So let us make it a tale to remember."

I smiled and rested my head against his chest. "You're such a bastard," I said fondly.

He chuckled softly and kissed the top of my head. "But I'm your bastard," he said, spinning me around one last time before leading us off the dance floor. "Always."

Can't get enough of the Summer King and his little mouse? Don't worry, I got you...

A secret bonus chapter is waiting for you! One that takes place after the book ends... from his point of view. The Summer King is most eager to invite you into his world.... Are you ready for it?

Thank you so much for taking the time to read *Captive of the Fae King.* Your support means everything to me as a fantasy romance author. I am grateful for each and every reader who has joined my characters on their journey, experiencing love, magic, and adventure along the way.

Special thanks to all those who have left reviews, shared my books with friends, and supported me in this writing journey. Your kindness and encouragement keeps me going.

About the Author

Silya Barakat is a chocolate-loving, travel-obsessed author of fantasy romance. She draws inspiration from her travels and weaves them into her magical stories that will transport you to other worlds.

When she's not creating enchanting tales, Silya can be found indulging in her love for cooking and trying out new recipes.

Despite living in a small town, Silya's imagination knows no bounds and she dreams of faraway places filled with adventure and romance. Whether it be through her writing or travels, Silya is always seeking new inspiration to fuel her stories.

Amazon

Goodreads

Tiktok

Website

Printed in Great Britain
by Amazon